A Spy Came Home

H. N. Wake

This is a work of fiction. Names, characters, businesses, places, events and incidents are either the products of the author's imagination or used in a fictitious manner. Any resemblance to actual persons, living or dead, is purely coincidental.

Copyright © 2014 HN Wake

All rights reserved.

For my Joe.

PROLOGUE

Picasso followed *Guernica* with his series of *Weeping Woman* paintings in which the woman's mourning continues, without end.
- Jonathan Jones, *The Guardian*, May 2000

For most of history, Anonymous was a woman.
- Virginia Woolf

Zurich, Switzerland

Zurich was the only city in the world that made her uneasy.

Near the mouth of the Limmat River, she looked across Lake Zurich at the church spires rising above wide promenades and grassy hills. Vacation homes dotted the foothills of snow-capped Alps. Out on the glistening cobalt water, white sails caught a crisp breeze. Somewhere in the medieval city, a trolley bell chimed.

This idyllic picture was discordant with her reality: hers was a world in which evil washed back and forth across continents.

She resented the Swiss their perfection and their isolationism. It was the potency of her resentment that made her uneasy.

Standing on the gravel path by the river's bank, she sucked one last drag from her cigarette, crushed it out in the public ashtray, and turned toward the city. She limped slowly down Bahnhofstrasse, passing bright red umbrellas at an outdoor cafe and magenta flowers trimming the Savoy Hotel. Bankers in blue, pin-stripped suits strode past. At the corner, she rested and watched two trolley cars cross in front of the stately, grey-stoned arch of the Credit Suisse headquarters on Paradeplatz.

She lumbered across the street toward the bank. In the lobby, she took quick note of the birds-eye security camera in the far corner, shuffled past, and settled into a chair at one of the customer service desks.

Looking up, a young banker saw a 70-year-old woman in an outdated green suit with white, bobbed hair and 1970s sunglasses. Her movements were slow, deliberate, almost heavy.

With stiff fingers, she took off the sunglasses to reveal a lined and well-lived faced. She smiled hesitantly.

He smiled in return. "Bon jour. Commet ca va bien, Madame?"

"Tout marche bien. Merci."

They continued in Swiss French.

He asked, "How may I help you, Madame?"

In a throaty, cracked voice she said, "I've come out today, only here, to pick up a package, my dear." She slid a slip of paper across the shiny wooden desk with a handwritten sequence of numbers.

He stood. "Certainly. Just a moment."

Within fifteen minutes, he returned carrying a letter-sized Credit Suisse envelope. "I have instructions only to check your ID, Madame Le Blanc."

"Of course." She carefully offered him a Swiss ID card for Madame Le Blanc, 357 Kilchberg Strasse, born 1/13/44.

He dutifully returned the ID and handed her the envelope. "Happy to be of service, Madame."

She haltingly replaced her sunglasses and pushed herself out of the chair. "Have a good day, Sir."

Arriving back at the lake, she unsealed the envelope and shook out a $1 million Credit Suisse cashier's check. She slipped it into her pocket. She dropped the Madame Le Blanc ID into the empty envelope, crushed it, and nonchalantly dropped both into a trash bin.

Later that afternoon, an undisguised Mac Ambrose sat on a hard laminate bench in a sleek art gallery. She was dressed in a black cotton sweater, fitted jeans, and running shoes. A messy knot of auburn hair topped her head. She felt relaxed, at home in the quiet stillness, alone with her thoughts.

Across the barren, white gallery, the receptionist read a book at a spotless, white desk: her job was to look like she didn't have a job. There was no movement on the cobblestone street beyond the gallery's window.

In the tomblike space, Mac gazed at a brightly colored image of a woman whose features were fractured and incongruous. The stark portrait hanging on the white wall was one in a series entitled *Weeping Woman* that Pablo Picasso painted after completing his famous work about the Spanish Civil war. The series explored the theme of suffering through the image of crying women.

Mac reached into her courier bag and pulled out her cell phone.

When she was sure the receptionist wasn't looking, she snapped a photo of the Picasso and attached it to a new text message.

"I'm in if you are," she wrote and sent.

As she walked out, she nodded to the receptionist and picked up a gallery business card.

At the corner, she pulled out a burner phone, turned it on, and dialed a US number from memory. Deep in the bowels of the CIA headquarters in Langley, a female operator answered. "Lunext Corporation."

"This is Susan Anthony."

"Go ahead."

"Message for William Penn." It was code. The message was for Staff Operations Officer (SOO) Frank Odom, her direct report in Langley. "I've got pen pals. I think in China." This was code letting him know she was being followed by internet crawlers, most likely of Chinese origin. "I'm going on vacation for two weeks." She was going offline for two weeks.

The operator said, "I'll repeat your message. Susan Anthony has Chinese pen pals and will be taking a vacation for two weeks."

"Great thanks." Otherwise known as affirmative.

New York, NY

In the galley kitchen, Freda Browne pointed the remote at the cheap, flat screen television and smashed buttons in search of news. Out the small kitchen window, the sun rose over the East Village. A faint hum emanated off early morning traffic on FDR drive.

Over her shoulder she shouted down the short hall. "M, that's your 30 minute snooze. I need you out of bed. Don't push me."

She paused on a local news broadcast, sipping her low-fat, soy latte. It was the same drink she made every day after the gym.

On the television, the newscaster started a new segment. "A shooting on Wednesday in a local market has left one dead and another person wounded." An image of an older Korean man flashed on the screen. "NYPD identified the gunman as Song Ho Kim, a former employee of the market. Kim opened fire in the late afternoon during a shopping lull, killing three people. The killer is being pursued by authorities."

She re-read the lead article in the folded *New York News* laying on the counter. Above the fold, the title blared, "US Senate Considers New Gun Legislation."

She stared blankly through the window for a long moment, then shook her head and turned her back on the news and the newspaper.

She pulsed a green protein shake in a beat-up blender, poured it into an out-sized glass, and marched down a photo-lined hallway, passing ten years of images of her grinning, wide-eyed daughter. A few of the photos showed them hugging. She banged once on her daughter's door as she passed.

"M, I'm serious, we need to get to school. I've got a lot on today," she barked.

Her cell phone beeped as she stepped into her sunflower blue bedroom. She read the message and opened the attachment, recognizing the painting as a Picasso. It was of a woman's face contorted in pain.

She quickly typed a reply. *"Yes! Let's do this!"*

Striding into the bathroom, she stripped off her sweaty jog bra and t-shirt from a very tight body. She peeled yoga pants off muscled legs that were already burning from her morning work out. As she stepped into her white, tiled shower, she leaned her head back and yelled toward the ceiling. "M, I'm serious. Chop. Chop!"

Penny Navarro was leaning on the marble counter as the morning sun drifted across the far side of the New York NoHo loft apartment and warmed the diamond-tufted leather couch into a deeper shade of yellow. Next to her, a top-of-the-line coffee maker percolated. Next to the coffee maker, a silent cell phone beckoned.

She picked up the cell phone, opened the photo for the fifth time, and stared at the image of the Picasso. She closed the image and slipped the phone into a robe pocket.

She poured a mug of coffee for herself with no milk, no sugar and a second mug with cream and sugar, then padded through the living room and into the first bedroom. Bending into the top bunk bed, she put her nose to her 13-year-old son's head, breathed in deeply of his kinky hair, and planted a kiss.

She whispered, "Time to wake up, Pumpkin."

He moaned and rolled toward the wall.

Leaning down into the bottom bunk, she repeated the kiss on her 10-year-old son's head, noticing his hair had gone a day too long without shampoo.

"Morning, Sweets. Time to get up."

She carried on down the long hall and into the cold, master bedroom. She set a coffee down on the far bedside table next to a framed photo of two young, black liberals on the steps of a college dorm; in the photo, a tall, confident Kenneth had his arm slung around the shoulders of a petite, self-effacing Penny. Her eyes stopped on the image of her younger self. Having weathered difficult pregnancies, aggressive bosses and grueling trials, she knew she was no longer that naive girl. She said, "Here's your coffee. I'm hitting the shower. Can you help with the boys this morning? They need showers. I've got an early meeting."

From under a tan duvet, her husband mumbled, "They don't need me. They've got it covered. Penny, I was up super late writing. I need some sleep."

She tamped down the frustration of a million similar moments; she had a far more pressing issue that required her focus. She turned without a word.

In the master bathroom, she started up the shower, pulled on a shower cap, and dropped her robe on the marble tiles. She heard the weight of the cell phone land on the floor. She stepped through the steam and under the showerhead, pressed her palms into her eyes, and turned into the pulsing waterfall.

Everything around her slowed.

The hot water hit the back of her hands, sluiced down her forearms, dripped off her elbows, and splashed, slightly cooler, onto the tops of her thighs. From a gap in the shower curtain, a draft of cold air slid up her spine. Goosebumps formed across her back. She concentrated on the sensations for a long moment.

In a burst of movement, her hands dropped, her eyes opened, and her chin lifted. Droplets bounced into her eyes. She quickly lathered, rinsed, and turned off the water.

Two minutes later, she wrapped her robe around her curves and pulled out the cell phone. She typed a reply, "*Count me in.*"

FOUR WEEKS BEFORE THE SENATE VOTE

It was as if, after documenting the disbelief and shock at the events at *Guernica*, he could not let go of the sorrow and was compelled to grieve the loss of the victims through these archetypal images of a suffering woman.
- James C. Harris, "Picasso's Weeping Woman", *Arch Gen Psychiatry,* 2012

I have learned over the years that when one's mind is made up, this diminishes fear;
knowing what must be done does away with fear.
- Rosa Parks

1

Arlington, VA

He was not a bored, uniformed cop drinking coffee in a donut shop, but ruefully he realized he resembled one in that moment.

Cal Bertrand, an even-tempered, 15-year veteran with the Bureau for Alcohol, Tobacco, Firearms and Explosives, chewed a dry cranberry scone and sipped a mediocre coffee while staring at the wall clock across the empty, open-plan fourth floor of a suburban business mall. His tall, angular body was relaxed at a desk that was surrounded by cardboard-box pyramids piled on standard-issue metal tables.

It was the start of the second week of the third month of a 6-month 'close-out' assignment for the ATF Mexican gun-running operation widely known as 'Fast and Frenzied.' 'Close-out' was a deceptively pleasant term for the interminable process of dotting millions of i's and crossing millions of t's on reams of paperwork destined for a warehouse, never to be seen again except maybe by an eager-beaver-criminal-justice-graduate-student who finessed the proper approvals out of the Bureau. Nobody wanted this particular operation revisited. Least of all Cal.

The minute hand on the clock ticked to 9:02 in the morning and the grey door opened on the far side of the desolate floor. The project accountant assigned by the Government Accounting Office - a thin man in his 30s with premature bifocals - shuffled to his desk near the door, switched on his computer, and settled in without a glance.

A dust moat floated by Cal, disturbed by the gust from the accountant's entrance.

Cal took the last bite of the scone and decided against pulling out his cell phone to play a quick game of Sudoku. His latest obsession frustrated him; it was a regular reminder of his compulsive nature and it felt wasteful, mundane. That it was more interesting than his current assignment depressed him further.

Just as he took the last sip of his coffee, Cal's inbox chimed with the arrival of a new email. His eyes snapped up over the cup's rim to the computer screen. Emails had been few and far between the last several months.

He didn't recognize the sender, Maar@hushmail.com. That was unusual. The ATF normally had a very tight spam filter. He did recognize that the address was from a private email system with significant encryption used by folks who wanted to stay anonymous.

Curious, he gently set down his coffee.

The actual email message was blank. In the far right corner was an icon for an attachment. He clicked on the attachment and quickly scanned it. He recognized it as a Confidential State Department cable from the US Embassy in Pakistan to the office of the Secretary of State.

He returned to the top of the cable and read it more deliberately.

SUBJECT: BLUE LANTERN - ROUTINE POST-SHIPMENT END-USE CHECK ON LICENSE 88088
Origin: Embassy Islamabad/AMEMBASSY ISLAMABAD
Classification: CONFIDENTIAL
To: SECSTATE WASHDC
Date: 10 August 2012

REF: STATE 88088

1. Blue Lantern Coordinator Islamabad has confirmed with Office of Defense Cooperation the receipt of 696 M4s approved for import under License 88088 to the Pakistan Army's Special Services Group (SSG.)
2. This shipment of 58 racks @ 12 weapons each was funded by the Pakistani Counterinsurgency Capability Fund.
3. In line with Blue Lantern review procedures, PolOff will confirm chain of custody, delivery and end use to SSG.

Investigation has commenced.

- BRADLEY

This was a routine State Department cable similar to many Cal had seen before. The Blue Lantern program monitored the end-use of commercial arms sales under the International Traffic in Arms Regulations of the Arms Export Control Act. Housed in US Embassies, Blue Lantern coordinators verified that exported defense equipment was used in line with US government regulations and was not ending up in the wrong hands.

Cal read the cable for a third time. There was nothing particularly striking in its contents. A Political Officer named Bradley in the US Embassy/Pakistan had confirmed that the Pakistani Army's Special Services had received just under 700 assault rifles. Bradley had planned to verify their arrival and proper use.

Cal picked up the phone and made a call.

A gruff voice answered, "Ben Atkins. ATF."

"Hey Benji, it's Cal Bertrand," Cal said.

"Holy shit. Cal. How are you?"

"Yeah, alright, alright."

"I saw your testimony on Fast and Frenzied. Wow. You either have gargantuan rocks or IQ amnesia. I'm not sure which."

Cal grimaced and replied, "Yeah. Me neither. Probably just straight up stupidity. Hey, you're still working Pakistan, right?"

"Sure."

"What's the low down on the —" he read from the cable, "Pakistani Counterinsurgency Capability Fund?"

"What's a Latin America guy doing asking about the PCCF?"

"Just curious. It came across my desk."

Benji chuckled. "Really? It came across your desk? Out in purgatory? The PCCF pops up over in the 'close out' sarcophagus?"

Cal looked around the bleak office, waiting him out.

"What will the universe think up next?" Benji asked no one in particular. There was a pause down the phone line. "Actually, the less I know the better. Well, let's see. It's the 3 Billion --"

Cal sat up. "With a B?"

"Yeah, it's the 3 Billion budget over five years. From 2009 to 2014. It's for the Pakis to get the standard shit. It was a carrot for them to go fight the Islamist militants in their tribal area. You know - Pushtan."

"So, how's it going?"

"Mostly copters. Those Pakis love flying around. I can't blame em. You ever been up in those mountains? Holy crap those are god forsaken. Nothing but scrub and mountains. A few goats. I mean, god-fore-saken."

"They order the full budget every year?"

"Absolutely. Wouldn't you if someone was giving you free military hardware?"

"What do you think about it? The PCCF? What's your personal assessment?"

Benji considered this. "By and large it delivered. The Pakis bought our equipment. And they got some training. But the entire relationship with Pakistan hasn't been smooth, as you know. Our issues with them are not exactly classified; the whole damn world knows those guys use and abuse us. So, what was intended as a PCCF carrot to get them in line basically turned into a spigot. They didn't really change their attitude but we keep sending shit. I hear the White House has pushed to kill next year's budget altogether."

"So the spigot is getting turned off next year?"

"That's what I'm hearing."

"Any funny business with the PCCF?"

"What do you mean?"

"No scandals? No skimming?"

"Nah, pretty much business as usual. USG buying arms from US manufacturers and sending it overseas to our Paki friends."

"That's a lot of money to US manufacturers."

"Yeah, I guess. Same shit different country. You know the drill."

"Got it." Cal hesitated. "And nothing weird going on with Blue Lantern in Pakistan last year?"

"I would think you Latin American guys have enough on your plate with Blue Lantern in Mexico to be worrying about Blue Lantern in Pakistan."

"Yeah, just covering all the bases."

Benji grunted. "The less I know the better."

"Just sniffing."

"Sniff all you like, but as far as anything I've heard, the PCCF is all systems go this year. And there are no issues with Blue Lantern."

"Ok, thanks, Benji. I appreciate the intel."

"Anytime. Cal, keep your head down over there for a bit. You're not exactly the Bureau's favorite guy right now."

"Yeah, that's the same advice the Director gave me."

"That guy's pretty sharp. What about those suits? Rumor has it he drops like a G on each. Can you imagine? Anyway, I recommend you do your time and then come on back in. We don't like to lose too many good ones. Even if they do narc on us once in a while."

After hanging up, Cal read the cable for a fourth time. Everything about the cable was routine. Nothing indicated a law had been broken. Nothing, in fact, in the content of the cable should have pricked an ATF agent's investigative curiosity. Especially a whistle-blowing agent currently on the back foot and hated by the Bureau's entire senior staff.

The fact that someone emailed him a Confidential State Department cable from a civilian, anonymous email was, however, astounding.

2

New York, NY

The doorman at the Bowery Hotel, wearing a long-tailed red jacket and a bowler hat, held the door as Mac walked into the lobby. She was instantly transported into a turn-of-the-century English manor. Dark, wood panels lined the walls. Chintz chairs and red velour sofas floated on a spacious oriental rug before a huge marble fireplace. A massive flower arrangement in reds and blues dominated a table by the front door. Soft, club music played in the background.

The Bowery Hotel is where the celebs go to hide out. As long as you are not a high profile celebrity, it's a good place to go unnoticed.

Mac stepped to the reception counter, slid off her wide, white sunglasses, patted her shoulder-length blond wig, grinned goofily, tilted her head and pitched her voice an octave higher. "Hi. Oh my God. There's a package here for me. Under Maar. M-A-A-R."

The receptionist returned with a small envelope. "Here you go."

Mac opened it, pulled out a license and a credit card and handed them back to the receptionist. With an exaggerated grimace and the same ditzy voice, she squeaked, "Oh my God. My wallet totally got stolen."

"Oh no!"

"Totally!" Another dramatic shake of her head and a wobble nod to the cards, she said, "But those are my replacements, so now I can check in."

The receptionist checked the new ID against her computer. "Well, welcome to the Bowery. You're all set."

Mac grinned widely, grabbed her room keys and wandered over to the elevators.

Inside the hotel room on the fifth floor, she pulled the duvet cover from the bed, folded it, and set it down on the closet floor. She glanced under all the lampshades and underneath the desk. She took out her cell phone, turned on the flash, and took a photo down the air vent placed high on the wall. The photo revealed an empty air duct.

Satisfied there was nothing overtly planted in the room, she picked up the bedside table phone, and dialed room service. "A jug of coffee, please. Thanks."

She threw her roller bag up on the bed, unzipped it, took out her cosmetics bag, and distributed her lotions and makeup along the marble and chrome console sink in the bathroom. She laid the shower mat down by the tub.

She placed her courier bag on the bedside table, dropped down onto the crisp sheets, grabbed the remote and flipped on the news. She unfolded seven *New York Posts* and set them across the bed. Flipping through the big, loose pages, she skimmed the stories.

Boy, 13, in gun attack: Brawl 'revenge'
A studious Harlem 13-year-old named Elmo coldly opened fire on a teen rival to avenge a humiliating beat down, sources said yesterday....

NYPD locks down Harlem neighborhood after fatal shooting
Metal barricades separate residents from street traffic. Visitors must pass through checkpoints manned by armed guards. Weary citizens feel like prisoners in their own homes....

At the knock on the door, she let in a waiter with a tray and handed him a tip on his way out. She peeled off her wig, settled back on the bed, poured her first coffee, and continued reading.

3   w o u n d e d   i n   H a r l e m   s h o o t i n g
A gunman shot three men across from a Harlem playground this afternoon, police said...

An hour later, she rummaged through her courier bag and

pulled out her laptop. She lifted the cover, logged into the hotel Wi-Fi, and clicked on Tor. The program would direct her internet surfing through a series of proxy servers and routers so that no one could track her IP address.

She pulled up the very boring Louisiana Secretary of State's official website, logged into the state database, and searched the names of private foundations. She did not find anything remotely similar to the name 'Julep Foundation'; she reserved it. She filled out Form 12:204, the Louisiana Articles of Incorporation, and used her new Visa card to pay the $75 application fee and the $30 fee for the 24-hour expedited process.

She clicked over to the IRS website and the online Form SS-4, an application for an Employer Identification Number. She filled out the application with the new Julep Foundation information and hit submit. A warning popped up on her screen: *"U.S. GOVERNMENT SYSTEM! Use of this system constitutes consent to monitoring, interception, recording, reading, copying or capturing by authorized personnel of all activities. Continue?"*

She hit the agreed button, smiling sardonically and thinking, *You have no idea.*

She poured coffee, leaned back against the bed's headrest, and typed in a new key word search. *"history US gun control"*

From behind a podium emblazoned with the New York City seal, Mayor Fisk was wrapping up a speech at City Hall to a room of journalists. He said, "This isn't an issue for tomorrow. It's an issue today. If Capitol Hill is hamstrung, we don't need to be. I'll take questions now." He scanned the crowd and nodded toward Freda. "First from the New York News."

"Thank you, Mayor." Freda held up her pen. "We've got new legislation making its way through the Senate. What do you say to those Senators that may not support it?"

"Good question. Two facts. One: the legislation coming before the Senate is common sense gun control. Two: a significant majority of Americans want common sense gun control. So, to any Senator against this legislation I would say, 'You aren't representing your constituents.' It's that straight forward."

The mayor fielded a few more questions then said, "That's all for today, folks. Thanks for coming."

Camera shutters clicked as he and his team exited. Journalists closed their notebooks and headed for the back doors.

Freda crooked her head to the young, intense woman next to her. "Let's go."

Ten minutes later, as the taxi fought its way up 8th Avenue, Freda said, "We need something on gun control."

Stacia's flat, Midwest accent was obscured by short, staccato bursts of speech. "There's a lot. A lot on gun control. Tired. Worn-out shit. On gun control."

"I know, that's the point. We need something fresh, leading up to this new assault weapons ban. We need to capture some attention."

Stacia pushed against the tortoise shell glasses on her small, pixie face and shifted in the stiff, black seat. "Please tell me... Please tell me you're not assigning me to bring the sexy back. To gun control."

"I am."

"This is what happens: there's a shooting in a school or a mall; the networks go on a frenzied, 24-hour cycle; ratings spike; people wait for gore and body counts; a day later they tune out. It doesn't affect them directly —"

"We need a new angle --"

"Unless it happens like three blocks away. Then maybe we pay attention. For 24 hours. Maybe. 24 max."

Freda regarded her patiently.

"Wait. Are you serious?" Stacia asked incredulously.

"Serious as a heart attack from the hundredth Big Mac. We need something new and intriguing on this"

A bike courier careened into their lane and the taxi driver slammed on the brakes, jostling them.

Sliding her glasses back up her nose, Stacia continued. "In no particular order. First, liberals have been fighting this fight - for what - a 100 years? Second, the Second Amendment says we can have guns. Third, the Society for Guns - SFG - is going to fight forever against any kind of regulation. Fourth, the SFG rates Senators and Congressmen on their gun records. Like report cards. Five, the SFG has a shitload of members and a shit ton of money. They're winning and it doesn't appear to change. That last one is number six. They're winning and that doesn't appear to be changing. What is new there? There is nothing intriguing about gun control. It's a lost cause."

It was end of the business day and crowds streamed from the back side of Penn Station forcing the taxi into stop-and-go lurches.

Freda softly said, "That's exactly what I would have said. But maybe they're not the elephant in the room we think they are."

"What are you thinking?"

"We assume their influence is huge. Maybe it isn't. Maybe it's smoke and mirrors. Let's dig into them. Let's start with the organization. How many active members? What are their demographics? Then let's look at their cash. How much do they really have? Where do they get it? Maybe they aren't as threatening as they claim to be." Freda looked over at Stacia. "I'm seeing potentially a front page series here. Yours."

"Jack won't let me. He's got it out for me."

"What?"

"He ignores me in Monday meetings. He walks right past me at the water fountain. He's never going to let me lead."

"He walks right past you at the water fountain?"

Stacia's jaw clenched. "Totally blanks me. Every time. I wait till he leaves his office then I hit the water fountain. He has to walk by me."

Freda's sarcasm dripped. "You could slip a note in his locker before gym class."

"I. Am. Not. Joking. You tell me how a 2nd year reporter on the city desk gets the attention of the Editor in Chief?"

"Wait, how old are you?"

"24"

"Jesus, what's the rush? You know how long I did local investigative before anyone moved me up to anywhere?"

"How long - in total - did it take you to get to be a managing editor?"

"15 years," Freda said proudly.

Stacia's face registered dramatic shock.

Freda protested. "I'm only 44! I'm the youngest managing editor the paper has ever had!"

"Practically 12 Years a Slave." Stacia gave a sad, slow shake. "A lifetime."

"Your generation…is so… impatient."

"And I bet if you were a guy, you would have gotten there faster."

"What do you mean?"

"It's still a man's world. That's all I'm saying."

Exasperated, Freda looked out the window.

Stacia mumbled, "I'll do it."

"Of course you will. It's a great opportunity."

"Jack won't like it."

"Leave Jack to me. It's my front page."

Stacia gave her a questioning look.

"Holy Mother of crap on a crepe," Freda responded. "It's my front page. How 'bout you just do your job and we get the story out there?"

"Ok. I'll do it."

"I know you will. I'm not asking you, by the way, I'm telling you."

"I said I'll do it," Stacia mumbled again.

"I know you will."

3

New York, NY

At 2 a.m., Mac opened the window, letting the fresh air chill her skin. She squeezed her strained eyes and soaked in the sounds of the city's nightly rituals. A vehicle revved loudly as it battled into second gear. Heavy wooden crates crashed onto the sidewalk. A block away, a warning blared as a delivery truck reversed.

She lit a cigarette and slowly blew the smoke out the window. Her mind settled around what she had learned.

The United States had only passed nine national gun laws.

The first was passed in 1934 (The National Firearms Act) during prohibition to rein in gangster violence, making it difficult to obtain especially lethal guns (sawed-off long rifles, shotguns and machine guns) and regulating concealed weapons.

It would take another thirty years and the assassinations of Jack F. Kennedy, Martin Luther King, and Robert Kennedy to reignite interest in regulating civilian gun use. A 1968 law (The Gun Control Act) established a number of regulations on civilian purchase and use: prohibiting convicted felons from owning firearms; requiring licenses to buy or sell guns; and introducing procedures to track serial numbers and control imports. Four years later, the Bureau for Alcohol, Tobacco and Firearms - initially a division of the IRS within the Treasury Department - was created to enforce these new regulations.

Five hours later she still hadn't slept.

She opened the window for another cigarette. On the television, the local newscaster was discussing another Harlem shooting. She turned up the volume.

She searched for the incident on the internet, scribbled down the address. She took a quick shower and threw on jeans, a t-shirt, a windbreaker and a baseball hat. She grabbed her courier bag, dropped in her cell phone, a notebook, a pen, her wallet, a bottle of water, and a protein bar.

In the heart of SoHo, on the corner of Broad and Waverly, she stepped into a healthy fast-food chain and ordered a salad full of quinoa and kale. Certain foods were hard to get overseas. She took a leap of faith and ordered a wheatgrass shot.

She sat with her tray at the corner window watching the morning crowd - an anonymous melting pot of whites, Asians, blacks, and Hispanics - stream by. She was mesmerized by the variety. A woman in a flamboyant combination of pink and leather stepped around a tall, dark man in a lumberjack jacket. Teen girls with enormous, dangling earrings and lengthy hair-weaves giggled past suited businessmen.

She picked up the shot of wheatgrass, stared at it a long time, then swallowed it back. The tangy, bitter aftertaste of a freshly mowed lawn lingered in her mouth.

This may be home, but much of it felt shockingly new to her.

Out on Broadway, the towering buildings blocked out the sun as she hailed a cab. The driver's accent was West African, probably Gabon.

To his reflection in the rearview mirror she said, "First stop: corner of 8th Ave and West 155th."

He nodded, unfazed, and pulled out into northbound traffic.

She added, "I'm going to need you for a few hours."

He nodded again.

"Take the side streets. I want to see the neighborhoods."

They traveled through midtown, then up by Central Park. The commuter traffic was heavy, hulking SUVs commanded many of the lanes.

She asked, "How much do you pay for a gallon of gas?"

"$4.50"

"How much is it to fill up this car?"

"About $50."

"How far do you get on that?"

"A few hours driving."

She did the math in her head. "So an SUV must pay like $75 for a tank and it gives them probably two to three hours of driving."

He shrugged. He wasn't a conversationalist.

She got lost in memories of Iraq.

When she looked up again, they were driving through Morningside Heights and past Columbia University. The sidewalks were busy with college students. Restaurants were squeezed between high-rise apartment buildings. Here, the all-night corner stores had bars on their windows.

She leaned her head back against the taxi seat. Her mind revisited what she had read last night.

It would be another fourteen years before Congress revisited gun regulation. A 1984 law (The Armed Career Criminal Act) enhanced penalties for felons using firearms if convicted of certain crimes three or more times.

In response to an overzealous ATF, a 1986 law (The Firearms Owners' Protection Act) actually eased restrictions on gun sellers and sales (licensed dealers could operate outside the stores, for example at gun shows; allowed ammunition sales without licenses; and excluded hobbyists from regulations.) The 1986 law, however, did ban the manufacture of fully automatic rifles - machine guns - for the civilian market.

In 1990, a new law established "drug-free school zones" and criminal penalties for guns near a school. It also outlawed the assembly of certain illegal semi-automatic rifles or shotguns from legally imported parts.

After a seven-year legislative battle, the 1993 Brady Handgun Violence Prevention Act was passed, requiring background checks for firearms purchases.

Two 1994 laws (The Violent Crime Control and Law Enforcement Act and The Youth Handgun Safety Act) increased fees and required photographs and fingerprints to obtain a dealer's license, banned possession of handguns for those under 18, and prohibited adults from transferring guns to juveniles.

Outside the taxi window, they had descended into Harlem's urban decay. There were no commuter crowds here. On the sidewalks, people walked with less impatience. Houses had been boarded up: some were torched, others were simply abandoned. Young teens cruised past on motorbikes, alert for drug buyers or police.

Unlike the times when she had walked down the red dirt streets of Johannesburg's Soweto or through the stench of Manila's Smokey Mountain landfill, today she was not a dispassionate observer. Today she felt more American, more invested, than she had in a long time.

The taxi driver slowed, pulled over at her destination.

She said, "Give me 10 minutes."

He nodded, put on the radio, and cranked back his seat.

She walked slowly towards the Polo Grounds Tower, a housing project complex of four, 30-story buildings that sat on a brown, scrubby lot next to the elevated Harlem River Drive. Now home to robberies, shootings, murders and gang activity, the lot used to be the home of the New York Giants.

She reached the black fence along the perimeter of the bleak towers and stared past a decrepit sign. She imagined the scene that must have unfolded yesterday in a 5th floor apartment.

Returning home early from school, 10-year-old Anna walked into a screaming match between her brother and mother. Anna's brother, his face contorted in rage, reached into the closet and pulled out a large, matte-black assault weapon. Anna froze by the door. Her mother wailed in fear. He shouldered the rifle, wrapped his left hand around the ridged barrel, and placed his right hand around the trigger. Cartridges sped through the barrel with a zap zap zap and spewed out the top. Her mother flew across the room, bullets slamming into her. Empty cartridges rained on the floor. The gun turned, pointing at Anna. The bullets ripped into her chest. The floor met her. A warmth spread across her stomach, a chill across her chest. In her ears, Anna's heart slowed.

At the fence, Mac stooped down and picked up a small, round rock. She slid it into her pocket and turned her back on the housing complex.

In the taxi, she said, "I need to go to Connecticut. To Newtown."

The last US gun law was passed in 1994. It banned semi-automatic guns that resembled fully automatic 'machine guns' in the sense that they had detachable magazines and two other characteristics (such as a telescoping stock or a flash suppressor.) It was called The Assault Weapons Ban. It had a 2004 expiration date.

Newtown, CT

Mac approached the school from across a green, sports pitch set among lush trees. Clover overran the field; tall stalks thrust up white, spindled flowers above the grass. Her foot struck a partially buried baseball diamond. With long, unhurried strides she carried on toward the empty parking lot in the distance.

She reached the drive and followed the arc of the bus route. At the fence, next to a demolition crane, she stopped and stared at the red brick building. The front had once been a wall of glass. Now it was boarded up with plywood. Stenciled metal letters read Sandy Hook Elementary. She listened for the sounds of birds or crickets, heard nothing.

Glancing back down the drive, she imagined the scenes as they would have unfurled that day.

A 20-year-old dressed in black shirt, sneakers and fingerless gloves, stomped toward the school, green utility vest swinging bulkily around his thin body. He reached the school, heard the sounds of playful screeches bouncing off tiled walls and bells chiming across the intercom. He lifted the weight of the matte black, semi-automatic Bushmaster rifle. He shot through the security door.

The principal and the school psychologist stepped into the lobby to investigate the noise. He shot and killed them.

Two other staff members were shot in the hallway.

Across the school, teachers heard the shots and ushered students into bathrooms and closets, hiding them and distracting them with reading and drawing

He entered two, first-grade classrooms in rapid order, spraying bullets from the assault weapon, as if on a battlefield.

In one room, he killed a substitute teacher, a behavioral therapist, and 15 first graders. A six-year-old girl that played dead was the only class survivor.

In another, he shot the teacher and killed five children. He shot a behavioral therapist and the six-year-old boy she had been shielding. Nine children fled. Two survived by hiding in a classroom bathroom.

The school's custodian ran through hallways, alerting classrooms. The school librarians hid 18 children in a storage room. One teacher and one reading specialists pulled children out of hallways.

Ten minutes after the carnage had begun, the 20-year-old placed a Glock 20 to his head and ended his rampage with one shot.

Mac blinked, her focus returned. She turned and began a slow march across the field. The research from last night looped in her mind. Following the shooting at Sandy Hook Elementary, the US Senate again failed to pass any new legislation governing guns.

In the middle of the field, Mac slowed to watch a cloud pass in front of the sun. Up ahead, the taxi driver watched her. Something caught her eye in the tall grass; a plastic, pink barrette rested among green stalks. It was an inch long with the imprint of a small flower. She picked it up and slipped it into her pocket.

4

New York, NY

The Italian restaurant on Bond and Bowery played to rustic Mediterranean roots with exposed brick walls, single candles burning on simple, metal plates, and deeply scarred wooden tables. The air in the small space was heavy with garlic, basil, and tomato. At the corner table near the kitchen, Penny and Freda huddled over red wine glasses and a ceramic bowl of olives.

They jumped to their feet when Mac walked through the door.

Penny gave her a tight hug. "Oh my God, it's been way too long."

Freda leaned in for an efficient hug and cheek kiss. "I can't believe you're home."

Mac was stiff and nervous, her movements jerky.

Penny motioned to the table. "Sit, sit, let me get you a glass of wine."

Mac forced her shoulders to relax. "Yeah, good I guess. It's weird to be here after such a long time. Twenty years. Some things are exactly the same. Some things are completely different."

They wanted to understand, but couldn't.

She shook off their confusion. "Let's start with you guys. That'll be easier. How are the kids? I want to hear it all."

An hour and a second bottle later, Penny turned confidential. "So. I guess it's time to ask. We've always suspected but never knew. You're CIA, right?"

Mac ran her finger over a large crack in the roughhewn table. The candle between them sputtered. The word stuck in her throat.

"Yes."

Penny said, "I knew it."

Freda's mind started running. "I have a million questions."

"I'm not sure I can answer them. A lot of stuff I can't tell you."

Penny asked, "So where have you been?"

"Mostly Asia. Sometimes the Middle East."

"Scary places?"

"Yeah, some of them."

"What can you tell us?"

Mac turned thoughtful. "Technically, I'm what is known as a Human Intelligence Operations Officer. I spend a lot of time building relationships with well-placed foreigners and eventually try to convince them to become agents for the US. If they do, then I manage them."

"You 'run' them," said Penny.

Mac smiled. "I gather information - information the President needs to defend this country. It's anything from security to military to tech to economic. Langley gives me directions and off I go. I'm alone a lot. I travel a ton." She shrugged, playing down the job. "To be fair, it's a lot of down time."

Freda shook her head. "Mac from Germantown, as we live and breath, sitting in front of us telling us she's a CIA agent. H to the hella."

Over her wine, glass Mac mumbled, "Officer."

"Right, I meant officer. The foreign guys are the agents."

Penny was subdued. "It's just like we've always suspected."

"Yeah, a bit weird for me too."

"Really?"

Mac admitted, "Yeah, it's not like I talk about this stuff all the time. It's a bit…no, it's a lot - disorienting. I've spent a lot of time concealing the truth."

"So did they train you in firearms?"

"They trained me in all kinds of things."

Freda asked, "Have you ever killed anyone?"

Her shoulders tightened. "Indirectly, yes."

"Does that bother you?"

"A lot of things bother me."

An hour later, a third bottle of wine was nearly empty. They had caught up on the gossip about high school friends and careers. Penny and Freda had shown Mac videos and pictures of their kids.

The front door of the restaurant opened and the three women watched two couples, laughing over a shared joke, enter the restaurant. The hostess seated them four tables away.

Penny asked. "Do they know you're here, in the US?"

"No. Not yet," Mac replied.

"How long before they figure it out?"

"I have a lot of room. That's the nature of the job. They think I'm deep cover in Asia. They'll reach out to me in about 2 weeks. When I don't answer, they'll start looking for me."

"Then you'll check back in?"

Mac shrugged. "I haven't decided."

Surprised, Penny asked, "You might quit?"

"I'm thinking about it."

Penny lowered her voice. "Did you get the money?"

Mac nodded.

"How did it go?"

"Swiss bankers are enormous kiss asses. I showed up, flashed a fake id, they handed me a cashier's check."

"As easy as that? Money is cleaned?"

"As easy as that."

Freda asked, "How did you know our donor would have a Swiss bank account?"

Mac said, "First of all I know the donor is Laura."

Both women were startled. Penny tried to cover. "What? Wait --"

Mac interrupted, "Don't tell me any more. Laura's secret is safe with me. And all rich folks have Swiss bank accounts."

Freda moaned. "God, I feel so poor. I should never have gone into journalism."

Penny assuaged her. "I'm a freaking litigation lawyer for a top law firm and I don't have a Swiss bank account. That's for the super wealthy only, Freda."

Mac interrupted their banter. "So, tell me what you're thinking."

"In theory, it's quite simple," Penny said as she sat upright in her chair. "Senator Martha Payne is introducing a new bill, an assault weapons ban. When it hits the Senate floor, we need to give the Senators the freedom to vote the way their constituents want."

Freda leaned on the table. "Mac, we need you to put the SFG out of commission long enough for the Payne bill to pass."

"What's my deadline?" Mac asked.

Freda said, "The bill is in the Senate Judiciary Committee. It's due to pass out and go to the Senate floor in four weeks."

Mac nodded slowly. "Ok."

In that moment, the restaurant went silent as the two couples started eating.

Freda and Penny stared at Mac.

Freda whispered, "Just like that?"

"My work will be done in four weeks."

Freda's eyes went wide. "Christ, I'm glad nobody else is hiring your type in the US."

Mac continued, "I'll do this on one condition. You tell no one. I mean no one. From this moment forward you never mention this. Not to your husbands or your boyfriends. No one. Ever."

Freda held up her hand. "Not a problem here."

"That means we did not have this conversation. I am a friend from high school that you hear from once in a while. These drinks, this night. Sure." She looked around at the almost empty restaurant. "We met up. We ate olives and drank red wine. We caught up on gossip and old boyfriends and who is married to whom. We never had any conversation about anything serious. We didn't discuss politics or guns. Can you do that? Complete lock down?"

They both nodded.

"If you break this code, I'll disappear and you'll never hear from me again. What we're talking about is illegal. If they find me, they'll find you and you'll go to jail and never see your kids again. We're about to irretrievably cross a line into some serious shit that I take very seriously and for which the US government has spent a lot of time training me very seriously. This is big girls playing with the real wolves." Mac stood up. "I've gotta use the bathroom. Take a minute and make sure you're in. 150%. If you have doubts, now is the time to pull out. We can go back to wine and charcuterie."

When she sat back down ten minutes later, Freda said, "You

know I'm in, of course. Penny's in too."

Mac hailed the waitress and ordered desert and coffee for the table. She pulled out two cheap cell phones and placed one in front of each woman. "From this point forward this is the only way you communicate with me. I've loaded them up. If you need me, text or call me. I'm the only number in there. If I tell you to get rid of the phone, immediately flush the sim card down the toilet, wipe the fingerprints from the phone, and drop it in a public trash bin. On the street kinda public. Not in your offices."

Freda grinned. "All spy-like."

"These are just basic precautions. NSA, NSC, CIA, MSS, phone companies, internet companies - they know everything. So we go basic: we stay off the grid. They don't have as many foot soldiers as they do tech guys these days."

Penny whispered, "Who is they?"

"All of them. Depends on whose business we disturb."

Freda eyed Mac. "Did you just say MSS - as in the Chinese?"

Mac nodded.

"Jesus. I'm a managing editor at the New York News and I'm sure - that compared to what you know, I'm a babe in the woods." She asked, "When do you start?"

"You don't need to know that."

Freda said, "We know why we're doing this. Mac, why are you doing this?"

Mac watched the smoke rise from the flickering candle. "Two reasons. First, my two closest friends asked me. And I learned last night that more Americans have been killed by guns in the US than have died in all of this country's wars. I didn't spend my adult life overseas defending a country that's killing its own damn self."

5

Lexington, KY

The low, red brick building sat in a valley between two rolling green hills, hidden from the road to Lexington. A long driveway meandered past a modern, Plexiglass signboard with brushed, silver letters that read Scimitar Defense Ltd.

In the lot, Mac pulled up next to a brand-new, tan Porsche Panamera parked in the single VIP spot. She stepped out of her red, rented sedan as a blue-eyed blond in a tight fitting pale pink sweater stretched across a C-cup. The sticky Kentucky summer heat enveloped her. She gently smoothed down a fitted, print miniskirt.

She sauntered through the glass door into a chilly reception area. A low hum buzzed from a distant manufacturing floor.

She reached the reception desk and smiled at the young woman. In a thick, southern Louisiana drawl, she announced, "I'm hear to see your CFO. I'm from the accountants." Just as the receptionist picked up the receiver on her desk phone, Mac leaned over conspiratorially. "But can I use your little ladies' room first?"

The receptionist smiled sympathetically and pointed down a side hallway. "Of course. It's just down that hall. Second door on your right."

Mac blinked her heavily mascaraed eyes. "Lifesaver! Thank you!"

She sashayed down the hall on tall, wedge heels, swinging her pink handbag.

Glancing back over her shoulder, she confirmed the hallway was empty and stepped into the bathroom. It also was empty. In the last stall, she unraveled half a roll of toilet paper and flushed it. Unsatisfied, she unrolled the rest of the roll and flushed this. On a third attempt, the toilet backed up, water roiled over, and a lake spread across the tiles, beyond the stall walls.

She counted silently to ten.

She slammed open the bathroom door and rushed down the hall. She turned the corner flapping her hands. "Oh my god. You have to come help me. The toilet! It's backed up!"

The receptionist jumped up, hurried past her, and dashed down the hall.

Mac squeaked, "Last stall. Oh my god."

The receptionist threw open the bathroom door and rushed in.

Mac quietly returned to the empty lobby, stepped behind the desk, lifted the phone receiver, and dialed an international number. On the third ring, a deep voice answered with an Arabic accent. "Hallo?"

Holding the receiver to her ear, Mac stretched the phone's cord as she peeked around the corner and down the hallway. From behind the bathroom door, she heard the receptionist pumping a plunger and muttering, "Stop stop stop."

In her ear, the male voice grew insistent. "Hallo? Hallo?"

Mac slowly set the receiver back down on the cradle. From the side pocket of her pink handbag, she pulled out the business card from the Zurich art gallery and carefully placed it in the receptionist's pen holder.

She walked out the lobby door, back into the summer heat.

Two hours later, Mac watched the tan sports car speed past her on the country road to Lexington. She set off after it in the rental car. Other than a few cars passing in the oncoming lane, the road was empty. She hung back and let the sports car take the curves out of line-of-sight. The road was a straight shot into Lexington with only dirt turn-offs; she wouldn't lose the sports car.

Ten minutes later, she watched the Porsche slow and pull into the gravel parking lot of a country bar. It was a ramshackle, wood planked building with peeling paint. High in the peak of the weathered roof, a neon light blinked weakly in the late afternoon sun announcing the bar's name as 'Homers'.

Out on the road to Lexington, she cruised past the driveway for another three miles then circled back. She pulled into the far corner of the parking lot, her tires crunching gravel.

Five minutes later, she pulled open the bar door and squinted into the dark interior. The bar was carpeted, dimly lit, and smoky. The banjo of an Earl Scruggs tune crackled through speakers set high on chipped walls. Above the bar, a small television was muted to a football game. Red helmets and white jerseys huddled on a lined field. The score read Alabama 42, Georgia 24.

She recognized him right away. He was sitting toward the back of the room, facing the door, with his arm stretched along the top of a brown, vinyl booth. His white button-down shirt was open at the collar. He was chatting with two men across from him.

He glanced up as sunlight momentarily streamed through the door. She held his gaze, inhaling and exhaling for two beats, long enough to convey her interest.

She closed the door behind her, sauntered up to the bar, and leaned against it slightly, lengthening her legs. She could feel his eyes on her.

The bartender was an older man with a huge grey beard and the blank look of someone who long ago replaced dreams with monotony. He took her order with disinterest.

She sipped her drink while scanning the bar, then followed the sound of a pool game into a back room.

The white button-down watched her pass.

In the back room, two young men looked up as she entered. She placed four quarters on the pool table rail, eyed them over her drink, and grinned around her straw. "I've got winners."

Fifteen minutes later, she had the two young men gossiping about their work at the gun factory.

The skinny redhead was more generous. "It's not a bad job. The owner's ok."

The shorter one smirked. "No he ain't, Sam. He's just as cocky as any rich man round here."

The redhead nodded to the bar room. "That's him out there."

"Where?" Mac asked.

"That one in the fancy white, work shirt."

Just then, the white button-down rose, palmed his drink, and turned. He stepped into the back room and nodded to the two young men. "Hi Johnny, Sam. How's it going?" Without waiting for an answer, he turned to Mac and offered his hand. "I'm Chuck Boare."

Squeezing his hand, she said in a perfect, polished Southern accent, "How do you do, Mr. Boare?"

"Please call me Chuck. Can I buy you a drink?"

Mac ignored the young, gaping men. "Absolutely."

Up close, she noticed he wasn't bad looking. He had really good teeth; they were incredibly white. But his brown eyes were red rimmed, his hair was thinning, his chin was weak and he had the mild bloat of someone who enjoyed the good life. She noticed his cell phone was clipped to the back of his belt in a tacky man-holster.

At the bar, he pulled out a stool for her. "You're not from here. We don't see a lot of DX ladies round here."

"DX?"

He offered a dramatic but insincere apology. "Sorry. I work in the defense industry. It's sector speak for priority."

She acted confused.

"Sorry, sorry. I'm a contractor to the Department of Defense up in Washington."

"Wow."

"My company supplies the military complex. DX is the designation for top priority items. The President can tell me an order is DX and I have to produce it for the Department of Defense first. As in pronto. You know, in the name of national security. When we sign those contracts it's stipulated that if our country, our boys, need something right away, we give 'em what they need. That's the way it works in times of war or peace."

"Department of Defense?" She turned her body toward him, touching his lower arm. "That's so, I dunno, manly."

"Let me tell you, it's a very, very necessary part of protecting the USA." His bluster amped up. "Protecting Americans every day. There are a lot of bad guys out there. Sometimes we feel like we're just holding back the tide. Then other days you feel like we're winning the war."

"Huh." She glanced at her empty glass. "And what kind of stuff do you make, if I can ask?"

He followed her glance. "Where are my manners? What are you drinking, little lady?"

"A rum and diet Coke would be lovely. Thanks, Chuck." Standing, she whispered in his ear. "Let me go powder my nose in the little girls' room. I'll be right back and you can tell me how manly it all is."

His breath caught. He didn't notice her hand unclip his cell phone.

In the bathroom, she scanned under the four stall doors. The room was empty.

She dialed the same international number from memory and the familiar male voice answered. "Hallo? Hallo?" She waited a few minutes, then closed the phone.

Back at the bar, she slide her arm around Chuck's thick waist, leaned into his ear, and whispered, "I'm staying at the Hilton in Lexington." She slipped his cell phone back in the holster. "I'm sure there is somewhere nicer in town for a DX lady like me and a hot-shot defense guy like you. Give me a ten minute lead time to freshen up? Meet you in the lobby?"

This time he didn't miss a beat. "Done, little lady." To the bartender he said, "You know what, Homer? Hold that order." Turning back to Mac, he said, "Wait, I didn't even get your name."

"Isn't that a cliffhanger?" She grinned, kissed his cheek, grabbed her pink handbag, and paraded out, all eyes on her.

Thirty minutes later, she dropped the red rental car at the Lexington airport and got the next flight New Orleans.

6

New York, NY

Penny stepped into the bright and airy Jean Gorges restaurant on 18th and Park and saw Laura Franklin at a far corner near a whitewashed brick wall. As she reached the table, she leaned in for a kiss. "My gorgeous Laura. It's been ages! How are you sweetheart?"

Laura, a heavyset black woman with fire in her eyes, planted a kiss on Penny's cheek. "Fine, fine. All good."

Settling into her chair, Penny eyed her. "Seriously, how's it all going?"

Laura released a long breath. "It's going, that's for sure."

"You getting any time off?"

"At this stage? Definitely not."

"Is the IPO that bad?"

"Endless. Bankers. Lawyers. Shareholders. Endless"

"How's the new house?"

"Huge. It's insane. I can't believe we bought it. What is a childless, black, lesbian couple doing buying a house on the white Upper West Side? When you coming up?"

"Right? And who's got time? Tell you what, you two have a house warming and I'll bring some insanely priced Napa wine."

"Deal."

A waiter recited the specials and they both ordered lunch salads. Penny asked, "How's Harriette?"

"Fine, fine, always fine. I've got her managing the contractors in the house. How's Kenneth?"

"Yeah, ok. He's working on a new script. His bullshit agent got him something…I dunno."

"So, same?" Laura shook her head sadly.

"Yeah, it's all the same."

"The boys? Good?"

"Crazy good. Thanks."

"The job?"

"Good. Tough. But good. We're getting in some interesting work. I just pulled in a new client that I should keep me really busy."

Laura took a sip of water, flashed her eyebrows. "And it's still good being the senior chick partner in the litigation department?"

"So far, so good. You still hear horror stories, but I think the boys are starting to take us seriously."

"From your lips to God's ears."

An hour later, over post-lunch lattes Penny mused. "I want to be happy. I'm just not sure I know what would get me there."

"Well, it can be, what? Home, job, hobbies, or family?"

"Right?" Penny gazed across the white tablecloths at the posh, smiling women 'doing lunch'. Her mind wandered to another place and time. A Princess Diana look-alike gracefully climbed out of a taxi, glided up the steps of a stately brownstone, breezed through a grand front door, and swept into a black-and-white marbled foyer. The socialite called out cheerfully, "I'm home!" A butler floated in with a pink cocktail on a silver platter. A cultured husband met her in an opulent library, heady with the smell of roses, where the two fell into a long, loving embrace. They settled into big chairs by the fire and regaled each other with their days' stories.

Laura broke through Penny's distraction and asked, "Right?"

Penny startled. "Right. So my job is fine. Home. Fine. Boys, check. It's just, you know, Kenneth. How many couples that have survived more than fourteen years are truly happy together?"

"What does 'truly happy' mean?"

"Like in the movies. Love."

They both paused, scanning mental rolodexes of couples they knew.

Penny looked over the table. "I know one couple out of all my friends that truly seem to still be in the kind of honeymoon love.

Not that totally fake Facebook-happy, show-and-tell shit. I mean, they really do love each other. They're happy to be together all the time, they aren't resentful."

Laura was shaking her head. "I don't know one couple I can say that about."

"You realize we just admitted neither of us thinks the other is still truly in love with their partner?"

They let the moment pass.

Laura mused, "Maybe it's about just settling in? I mean, maybe it's not so bad to be comfortable and settled. Maybe that honeymoon love isn't a brass ring you can actually grab. Maybe it's something you aim for, but in not getting it, you find some comfort in the trying? I don't know."

A waiter swept past them with a loaded tray of food for another table. Laura changed the subject. "How's *it* going?"

"So far so good. Except…"

"What?"

"She guessed that you're the bank roll."

Laura let out a deep, heart-felt laugh that crinkled her eyes and pushed up her round cheeks. "Well at least we don't have a *dumb* CIA spook on the case. She always was a quick learn, from what I remember."

"You're not pissed?"

"Pissed? Moi? Nah, I'm ok with her knowing." Laura grinned. "Who she gonna tell?"

"Are you nervous?"

Laura considered this. "I would normally be. But over the last year or two I've realized you have to take risks. Avoiding risk means you avoid opportunity. I would like to believe the risk on this one is minimal. It will be very difficult to prove it was my money. And I've got lots of folks I can throw at the problem if it does erupt. End of story." She gave Penny a meaningful look. "You, however, have fewer resources and are a direct link to Mac."

Penny set down her napkin, avoiding the comment. "You watching the legislation?"

"Of course. They think it has another three weeks till floor vote, right? She's on it, right?"

Penny nodded.

"What's our weak link?"

Penny paused. "I'm actually not sure. If she gets caught, it would be Mac."

"What happens if she does get caught?"

"I don't know."

"Do you know her plan?"

"No. I don't. I don't even know if she has a Plan B."

"Do you know if she has an escape route?"

"No."

"We don't know much, do we?"

"No." Looking directly at Laura, Penny said, "Maybe that's not such a bad thing."

"Did she get the funds?"

"Yes. Thank you." Penny placed her hand on Laura's hand. "Sincerely."

"Don't mention it. Except around Mac." Laura winked. "Since she already knows and all."

The new New York News building was a modern glass structure in Midtown. Inside, the newsroom was a brightly lit, open-plan floor topped with a two-story atrium. The space was dominated by splashes of red and white across walls, floors, and desks. Reporters were either talking loudly into phones, slurping coffee, banging on keyboards, or rubbing foreheads. A television droned in a far corner.

In a cubicle in the middle of the newsroom, Stacia's eyes were watery from the strain of staring at an endless stream of websites. She had started researching early this morning and it was already 6 p.m.

On her screen was the home page for the SFG. Across the top of the screen were tabs for additional open sites. In total, the SFG had 45 separate websites. The main portals were the SFG home page, the site for the lobbying arm called the SFG Lobby, the SFG Foundation, the SFG Museum, the SFG Legal Fund, SFG Insurance, and the SFG Store. There were also sites for SFG country music, SFG television programming, and the *SFG News*. And yet another separate site was dedicated to an annual meeting.

It had taken her three hours to read through them all. She was engorged with information and seeped in resentment.

She stood, placed her Mont Blanc pen in her jeans' pocket, grabbed her wallet, and headed to the elevators.

On the 7th floor, she walked into the cafeteria, passing dozens of empty, white, round tables buoyed on an expanse of red carpet.

Back in the elevator heading up, she sipped a low fat latte and read through her cell phone. She had gotten a text from her scatterbrained - yet incredibly smart - roommate Charlotte. *"Happy Hour @ Ninos."*

She typed back, *"Can't. Working a lead."*

"Hotshot reporter. :(Don't work too late."

She opened up Facebook and saw Charlotte had posted, *"Any and all - heading to Ninos Happy Hour."*

She posted, *"Slackers."*

Heading back through the packed newsroom she proudly soaked in the cacophony; it seemed like there were reporters here around the clock.

Two years ago, interviewing with five reporters and ten department editors, she had pushed - her voice trembling at points - to position herself as the thoughtful, focused side of the new, distracted generation. They had liked her college investigative reporting on food waste. They had been impressed with her "Punk Politics" blog expounding on the political messages in punk and grunge music. Freda had liked her spunk, her grit.

In the end, she knew it had also been part luck and part good timing that had gotten her the job. She was glad she got in when she did. Now, rumors were flying through the 1,000 New York News reporters that more 'ambush layoffs' are coming in the face of downturns in both print subscription and digital revenue.

Despite the rumors, Stacia was hungry to move up the ladder, to prove herself. It was ambition mixed with raw passion. She woke up every morning churning ideas about how to better distill the news and how to better clarify the confusing for a generation that worked on sound bites.

At her desk, she gently placed her coffee and pen on her blotter. Her very traditional industrialist father had gifted her the pen from its regular spot inside his business suit jacket. It had been his sign of respect for her move to the big city.

She slowly bent over, setting her hands on either side of her feet. A few older reporters looked up in amusement; this wasn't the first time she had done yoga at work. She walked her hands forward along the grey carpet in front of her desk and held a Downward Dog for five minutes, concentrating only on her breathing, allowing her brain to clear.

Standing, she snapped each of her fingers one at a time, stretching out the stiffness.

Then she sat down with a quiet mind.

There were only four reasons a membership non-profit organization would have such a dizzying array of sites. She picked up the Mont Blanc and broke ground on the blank paper in front of her:

1. To confuse their members.
2. To confuse the public and their opponents.
3. To confuse the IRS.
4. To appeal to a broad audience: each audience only gets part of the messaging

On her screen, she pulled up a new folder and gave it a name, '*SFG Research.*' With quick, sharp keystrokes she started conceptualizing her sound bites based on the day's research: *Franchise. Opportunistic. Delusions of Grandeur. Dominance. Monopoly. Shadowy.*

Two hours later, while chatting on the phone and looking through her office window to the building across the street, Freda felt the nagging sense of a presence in her office. She slowly spun her chair. On the office guest chair, Stacia sat crossed legged with both hands resting on her knees, middle fingers to thumbs, eyes closed, her glasses pushed up into her spiky, black hair.

Freda spoke softly into the phone. "Uh, listen, someone's just walked into my office. I've gotta take this. I'll call you back." She hung up, shaking her head at Stacia. "Ok stealth yogi. What is it?"

Stacia opened her eyes slowly and said, "Just trying to keep you posted on the big SFG story."

"Ok, go ahead."

Stacia dropped her hands to grab a document off a table and handed Freda a printed timeline. "First of all, looks like the radical, zealous gun rights group we know today as the SFG, wasn't always so radical or zealous or hell-bent on opposing gun restrictions."

Freda read through the timeline.

Stacia continued, "In fact, the SFG supported controls on guns all the way up to about the 1980s at which point they seized on the language in the Second Amendment as their raison d'être. They spent the 80s and 90s focussing on legislation and preventing gun control."

Freda faked anticipation: none of this was new to her.

"In 1998 they elected the current CEO, Charles Osbourne." Stacia looked up. "Who we know is a bit off script --"

"I need something new other than Osbourne is a jackass." Freda looked at her expectantly.

"That's what I've got so far on their history."

Freda sighed. "I'm not sure you should have interrupted me for a history lesson. That was mildly interesting but nothing really new."

"Well, then let me give you some numbers. In 1973 a half of all American households had a gun. Now it's only one third. That's a significant decline. Of that, only about 6% of households own 65% of those guns."

"So civilians interested in guns in America is declining? That's also only mildly interesting."

"And hunting? Forget about it. Only 6% of Americans hunt even once a year. Nobody, nobody, hunts anymore. It's not clear to me why the SFG keeps blathering on about hunting." She read from her notes. "An astounding number of Americans support some regulation. One poll found 92% of Americans support background checks for gun purchases. Even gun owners want better regulation."

Freda waited impatiently.

"So here's what's really interesting: just as Americans are buying, owning and using less guns, the SFG's power is on the rise. Their budget quadrupled - quadrupled - in the 2000s. The SFG is now the one of the most influential lobbyist on Capitol Hill. They power is disproportionate, steady, strong, and consistent. Their increasing influence is actually counter-intuitive to what is happening on the ground in terms of gun ownership."

Freda tilted her head with an 'and then?' gesture.

Stacia looked at her notes and shrugged. "That's it so far."

Freda steepled her fingers, her condescension was thick. "So thanks for that history lesson, my young Jedi. None of that is news or investigative journalism. Please go back to your desk and find me the messy. Go attack this like a garbage bag on a Christmas wreathe."

Freda picked up the phone, spun her chair, and dialed back her previous caller. As the call rang through, she held her hand over the receiver and yelled over her shoulder to Stacia's retreating back, "We need to know how these guys have such a stranglehold on America *now*!"

7

New Orleans, LA

Mac had extensive training in firearms, but she had never been to a gun show. She stepped into the air-conditioned hall and did a quick assessment of the 100 tables neatly laid out in rows inside the 60 x 60 square foot room. Over 80 customers, pallid in the bad lighting, walked slowly down the aisles, speaking in hushed voices. The air was ripe with the smell of metal and beef jerky.

She made a wry face when her mind connected sport hunting to beef jerky.

Across the hall, men lifted and sighted guns with a confidence born from watching Hollywood action movies. Most of them fit into stereotypes. The shuffling Louisiana hillbillies stood out right away; they were gaunt, dirty, tattooed and unshaven. The old timers wore outdated gear and congregated by the antique paraphernalia. The preppy bubbas sported bright golf shirts and conversed animatedly with the sellers about gun specs. There were a few military and outdoorsy types. At one table, a trio of well-dressed black men were getting background checked by a white guy wearing a Nazi t-shirt.

She passed a hulk of a man explaining the virtues of a particular box of ammo to a customer. His voice was scratchy. "These are the best from Nevada. You can shoot for an hour straight and no failures."

She stepped between two men to examine a table of assault weapons. The young guy to her left hefted up a rifle, shouldered it, slanted it sideways, and pantomimed slapping a magazine in the chamber. His movements were practiced, precise. His arms were sleeved in cheap tattoos.

At the next table, she looked over the 100 handguns under a black netting. The seller glanced up. "Let me know if you want to look at anything. I can get them out."

She pointed to the Berretta M9.

He placed it in her hand.

She moved slowly, disguising that this was, in fact, her gun of choice. She lifted the two-pound gun up and down, holding it awkwardly, faking a look of amazement. "How many rounds can I put in the clip?"

"That's the standard M9. Magazine comes with 15 rounds."

She straightened her arm and looked down through the sight. "What's the range on this type of gun?"

"Maximum about 1800 meters but it's most effective at 50."

"What do you think of it?"

"It's the standard military issue so you know it's reliable. It works in temperatures from -40 up to 140 and only has commercial ammo failure in like every 35,000 rounds."

"How much is it?"

"That one's new. It'll cost ya $680."

"If I wanted this today. Could I have it?"

"Yes. You have Louisiana ID?"

She nodded.

"We do a background check." He tilted his head toward his girlfriend - a bleached blond in stretched Lycra - sitting at the end of the table, speaking into a cell phone, and reading from a clip board. "We call it in."

Mac rotated the gun over and under. "How long does that take?"

"15 minutes."

She eyed the table with the assault rifles. " And those?"

"Same."

"15 minutes?"

"Yup."

She handed him the handgun. "Let me think about it."

On her way out, she slowed by the SFG booth. A 19-inch flat screen was displaying a looped, 'best of' video. In the first clip, Charles Osbourne stood on stage before a cheering SFG annual convention. He yelled, "The Payne ban on semi-autos flies directly in the face of our Second Amendment rights. It would allow the government to invade our homes and seize our means of protection!"

Mac glanced at the kid manning the booth. "Can you turn up the volume?"

On the screen, political celebrities crossed the stage. Sarah Palin bleated, "If you ban guns, you take them away from responsible people." Glenn Beck gave a Sieg Heil salute and bellowed into the microphone. "SFG members unite! Americans unite! Those before us fought for our rights! We shall be victorious!"

On the screen, the audience was uproarious.

In the final clip, Charles Osbourne introduced a speaker. "I'd like to welcome our single largest supporter from the gun industry: Mr. Boare and Scimitar."

From behind the microphone, Chuck Boare cautioned the crowd in a somber tone. "Now is not the time to capitulate. We are fighting a battle over the Second Amendment with dark forces in this country! We will not give an inch!"

The crowd thundered as Osbourne and Boare pumped AR 15s into the air like prizefighters.

Mac noticed the redneck youth manning the booth was leering at her. She turned toward him and stared blankly. He wagged his eyebrows in a comical 'come on'. She remained unblinking.

Slowly, he lost his grin.

She stood stock-still.

His eyes hardened.

She held his gaze, immobile.

Finally, he flinched, glancing left.

Twenty minutes later, Mac road an open-air streetcar with a city tour book on her lap. She flipped through the images of the city's French, Haitian and Spanish inhabitants. Photos displayed steamboats plowing through the Mississippi river, horse-drawn carriages rolling along wide streets, and plantation slaves working cotton fields.

The trolley rumbled on the tracks. Up ahead, she saw the sign for the Audobon Garden and pulled the bell, jumping off at the golf course.

She walked along the west side of the course through huge, branched trees blanketed in Spanish moss. Runners rushed past. The smell of pungent mold tickled her nose.

At Prytania Street, she peeled off from the park. Two blocks in, she stopped before a large, white-columned house. Four whitewashed rocking chairs sat on the veranda. A bright red welcome mat lay at the step before a huge front door with a round, brass knocker.

She reached into her courier bag and pulled out a well-worn Saints baseball hat. She tiptoed up the large steps, stood on the red mat, pushed open the mail slot, and quietly pushed in the folded hat. She placed her fingers on the brass mail cover, closed her eyes, and said a small prayer.

There was only one last task to do in New Orleans.

Mac sauntered into the Canal Street Wells Fargo. The AC was on full blast and the LED ceiling lamps bleached out the room; it was like being in a walk-in freezer.

She spotted the manager's desk and headed for it. She sat down in front of the older, black woman who looked up and saw a trim, blond woman in a light blue cardigan over a khaki skirt.

The manager said, "Good mornin! How can I help you, my dear?"

"I need to open a bank account for a family foundation." Mac's southern accent was drawn-out but concise.

By contrast, the bank manager's accent was thick and sugary. "Sure thing, honey. I'll just need your ID, Employee Identification Number and your certified Articles of Incorporation."

Mac slid the documents across the desk.

Looking up, the manager asked, "Ok, Ms. Maar, are you the signatory on the account?"

"Yes. I will be."

"Right. What type of deposit will you be using to open the account?"

"I have $500 in cash and a cashier's check." She handed her both. "How long will it take the check to clear?"

The bank manager was surprised by the size of the Credit Suisse cashier's check, but replied calmly, "This one should be about five days."

"Perfect."

"Ok, well, this will only take a moment. Sit back, relax and I'll be right back now."

A few tellers looked out from behind Plexiglass windows; each window offered a rainbow of lollipops in small, glass jars. Two surveillance cameras peeked out from high corners. Customers used the ATM near the door.

The bank manager returned ten minutes later with official documents. "Now, what will you need for this account? Checks?" She indicated a line for Mac's signature.

Mac signed the document. "No, actually. "

"Will you be needing a debit card?"

"We'll mostly be doing electronic transfers, so no need for any cards, really."

"Ok, well is there anything else I can do for you?"

"What will I need to set this account up online?"

"You just type in your account number at our main web page and this pin." She pointed to a number on one of the documents.

"Ok. You've been super helpful." Mac smiled widely. "Thanks so much."

"My pleasure. Thanks for banking with Wells Fargo. Now you have a great day, ya hear?"

The Julep Foundation was locked and loaded. Everything was in place.

THREE WEEKS BEFORE THE SENATE VOTE

When you are inside this picture you are inside pain; it hits you like a punch in the stomach.
- Jonathan Jones

How wrong is it for a woman to expect the man to build the world she wants, rather than to create it herself?
- Anaïs Nin

8

Arlington, VA

The wall clock clicked over to 7:58 in the morning, momentarily interrupting the silence hanging over the fourth floor of the business mall. The *New York News* was on the computer screen, Cal's weathered boots were propped up on the desk.

He bit into a toasted 'everything' bagel with cream cheese, half wrapped in stiff wax paper, and the blackened, burned edges scraped the roof of his mouth. He took a sip of coffee to relieve the pain.

It had been a week since he had received the Confidential Blue Lantern cable.

At first, Cal had tried to convince himself the email was a mistake. Maybe Maar had intended to send it to someone else. Maybe it had gotten waylaid in Cal's inbox by accident. It hadn't had an explanatory cover letter; perhaps someone had been expecting it, someone who knew what to do with it.

But Cal hadn't been able to convince himself Maar had made a mistake in the recipient of the email. Cal's email address was not publicly available; Maar must have typed it in.

Cal had tried to ignore the email, pushing it out of his consciousness. But it had returned on a regular loop, its sentences hovering in front of his eyes like a projected slideshow.

Finally, he had accepted the assumption that Maar had sought him out. So every few hours he searched on the internet for new variations of Pakistan, arms, export, purchase, PCCP, and Blue Lantern. He hadn't learned much. Actually, he hadn't learned anything. Without additional background, Cal was stumped.

The wall clock ticked to 8 a.m.

His email inbox chimed.

He stopped chewing. He stomach tightened. He dropped his feet, set down his bagel and toggled his screen over to his inbox.

A second email from Maar had arrived. Like before, there was no cover message; the email only included an attachment. He quickly double-clicked on the attachment icon.

It was a second Confidential Blue Lantern cable.

SUBJECT: BLUE LANTERN: POST-SHIPMENT END-USE CHECK ON LICENSE 88088
   Origin: *Embassy ISLAMABAD/AMEMBASSY ISLAMABAD*
   Classification: CONFIDENTIAL

To: SECSTATE WASHDC
Info: AMCONSUL PESHAWAR
Info: AMCONSUL LAHORE
Info: AMCONSUL KARACHI
Date: 15 August 2012

PRIORITY

REF: STATE 88088

1. Blue Lantern Coordinator Islamabad has been unable to verify end use of 696 M4s imported under License 88088. Pakistani military officers confirm receipt but do not have documentation for follow-on transfers.

2. The arms have been diverted.

3. Post has growing concern that end use of cargo may not be resolved satisfactorily.

4. Post has requested support from Blue Lantern Coordinators in Peshawar, Lahore and Karachi for further investigation. Further investigation has commenced.

- BRADLEY

Four thoughts stampeded across Cal's brain:

1. Last year the Pakistani Army lost 696 US-made M4s.
2. Maar is intentionally leaking these to me.
3. Maar understands Blue Lantern checks.
3. Maar is someone who has clearance to classified State Department cables and who can get them from a classified server to a civilian email.

Time to start sniffing. And by sniffing, he meant doing this very quietly under the noses of his superiors. Because he was assigned to a dismal 'close-out' and he was sure as hell not authorized to investigate guns that had gone missing in Pakistan.

The Arms Export Control Act strictly controls the sale of US-made defense items to overseas buyers. The US manufacturer must first register with the Treasury Department. This involves a background check on legal status, export eligibility, foreign ownership, personnel, and products. Once registered, manufacturers then apply to the State Department for an export license for the sale of a particular item to a designated user. These license applications are matched against a 'watch list' of known or suspected export violators. Resale or transfer by the end user is prohibited. Once a sale is approved, a license number is assigned to a shipment.

On his desk phone, Cal dialed a well-known number. Over at the ATF headquarters on New York Avenue near Capitol Hill, an optimistic, cheerful woman who had been with the Bureau for over 15 years answered, "Ruby Shelton."

"Hi Ruby, it's Cal."

"Cal, how are you? How's the annex? We miss you around here."

Cal grimaced. "We, huh? That include the boss?"

"Ok, well, I miss you. The team just isn't the same without you."

"Thanks, Ruby. It's fine over here. Really."

"Well, if you say so. What's up?"

"I've run across something and I just wanted a check on a DOC license number."

"Sure, Cal. What's the number?"

He glanced at the screen. "88088."

"Could take a while. The State system is slow."

"No problem. Thanks, Ruby."

"This part of your 'close-out'?"

All over the world, the wheels of government bureaucracies are greased by small, white lies. "Yes, related. Thanks, Ruby."

"No problem. Hey, Cal, good to hear from you. Hope to see you back here soon."

"Me too, Ruby, me too."

Once a licensed arms shipment sets off, the State Department relies on the cooperation of a number of agencies including the ATF, Customs and Border Protection, and the CIA to check on the products and the end user. It is common for the documentation to flow through the various information management systems.

Cal dialed a second number.

Five years ago, the Bureau had sent Cal on an introductory course called 'Tech Counter Infiltration' taught by a lecturer named Rautum Gosh. An Indian with American citizenship, startling intelligence, and unlimited energy, Rautum - nicknamed Ranty - worked in counter intelligence in the CIA. To drain some of his intensity between operations, his bosses often bartered him to other agencies for training. He and Cal had become good friends during the five-day course.

Somewhere in the bowels of Langley, Ranty responded, "Cal! Absolutely splendid to hear from you, my friend. To what do I owe this honor?"

"How're you keeping these days?"

"Superb, superb, Cal! My first is going to high school in a month. I'm absolutely astounded that I am old enough to have a 13-year-old. My second is just a genius, genius. I'm going to put her on the medical route as soon as she's in high school. And of course my wife is happy and healthy. What more can a man want? How are you, my friend? It's been a while. Have you found a nice partner yet? A woman I mean?"

"All good here. But no, working too hard for that."

"Ah, yes, yes, I completely appreciate that."

"How's the 'deep, deep' work going?"

"Superb as always. Although I'm forever trying to convince the Mandarins up on the top floor that we need new crawler programs. Always new threats from afar. Programs I can write, mind you. Not something they have to contract out. But they just refuse me any sort of leeway, leash, what have you. It's an odd thing over here. They always want to be seen spending. Must spend out their budgets. Can't have our in-house experts do it; don't want to get caught saving any taxpayers' money. Must bill it out to the highest bidder. Congressional oversight what it is these days. Did I just say that out loud? I must be losing my mind down here. Where were we?"

"Always the same. Am I right?"

"Absolutely. What can I do for you?"

"Do you think you can you grab a coffee later today?"

"Sure! Let's do our coffee shop in Dupont?"

"Five p.m.?"

"Done. Splendid. I like the intrigue! We don't get enough down here in the caverns. Slight hyperbole as I'm sure you understand."

"Indeed I do, Ranty. See you at five."

Cal set down his phone, narrowed his eyes at the second Blue Lantern cable shining from the screen.

"My, my. Missing M4s," Ranty whispered to himself while looking over the two cables.

He and Cal sat under the blue awning of an empty Dupont Circle coffee shop. The cooler day had broken one of the summer's heat waves. Taking advantage of the temperature, evening commuters were strolling along the sidewalks.

"Let us begin by dissecting the content." Ranty held up a finger. "First, Blue Lantern inquiries are very routine. Nothing extraordinary about that. These appear to be in order."

"Yes." Cal knew 'yes' was the best word in the English language. It was open enough to encourage, short enough to not interrupt, and ambiguous enough to place the onus of the conversation on the other person.

"We know State Department doesn't check the end use of every arms exported under license. Or military components for that matter."

"Yes."

"We also know Blue Lantern coordinators mostly check target key areas. Let us say, counter terrorism, for example. In, well, let's say Pakistan."

Cal nodded.

Ranty tapped the edges of two documents together on the table.

"We also know that out of all the items we export in the defense sector - helicopters, grenade launchers, high-tech satellite components - that small arms shipments are probably the easiest to lose."

"Yes."

Ranty placed the documents flat down and laid his hand across them. "So. The fact that there was a Blue Lantern check on these M4s in Pakistan is no big deal."

"Agreed."

"But. Last year it appears that this Coordinator - Bradley - assigned to the US Embassy in Islamabad, was doing routine end use checks and stumbled onto the fact that these M4s were missing."

Cal nodded.

"So, something was amiss in Pakistan with a particular defense shipment. Now. I imagine 700 M4s is a lot. How big a cargo pallet would that be?"

"I estimate a shipping container."

"Ok, so if these did go missing, it would require paying off people all along the chain of custody —" A stream of people passed by on the sidewalk and Ranty waited for them to recede. "Some kind of schedule to get these out of the Special Services warehouse, then a safe house to hide the guns. All in all, this isn't petty theft. This had to have been quite organized." Ranty tapped his fingers again on the documents. "All interesting facts. But as I'm sure you've surmised, the biggest question is why this fellow Maar - who is clearly on the inside - is sending these cables to you? One could hazard a guess --"

Cal beat him to the conclusion. "Fast and Frenzied."

"Indeed. Maar knows you're the type of ATF agent to pursue something, to do the right thing, all the way to the end. He wants you to investigate what happened to these missing M4s. This is all very interesting." Making up his mind, Ranty said, "Well, my friend, let me suggest next steps. I verify these are authentic and logged into the State and CIA systems. Let me see if they are being pursued. We only have two cables. Perhaps the investigation was already properly resolved."

"You have that clearance?"

"Cal, let me just say, it's absolutely charming that you would ask that. I am one of the Agency's key tech aficionados. One of perhaps three, if I had to hazard a guess. Likely, not to put too fine a point on it, the best. Although I'm sure the other two would like to think they are superior to me even though I best them at every turn. Even the top, and I do mean the top, have seen the fruits of my exquisite work." He leaned in conspiratorially. "Top, my friend, means down at the WH. White House. My signature goes directly. But I digress. My point, Cal, is that if anyone is going to chase the authenticity of these cables, it will be me, and no one in the Agency will ever be the wiser."

"That's more than I could ask for, Ranty. Thank you."

9

Philadelphia, PA

The rising escalator delivered Mac and the other Washington Amtrak passengers up into the arrivals hall of 30th Street Station. The shops and cafes along the perimeter bustled with waiting passengers. The early morning sun beamed through towering windows. From the huge old-fashioned timetable board, arrival and departure times toppled like dominos, echoing off the blond granite walls.

She passed under the soaring sculpture of Michael the Archangel holding a fallen soldier, past blue uniformed policemen with service dogs, and out the West colonnaded exit.

In a spot designated by the private seller, tucked up by the chain link fence of the far corner of long-term parking, she reached under the left back tire of a red 1968 Alfa Romeo two-door 1750 and retrieved its key. She unlocked the trunk and stowed her roller bag. She unlocked the driver's side door, dropped her courier bag on the passenger seat, and settled in.

It took the old motor 15 minutes before it purred properly, smoothly.

Dropping the race car into first, she gunned the motor and pulled out onto Market Street. She crossed the highway and headed into Center City, the Alfa's exhaust roaring.

The traffic was light as she skirted around Rittenhouse Square. With a feeling of unusual freedom, she made an instantaneous decision and guided the Alfa toward South Street. The famous street had changed, but its gritty tenor remained: tattoos, piercings, bondage sex shops. She passed what used to be the punk record store.

Back up Broad Street, she circled around City Hall, America's most expensive city hall and the world's tallest masonry building. The construction fences circling the foundation made her smile; she couldn't remember a time City Hall wasn't under construction.

Since she had been gone, Philadelphia had become the world's city of murals. Over 3,600 gigantic images in amplified colors covered whole sides of buildings, telling the tale of the city's history and celebrities including Mayor Rizzo, Julius Irving, artists and activists. The Alfa growled down streets and past enormous artwork.

On Museum Row, she cruised down Benjamin Franklin Parkway, past the Franklin Science Museum and the new Barnes Foundation. Ahead of her, the colossal Art Museum rose above the stairs made famous by Rocky.

Mac downshifted the Alfa into second gear, hugged the curve below the Art Museum, and accelerated into East River Drive's straight away.

The Schuylkill River is one of the city's defining features. Before it meets the larger Delaware River out by the airport and the Navy Yard, it winds along Route 76 through the expansive Fairmont Park, passes Boat House Row, and curves south below the Art Museum. The drives on either side of the river, set among lush parkland and connecting many of the city's 1,000 bridges, deliver commuters to the wealthy, Western suburbs.

Mac breathed in the summer air, letting very old memories wash over her.

23 years ago

Mac and Joe stepped out of Bachelor's Boathouse in rumpled sweats and thick winter parkas. Over the grey river, a misty haze filtered the sun, threatening snow. At the curb, they folded gangly teen legs and arms into a 20-year-old, army green, BMW 3.0CS.

She settled into the passenger seat and installed her feet on his dashboard. He started up the car. Simple Minds blasted through the speakers. "I'll be alone, dancing you know it baby." Grinning, she turned down the volume.

The wiper sliced through the accumulated mist. He gassed the motor, belching black smoke out the exhaust pipe and sending carbon wafting through the interior. He waited for her to fasten her seat belt then surged the car neatly into the traffic.

She picked up her Big Gulp from the center console, took a huge swig, and threw her head back dramatically against the head rest. "God, he's such a dick. He's always working the anger angle. It's hard enough to row in the cold. My hands are frozen icicles. We don't need his shit."

Joe quickly downshifted, hugged the East Drive curves. His feet worked the pedals like a professional driver.

She was oblivious to the high speed. "I mean, aren't we supposed to be a team? Fuck. He's making each of us in the eight mad at each other. What's up with that?"

"Maybe he knows what he's doing."

"Fuck that. We're allowed to question a coach." Calming down, she took another huge sip, the sweetness swirling down her throat. A rusty hole in the foot pad on the passenger side sporadically sprayed a fine mist of water.

She asked him, "How'd you decide on this car?"

"I could afford it."

"Where'd you get the cash?"

"I worked for it."

"Where?"

"My dad owns vending machines around town. He lets me restock them. I get to keep the coins."

She studied him. Loose, light brown hair hung just above intelligent, soulful blue eyes. His scrubby five o'clock shadow was emerging across his chin and up his cheeks. She'd met his dark-haired Armenian father and his Quaker mother. As the singular son among five sisters, he was probably the only American male with that particular genetic combination.

The BMW roared along the drive.

She tilted her head. "I can say something to her."

He glanced at her. "What?"

"If you want me to. I can say something to Freda."

He pulled to a stop at a red light. She watched him, waiting, while taking another sip.

The light switched to green. He gunned the car, then quickly released the brake. The BMW exploded forward. The cola in her Big Gulp crested against the lid and arced out across her chest. He snorted with laughter.

She screeched, "You did that on purpose!" Her shock was turning to laughter.

The BMW raced over a bridge. Simple Minds blared on.

Calming, she smiled. "I can't believe you just did that. It's called respect, Mr."

Thirty minutes later, the BMW pulled up to her big house in the sleepy Chestnut Hill suburb.

She reached for the door handle. "Thanks. Same time tomorrow?"

He looked forward through the windshield. "I never said it was Freda."

"What?"

"I never told anyone I liked Freda."

Mac's hand hovered over the handle. "You don't like her?"

"I mean, I like her fine. But I'm not *into* her."

"So who do you like?"

He shrugged, stared ahead. "You."

Her eyes widened, glanced away, and fixated on the long, dark street. She pulled down on the door handle and unfolded out of the car. He looked over as she shut the door. She stared back at him through the window, confused, speechless.

He watched her wander up the walkway and saw her open the front door. He waited while she closed it.

Present day

Manayunk, long a working class enclave, was originally home to the workers from the textile mills along the Schuylkill River. Now, many of the city's young professionals and students had mixed with the locals, moving into the town homes that rose up the hills and looked down over Main Street.

She sat on a bench in the middle of Pretzel Park between two Catholic churches, St. Josaphat's and St. John the Baptist. Instinctively she knew it was noon. Her internal clock was almost never wrong. A few minutes later that was confirmed when noon bells began in both churches. These two old churches had stared at each other across the green park for generations; they had learned to synchronize their bells.

In the quiet that followed, a car rumbled along Cresson Street's cobblestones and a SEPTA commuter train shuddered past on the turn-of-the-century, elevated tracks. She stared across the street, above the tracks, at a sign that read "Space for Rent' in one of the tall windows of a vacant warehouse.

A young real estate agent in a cheap suit led her through the second floor of the warehouse. It was laid out for a modern office; cubicle walls neatly divided an expanse of grey carpet. She pretended to be interested as he rattled off the specs.

He droned, "All the phone jacks are in. It's wired for at least 100 computers. Fully renovated a few months ago. Perfect for a medium sized company with a nice, modern brand --"

She interrupted, "What's the top floor look like?"

"Oh, that hasn't been renovated yet. The owner is working up one floor at a time."

"Can I see it?"

Slightly startled, he responded, "Sure."

Up on the top floor, he fumbled with the keys and opened the door to a cavernous space of damaged raw floors, faded walls, and exposed ceiling beams. The air was still and hot. A clawfoot bathtub, an ancient toilet, and a stained sink were hemmed in on three sides by poorly constructed drywall. A rectangle of grey linoleum demarcated a kitchen, home to a stainless steel sink and a battered refrigerator. An architect's drafting table, layered in dust, sat flush against a wall of dirty, paned windows. Across the street, a brick building - the original painted sign read the 'Manayunk Bottling Works' - was now an interior design showroom.

The real estate agent stood by the door as she walked the length of it, the wooden planks creaking under her feet. She tested the kitchen and bathroom faucets. Cool, clean water ran out. "Is this space available?"

"What?"

"We're a tech start-up, a small team, we need the space and the creativity. This is perfect."

"Uh, let me make a call."

"Ask him about the wiring. I'll need electricity." As he stepped into the hallway, she wiped her finger across the thick dust on the green drafting table.

Two minutes later the agent stepped back in. "He said, sure, if you want it. He's willing to do six months up front. He said the wiring is fine. He can flip the switch today."

Staring through the spattered window to the park below, she said, "I'll take it."

Six hours later, the loft was spotless. The floor had been mopped, the porcelain in the bathroom nook had been bleached, and the kitchen had been scrubbed. A broom, a bucket, disinfectant, and a mop stood in the kitchen corner. Gleaming windows were open to the summer breeze and the setting sun.

A brass lamp sat on the floor next to an old metallic fan noisily blowing air across the 1000 thread-count sheets on a single, twin mattress. There were no curtains on the windows. She had no intention to hang any.

Along the bank of windows, the newly shining drafting table hosted her 13-inch laptop with a hard drive, speakers, and a mobile hotspot drive tied to her new alias and the address of the Manayunk Bottling Company. The connection in the loft was strong, lighting up three bars.

Next to the laptop were two cellphones, each identified with hand written labels on masking tape that read 'SFG' and 'NYC'. Next to the phones was a well-worn leather envelope the size of an airplane pillow. Inside were escape documents - clean passports, credit cards, and ATM cards to hidden bank accounts.

Sipping a beer, Mac pulled up Tor and got online. She typed in a website address, logged into a private chat room, and left a message. "*42 here.*"

A response appeared almost immediately. "*Hey 42. It's 89. How goes it?*"

"*All good. Thanks for La Blanc. She fit right in. I liked her hair.*"

"*Of course.*"

"*Sent you an email under the new Maar Hushmail. Can you re-*

check that it is clean?"

He pinged her, *"Ye of little faith. Of course."*

As she waited for him to check her Hushmail account, she sipped the last of her beer.

She stood up, padded across the loft, and reached into the refrigerator for a second beer. Condensation had formed on the brown bottle and it slipped through her hands. She caught it mid-air.

23 years ago

Ella's Bar was small and smokey. A long wooden bar dominated the entire space. A neon sign out on the street shone back through a high, small window and cast a blue haze across the smoke.

Mac stepped in behind Dusty.

She immediately saw Joe at the bar. He was smoking, drinking a beer, and talking quietly to Ella the bartender, a curvy, gregarious woman with frizzy blond hair. Ella looked up, spied Dusty and Mac, and raised her eyebrows. Joe turned.

Echo and the Bunnymen played on the jukebox.

Dusty's wave was goofy, long limbed. He ambled over to the bar, his voice scratchy and deep. "What's up cats?"

Joe's eyes were darkly circled, his hair unusually unkempt. Ella set two beers on the bar. "You kids are lucky I like you."

Dusty began regaling his latest drama, his hands billowing around him as he talked. Mac pulled out the bar stool next to Joe.

The noise around her merged into a soft buzz. She could no longer distinguish Dusty's voice. Below the bar, she tentatively took Joe's hand.

Instantly, his fingers wrapped around hers.

With her free hand, she lifted the bottle of beer. It was cold and slimy with condensation and it slipped. She dropped Joe's hand to grab the bottle with both hands, but it hit the wooden bar and sent foam gurgling up through the neck. She quickly took a large gulp. The foam expanded in her mouth, threatening to explode through her nose. In a panic, she swallowed. The beer burned her throat and forced her to release a loud, phlegmy cough.

Next to her, Joe stared ahead, politely ignoring her shame.

He placed his hand up on the bar. She reached over putting her hand on his, for all to see.

Present day

Five minutes later, 89 pinged her back in the chat room. *"The closest I got was Peru. Given what I've recently sent you, I'm taking it you're not in Peru."*

"Indeed. I'm not in Peru. Thanks." She lit a cigarette. *"I also need an email worm. Maybe Straight Jacket? Non traceable. It will be discovered."*

"Roger that. I'll send to your new Hushmail. Can only be used for about a week, on one target. Lasts maybe five days then disappears."

"Perfect."

"It's not cheap."

She grinned. *Gotta love hackers.* *"Understood. How much?"*

"10"

Translation: $10,000. *Seriously gotta love hackers.* She typed him back, *"Will send tmrw."*

"And per our last convo: my clients are really pushing for some new talent. They have big money. Guarantees of no wet work."

She typed, *"Bad timing."*

"Well, good luck with your current endeavor. At least your email is clean as a whistle. For now. I heard NSA is sniffing hard on Hushmail."

"Let me know when it's not clean."

"That's another 10."

Classic. She replied, *"Roger. Will send that tmrw too."*

"Live long and prosper."

All fail-safes fail at some point. The key is to know when. Law enforcement will catch up with the account but she'll have dumped it by then.

10

New York, NY

"Hi, Jimmy. Good morning to ya. Listen. I'm doing a piece on the SFG." Stacia held the receiver to her ear in one hand and twirled her Mont Blanc through the fingers of her other. Around her, the New York News newsroom was loud. "Do you mind if I ask you some off-the-record questions? I just want some color."

Jimmy, a friend from college, was now the Communications Director for the junior senator from Arizona. His reply was measured. "Stacia, careful who you mess with."

"Right? Funny you say that."

"I'm serious. Those are some heavy dudes."

"That's just it. Seems like everyone is afraid of them."

"Probably because we are. This all off-the-record?"

"Absolutely. So how are these guys so powerful?"

"All I can tell you is that they are. When they come around to our office… kissing ass to them is the worst part of my job."

"Do they make threats?"

"They don't need to. They let you know that they are making a scorecard on a particular bill."

She gazed through the atrium. "Just like that. They mention a scorecard and —"

"You can bet my boss will fall in line."

"Wow."

"I'm not the only one with that experience on the Hill."

"Yeah, I bet not. Ok, thanks a ton, Jimmy. Chat soon."

She set down the phone and wrote 'scorecard' on her pad. She looked up a second number and dialed.

"Senator McClaran's office. Melody Hallwell speaking." Melody was a contact she had met at a networking function last year.

"Hi, Melody. Stacia DeVries from the New York News."

"Hi Stacia. What's up?"

"Yeah, I'm doing a piece on the SFG…"

Melody let out a loud cough.

Stacia rushed on, "Right? You're not the first with that reaction. I'm trying to get some background. All off-the-record."

"Well, listen, I'm going make my comment short and sweet. My boss is a Democrat in the middle of a red state. He absolutely wants a 100% on all SFG scorecards."

"So that's it. He votes what they tell him to vote."

"I didn't say that exactly, but you can go there if you want."

"Got it. Thanks, Melody."

Stacia hung up and underlined 'scorecard' on her notepad. She dialed a third number. This call was to a cousin working for a Republican Congressman out of Oklahoma.

He chuckled sadly. "You know, Stacia, that there's the new Senate bill coming up on assault weapons, right? So I asked my boss this morning what he thought about the SFG. He said he can't remember the last time someone took them on. He thinks it was maybe way back in the early 90s. They're just too powerful, too big."

"What if that's all bluster? They claim six and a half million members. But other sources put that number closer to one million. By some loose and generous math we can say the SFG represents only 4% of all gun owners and less than 1% of all Americans. That is a *tiny* constituency."

"Yeah, but they get em out to vote. We're all afraid of them."

"So you don't think the Payne bill is going pass the Senate?"

"No way. The SFG is already out doing the rounds. I saw their lobbyist, Neil Koen, walking past the Senate cafeteria last week."

On the other side of atrium, Freda walked slowly up to the Editor in Chief's office and leaned on the doorframe. "Knock, knock."

Jack Diamonte was a thick man with a head of full, white hair, a square jaw and reading glasses that sat low on his nose. He rarely smiled even though his humor was quick and often painful. He didn't look up from his document. "Yes?"

"You see the gun hearing?"

"Of course."

"I've got Stacia DeVries working on a profile."

Jack redlined the document. "All right."

"I'll keep you posted."

He made another edit. "I know you will."

Freda lowered her voice. "I'll keep an eye on her."

"I know you will."

"Maybe we make her point on other leads."

Jack finally looked up, the red pen hanging in the air. "We'll see."

Penny's 55th floor office looked out over Times Square and down Broadway. From her desk, she heard a group of young staff in the hallway chatting about the latest movie. She had never heard of it.

Cliff Tripp, another partner in her practice, popped his head around her door. "I just heard the price fixing issue is back on the front burner for our publishing clients."

She jumped in her chair. Cliff had the demeanor of a college kid despite being a few years older than her. His joviality never seemed to wane. Even delivering bad news, he smiled.

She said, "Oh. Really? Crap."

"Yeah. I think they'll call us in the morning. You feel up to speed on it?"

She hesitated. "That's such a bear. I can't believe they're bringing that up again."

"You got it? I can help tonight if you need me to."

She shook him off. "No, no..." In that instant her mind wandered. She was a polished, svelte version of herself calling a team of lawyers into her office. Wearing a fur-collared Chanel suit, the impeccable Penny poured a glass of champagne for herself. She pointed long, red fingernails at each of the team members. Heavy gold bangles clanged on her wrist as she assigned them menial research on the antitrust case. She sipped from her flute, her lipsticked mouth curling into a Anna Wintour half smile.

At her door, Cliff coughed.

She reddened. "Got it. Thanks for the heads up, Cliff."

He winked, turned and disappeared down the hall.

She chuckled to herself. *Did he just wink?*

She picked up the phone, waited as it connected, and said, "It's me. I'm going to have to cancel."

"What?"

"Something just came in."

"You've got to be kidding me. I'm showered and shaved. The babysitter is on her way. The boys are ready."

"I've got a big case, Kenneth. Something just walked in my door 5 minutes ago. I've got to get on it --"

He hung up on her.

On the window sill, a photo of her two smiling boys backed up to a view from the top of the world.

Stacia stepped into Freda's office as the sun began to set. She sat in the seat opposite the desk, closed her eyes and templed her fingers in front of her chest. The room smelled like expensive perfume and a fresh piece of Dentyne.

Freda looked up. "Ok, Dalai Lama, let's get to it."

Stacia opened her eyes, dropped her hands. "Just focusing my thoughts."

"I don't have all day."

"Ok. I've spoken to six contacts on the Hill. All of them say their bosses are afraid of the SFG."

"Well, my, my. Investigative reporting at its finest."

"Why do you bust my balls so much?"

"Cause you yank mine. Please get to the point."

"Ok. The main point is that they didn't really know why or how the SFG is so powerful."

"Don't they think it's cause they have gobs of cash at their disposal?"

"They didn't know. So I dug into the SFG's finances."

"Now you're talking my language."

"I found some very interesting facts about the SFG and their money." Stacia settled into her story. "The SFG has ten separate legal entities. The largest of the five nonprofits - the big whale if you will - is designated a 501c4. 501c4s are also known as 'social welfare organizations.' The SFG big whale raised $300 million last year."

"Yup, gobs of cash. Where does this war chest come from?"

"Well, interestingly, 501c4's do not have to identify their donors."

"So the big whale raised hundreds of millions and we don't know from whom."

"They pull in from membership dues and ad sales, royalties, and subscriptions --"

"Ad sales and subscriptions?"

"The SFG has magazines and their own store."

"Please be joking."

"You can buy a gun holster with an SFG logo that clips onto your bra."

"May I never hear those words uttered out loud for the rest of my life." Freda shook her head. "Go ahead."

"Now get this. Because of their designations, the big whale can't spend more than 50% on politics."

Freda's jaw slackened, stranding green gum on her back teeth.

"Exactly." Stacia flipped her pen back and forth between the tips of her fingers excitedly. "That being said, they claim they spend almost $100 million a year in 'membership outreach' such as newsletters, emails --"

Freda held up a hand, stopping her. "Woah, woah. Newsletters and emails on gun issues? Surely that's political?"

They look across the desk at each other.

"Exactly." Stacia continued, "They also spend another $100 million a year on advertising."

"Advertising on and around the issue of gun freedom." Freda crooked her head. "Also political."

Stacia nodded.

"So they're spending a crap load millions on newsletters and advertising but claiming it's not political."

Stacia waited for Freda.

"If it were determined that it was political, would they lose their non-profit status?"

"Absolutely."

"So who determines if their spending is political?"

"The IRS."

Freda summed up slowly. "The IRS determines if the SFG entities, as registered non-profits, are spending on politics?"

"Yup."

Again, they stared at each other.

Freda's voice dropped. "When was the last time any SFG entity was audited by the IRS?"

"From what I can tell, the IRS look into them back in 1993. It made the headlines. Nothing since then that I could find"

"Some of the largest non-profits fighting one of the most politically charged issues in America under one umbrella and the IRS hasn't audited any of them in over 20 years?"

"These guys have powerful friends."

11

Arlington, VA

It was ten minutes before 8 a.m. and the fourth floor of the business mall was silent. The accountant wasn't due for another hour.

It had been two days since the second Confidential Blue Lantern email had arrived and Cal was anxious in anticipation of Maar's next move. As he reached across his desk for his coffee, his inbox pinged.

His heart raced.

It was a third email from Maar.

SUBJECT: BLUE LANTERN: POST-SHIPMENT END-USE CHECK ON LICENSE 88088
Origin: American Consulate Peshawar/AMCONSUL PESHAWAR
Classification: CONFIDENTIAL

To: SECSTATE WASHDC
Info: AMEMBASSY KABUL
Info: AMEMBASSY ISLAMABAD
Info: AMCONSUL LAHORE
Info: AMCONSUL KARACHI

Date: 20 August 2012

HIGH PRIORITY

REF: STATE 88088

1. Blue Lantern Coordinator Peshawar has confirmed from local post contacts that a shipping container with contents matching description of diverted M4s imported under License 88088 - 58 racks @ 12 weapons each - entered Afghanistan by truck via Towr Kham crossing two days ago. Destination unknown.
2. It has been confirmed that cargo was shipped over land by intermediary Khan Trucking Company (English translation), headquarters Peshawar.

- *SINGER*

Cal swiftly reviewed what he knew:
- 696 US-made M4s were sent to the Pakistani Army.
- The M4s went missing from Islamabad.
- The M4s were later seen being transported through Towr Kham into Afghanistan.
- A company named Khan Trucking was involved.
- Ranty is verifying the legitimacy of the cables.
- Ruby is tracking down the DOC license number 88088.

His phone rang and he answered quickly. It was Ruby.

"Whatta ya got?" he asked her.

"Sorry for the delay, but I've got that company on the DOC license number you asked for a few days ago."

He grabbed a pen. "You never owe me an apology."

"It's a company out of Lexington, Kentucky called Scimitar Defense Ltd."

He jotted it down. "Thanks a million, Ruby."

"Good luck with your 'close-out,' Cal."

"Thanks. It's just getting interesting."

From an internet search, Cal learned that Scimitar Defense Ltd. was a relatively small, privately held, licensed manufacturer of firearms and firearms parts. It produced guns for the US government, Department of Defense, state and local law enforcement and consumers. The company was best known for manufacturing the M4 rifle.

They have had consistent annual growth, growing year-on-year by about 115%. They had 148 employees, all based in their plant outside Lexington. Their latest revenue was reported at $33 million.

That was a pretty, shiny penny.

The company website was slick. Glossy images of guns were set against a dark grey, metal background. Downloadable PDFs listed the various options and prices for customizing a gun.

The company was founded by Chuck Boare, the current CEO, in 1995. He was a local press darling with over 30 articles describing him as a home-grown success story, a Robin Hood for guns. All the articles contained a photo of a nice looking guy with soft jowls and swept hair. He was always cleanly dressed, holding black assault rifles. Boare was never in camouflage, never behind sunglasses; he was approachable, white, shiny teeth widely visible.

A linked video showed Boare confidently walking on stage at an SFG convention, pumping an M4 in the air and roaring into the microphone. "The Second Amendment can not be ripped from us. We will defend our rights."

In a second clip, Boare spoke with a female reporter by the side of the stage. He openly flirted with her. "I supply the finest tools in this fight. I'm the maestro - yes I like that - I'm the maestro for the music of freedom."

He turned and flashed a smug smile into the camera.

As an investigator, Cal had learned to trust his instincts. Early in an investigation, instinct is often your only guidepost. His instinct told him that Boare had the perfect profile - a megalomaniac with influence and wealth - of someone who thought they were above the law.

Cal placed the two videos side by side on his screen. He played them simultaneously in slow motion, catching glimpses of the man's true character. Boare stepped up onto the stage and paused, reveling in the crowd's roar, and smiled to himself. His head was held high. On stage, he brandished the M4 above his head, eyes wide. Later, off stage, Boare leaned in close to the female reporter who instinctively took a small step back. Boare leaned in further, pushing her boundaries.

Cal sat back in his chair and stared at a frozen image of Boare.

In the still-frame, Boare was facing the camera directly, ego and self-satisfaction glinting in his eyes. He had an unmistakable smirk on his lips. Behind him, the female reporter was backing away further.

12

Manayunk, PA

Early the next morning, Mac pushed open the door to the yoga gym and stepped into a deep orange room with the smell of burning, pungent incense. The store's logo was branded across mats and workout clothes. The combination of capitalism and self-discovery jarred her, made her feel like an outsider.

The receptionist flashed a huge smile. "Welcome. Are you new here?"

"Practically new."

"Great, then just sign up here and we'll get you into the next class. Trial classes are free." Her energy was addictive.

Upstairs, the yoga room was humid and heavy with sweat. Mac rolled out a mat in the back row just as the yogi started the class.

In a very low baritone, he said, "Good morning. Let's start with a warm up. And, into Downward Dog."

Mac leaned from her waist and held the pose, following the yogi's instructions to pace her breathing.

The class moved through a slow, deep yoga moves. Mac stretched her muscles, focused on her breathing, and settled her mind.

A half hour into the class, the yogi said from the front, "Now please go find a partner."

Her calm evaporated.

"This next exercise is with a partner."

She felt an unusual twinge of anxiety. Around the room, people paired off. A young man appeared next to her and gestured that they should be partners.

Following the yogi's instructions, Mac and the young man moved into a standing pose with arms raised wide, one foot placed on the inside of the opposite knee. She bit her lower lip as she found her balance. Across from her the young man was already balanced and was standing, calmly gazing at her, waiting.

Mac looked into his eyes.

Her heart started to pump.

A stream of sweat dripped down her back, inside her yoga tank.

Her standing leg trembled.

She heard the yogi say, "Into Temple pose."

Around them, couples placed their feet on the floor and rested forearms against each other. Mac and her partner slowly moved into position. His intense eyes moved closer to her.

23 years ago

Joe, shirtless in front of a steaming sink of water, lathered mentholated shaving cream across his cheeks and chin. He splashed a silver razor through the water and sliced a single swath across the foam on his cheek. Crossed-legged on the dusty, cluttered bathroom counter, Mac was fascinated.

He laughed. "It's just shaving"

"But it's so weird! On your face!"

"You've never seen a guy shave before?"

She rolled her eyes dramatically and teased, "Yeah, totally. All my million last boyfriends let me sit and watch as they shaved."

He grinned at her.

"You do this every day?"

"Yup, that's the idea."

"Does it hurt?"

"Nope." He stretched out his neck, the razor tracking across his skin. His eyes met hers in the mirror. "Is it true you're related to Pocahontas?

The music from his bedroom played loudly through the silent, empty residence.

"Yeah. My grandma did some family chart. Apparently Pocahontas is like my 8th great grandmother. My mom makes a huge deal out of it. It's like we're somebody, because of it. Like we're better people. Annoys the shit out of me."

"It is kinda cool."

"Yeah, just not when my mom says it."

She stared at his chest. She hadn't been around his bare chest this much. Mostly they had explored each other in the dark. It stood before her, vulnerable in its skinny paleness, a smattering of chest hair. Under her scrutiny he hunched his shoulders forward.

She reassured him. "It's nice to be next to you practically naked. You're hot."

He stared at her intensely. She joked it off with another wide eyed expression, this time of innocence.

Present Day

In the humid yoga room she suddenly dropped her hands, straightened up, and said to her yoga partner, "I'm sorry."

She rushed down the stairs and out onto Main Street. A block away, she slowed, placing two fingers against her carotid artery, checking her pulse, feeling its tempo. The rapid beat was unnerving.

She passed the open door of a bar and saw a pool table in the far corner.

23 years ago

The back room of the second floor of the mansion was dedicated to his father's pool talent. An oversized pool table with thick legs and green felt sat under a rectangular, stained-glass lamp that cast greens and blues in an otherwise darkened room. They were smoking and drinking sodas.

Joe leaned over the table, lined up a shot, and slid the cue stick gently through curled fingers. The cue ball banked off the far bumper, spun left, and kissed the red 3 ball which dropped neatly into the corner pocket. The white cue ball continued to spin down the table.

She was impressed. "How'd you learn to do that?"

"My dad taught me a lot. Then it was just practice."

"How much practice?"

He shrugged, lined up his next shot. "I dunno."

"No, really. How much?"

"I come in here a lot and play."

"How many hours do you spend in here?"

"I get lost in it. It's easy for me to lose sense of time when I'm…I dunno…focused."

"Ok. Like how many hours at a time?"

"Maybe five? Six sometimes."

"At a go?!"

"Yeah."

"God. I'd smoke like two packs if I did that."

He made his next shot easily. "My dad used to do really well down in competitions in Atlantic City."

"Wow."

"But he would always lose near the finals. Because he had a job, a company, and the other guys were like full-time professional pool players. They slept during the day to be ready to play at night. Those competitions would go through the weekend. He told me that the competition was with himself, not with the other guys. I get that. I just want to make a certain shot and I work at it until I get it."

"Do your sisters play?"

"Not so much. Sometimes."

"Where are you sisters?"

"I dunno. Out."

"All five of them?"

He glanced through open door into the empty hallway. There was no noise in the large house. "Yeah. I guess."

"Is it weird to have five sisters?"

"It just is." He made his third shot with a clean, smooth stroke.

"Are they mean to you?"

"Sometimes. Maybe a normal amount of time?"

"And where are your parents?"

He shrugged again. She waited. He didn't look at her, but he could feel her waiting. Finally, he admitted, "They're out a lot."

"When did you last see them?"

"What do you mean?"

"When did you last eat dinner or whatever?"

"I dunno, maybe a few weeks ago?"

"A few weeks? So you pretty much take care of yourself. Like food and all."

He shrugged again and made his fourth shot.

Present day

Mac let herself into the loft. She poured a glass of water, slipped out of the wet yoga gear, and pulled on a t-shirt and shorts. Her heartbeat was back to normal.

In an effort to move past the strange, earlier anxiety, she sat down at the architect's table, pulled up the SFG's main website, picked up the 'SFG' tagged burner phone and dialed the SFG's main number.

A nice lady answered. "Good morning. The SFG. How can I help you?"

Mac assumed an older, disoriented Southern accent. "You know, I'm quite concerned about our Second Amendment rights."

"Yes, of course."

Her sing song was hushed. "My husband, rest his soul, was a very avid sportsman and hunter. He always said to me, Vi, you make sure you take care of my interests when I'm gone."

"Yes, of course."

"So, as you can imagine, I want to do right by Russell now that he's passed."

"Yes Ma'am."

"He's left me quite well off and I'd like to pay that back. In his memory. As a donation. From the family foundation - the Julep Foundation."

"Yes, Ma'am. Do you have any ideas about how you would like the donation utilized?"

"Well, let's see...I'm very keen to hear about what the SFG legislative side is planning this year."

"I'm sure we can arrange something with the SFG Lobby."

"Would it be possible for you to set up a meeting with the folks there?"

"Of course! Let me give you the number of the DC office of the SFG Lobby. They will be happy to help." She read off a DC land line number.

"Thank you so much. Can you let them know that Dora, my assistant, will be calling tomorrow?"
"Absolutely, Ma'am. Now you have a great day."
"Thank you, my dear."

13

New York, NY

Stacia came up quietly and leaned against Freda's doorframe, her pen tapping against her cheek, her brain churning. Behind her the newsroom was loud and chaotic.

Freda turned. "What's up?"

"It just keeps getting curiouser and curiouser." Shaking her head, Stacia took a small step into the office. "In 2012, Neil Koen spent $20 million to influence House and Senate races. And of course against our fine Democrat President. Koen's standard MO is to buy television ads trashing gun control candidates."

"Opposition ads."

"Exactly. For example, he spent over $1 million opposing one Democrat in Iowa."

"Ok?"

"But that Democrat won." She sat down on the back of the guest chair. "Here's the weird thing: Koen lost almost every election he put money into."

"What?"

"The SFG Lobby only had a 3% success rate."

"What?"

"Koen consistently bet on losers." Stacia slowed dramatically. "Not just consistently. Almost completely."

Freda's brow creased. "Why is Neil Koen betting on the losers?"

An email pinged into Freda's inbox. A phone bleated on the newsroom floor. Neither moved. They were lost in thought, staring into the distance.

Stacia ruminated. "For a membership association it is not in the interest of their members. Or their donors for that matter. That's a lot of money to be throwing away."

Down the hall a door slammed.

Both their heads snapped up at the same time.

Freda asked, "What's the number one reason people give to the SFG?"

Sacia was quick. "Fear. Gun owners are afraid to lose their guns - their symbol of American freedom."

They looked at each other, both reaching the same conclusion.

Stacia said it out loud. "Koen is intentionally losing elections to manipulate gun owners' fear."

Across town in her office, Penny read a text from her eldest son. He was at the basketball game with Kenneth and his brother. The text spun her off into a daydream in which her son ran in sync with his taller teammates in red and white uniforms across the wooden, middle school basketball court. Someone snapped him the ball. He dribbled, shot, the ball silently swooshing into the net. The kids in the stands went wild. The team hefted him up on their shoulders. The badger mascot jumped in crazed jacks. On the sideline and behind the raffle table, Penny, decked out in red and white, clapped furiously. She launched raffle tickets into the air. The raffle ticket confetti fluttered down, crowning her son in tiny paper flecks. He turned and beamed at her. All the women in the stands cooed at his show of affection.

Cliff popped his head through her doorway and grinned at her. "What's that about?"

"Oh, hi, Cliff." She felt herself redden again.

"You're a million miles away."

"Oh, yeah." She held up her cell phone. "Just something from my son. What's up?"

"Yeah, what's he say?"

"Oh, nothing."

"Well, it's good to have stuff not work related. You know… personal"

She gave him a curious look.

"I mean…good for you to have outside interests." His statement hung awkwardly in the air like a shrunken, partially deflated balloon. He stiffened and stiffly added, "Just checking if you needed me on anything for tomorrow in court."

"Not anything other than the checklist from this morning's meeting," she said, puzzled.

"Right, right. I'm on that." He stammered, turned and disappeared down the hall.

14

Arlington, VA

"Cal, it's Ranty here."

"Hey, Ranty, I was just about to call you --"

Ranty cut him off. "— I've found a third email in the system."

Cal read the email on his screen. "Dated August 20? From a guy named Singer in Peshawar --"

"Yes! Wait. Did you get sent a third email?"

"I've got it here up on my screen. Maar sent it this morning."

"Ah, ever, clever fellow, our Maar is."

"What did you find out about the cables?"

"Well, my friend, these cables are indeed legitimate. All three were logged into both the State and CIA systems."

"So the shit is real."

"Yes, yes, indeed it appears so. But there is one thing --"

"Did you find any other cables?"

"Well, that's the thing. From what I can tell, this third cable from Singer in Peshawar is the last cable related to license number 88088."

Cal filled in the thought. "Which is odd since Singer has identified that the M4s were transported into Afghanistan."

Ranty quietly replied, "Well, that's exactly right. There should be follow up emails. The Blue Lantern coordinator clearly has identified missing defense equipment. The trail of cables should not end with this third one."

Cal looked out over the empty fourth floor of the business mall. Outside, the day was turning grey. "They just dropped it."

"It appears that may be the case."

"Probably because Afghanistan is a quagmire. Maybe it got too difficult?"

"Perhaps, perhaps," Ranty said almost in a whisper.

"That's why Maar is mad. He's mad this got dropped."

"So it would seem."

"And he wants me to chase down the missing M4s."

"That would be my assumption. Yes, Cal, yes."

A long moment of silence passed between them.

Cal broke it. "Well, he chose correctly. I, for one, am not going to drop this."

"I feared you might say that. I'm afraid your high level of curiosity may outweigh your self-preservation, Cal."

"So it would seem, Ranty."

Ten minutes later, Cal looked up the main number for Scimitar Defense outside Lexington.

A woman answered, "Good morning. Scimitar Defense."

"Hi. This is Jack Deers." The lie rolled off his tongue easily. "I'm a friend of Mr. Boare from college. I'm afraid I've lost my cell phone and Chuck's cell number along with it. Would you mind giving me his cell number again?"

"Sure." She rattled off a number.

Cal hung up and called Ruby. "Ruby. Hi, it's Cal again."

She chuckled. "Ah, two for one today, eh Cal?"

He tempered himself. "Yeah. You know how it is. You want to just get things cleared off your desk so you can move on to more exciting paperwork."

"Cal, never one for the sarcasm, eh? What is it you need this time?"

"I need a court order for some phone records."

She grunted. "No ya don't, honey."

"What?"

"Since you've been exiled, we've gotten Prism."

"Prism?"

"Technology and surveillance. The Bureau has access to records from all the phone companies going back 12 months."

"Wait. What?"

"Anybody who is using a phone company is in the metadata. It's pretty routine now. We request all phone records over three month periods from each of the phone companies."

"So, I can just give you a telephone number - anywhere in the US - you've got all their records?"

"Yup."

"Wow. Ok, I need the records of two numbers."

"Shoot."

He read off Scimitar's main office number and Chuck Boare's cell number.

She asked, "How far back do you need?"

"Uh…"

"I've only got back 12 months"

"Ok, as far back as you can go. I'll take what I can get."

"No problem. I'll send a spreadsheet as an attachment. Cal, this is still about the close-out, right?"

He got it; she was just covering her ass. No need to pull anyone else into the mire of the Bureau's shame along with him. "Yes, Ruby, close out. Thanks."

"No problem. Sorry, Cal. You know I had to ask."

"Absolutely."

He typed in an internet search for Khan Trucking Company based in Peshawar Pakistan. The screen filled up with Arabic looking alphabet soup, probably Urdu.

He dialed Benji. "Hi, Benji. It's Cal again."

"Hey, Cal. How's it going? Two calls in, what? Two weeks? You must be on to something. And let's be clear, I don't want to know about it."

"Absolutely. Another favor. I've got a trucking company in Peshawar and I need their telephone number. I can't read Arabic. I'm at a loss."

"Huh?" Followed by a long pause. Finally Benji asked, "What's the name?"

"In English it's Khan Trucking Company."

"Ok, let me find it."

Ten minutes later Benji called him back with an international number 92 91 234 54678. "And, Cal?"

"Yeah?"

"I think maybe you shouldn't call me anymore about this Pakistani stuff."

"Understood. Thanks, Benji."

Cal stared at the desk phone suspiciously, remembering Ruby's words about Prism. He slowly punched in the Pakistani number.

A deep, male voice answered. "Hallo? Hallo?" This was followed by a string of Urdu.

Cal gently hung up his phone.

A new message arrived in his inbox from Ruby. The subject line read *Phone Records*. Adrenaline surged through his limbs as he clicked open the attached spreadsheet. Two files contained hundreds of lines: one was the 12-month log of all calls made from the main line of Scimitar and one was the log of Boare's cell number.

Cal's eyes raced down the first page, but he quickly become overwhelmed.

Moving slower, he placed the cursor in the upper right search window, typed in the number from Jack - the Khan Trucking Company telephone number, 92 91 234 54678 - and hit enter. Immediately, the spreadsheet highlighted two calls made to the Pakistani number last week.

One call was made from Boare's cell and one was from the Scimitar main number.

Cal's instinct was right. Boare was involved with Khan Trucking and the disappearance of his own M4s.

In ATF parlance, that was known as gun trafficking.

15

Manayunk, PA

A fresh voice answered the line, "SFG Lobby. Good evening."

"Good evening, I'd like to speak with Neil Koen's office please." Mac had affected her Southern accent.

"I'll transfer you now."

A moment later, a different female voice said, "Neil Koen's office."

"Yes, hello. This is Mrs. Bodie's assistant, Dora, calling."

"Yes, Dora, we were expecting your call."

"Mrs. Bodie is quite keen to help out the SFG Lobby. She believes the political work you are doing is exactly the type of thing her late husband would approve of."

"Well, perfect. We aim to please."

"Mrs. Bodie is looking to commit some additional funds."

"Isn't that fantastic news?"

"She wants to make sure that your advocacy efforts are top notch."

"Of course."

"Well, let's just say they're a respectable family for a number of reasons here in New Orleans."

"Of course."

"They do their homework, you see."

"Understood and quite understandable, really."

"Let me speak plainly, if I may. She'll want some hand holding, white gloves preferably, by Neil Koen personally."

"Ahhhhhh, understood."

"Would it be possible for me to have an initial meeting with Mr.

Koen?"

"How does tomorrow work at 3 p.m. for you?"

"It works just fine. See you then."

Mac reached the end of Main Street where it met the Belmont Avenue Bridge. The cars passed over the bridge seamlessly, out of Philadelphia and into the wealthy, Main Line suburbs where the houses were larger and the streets were better paved. In Manayunk, the potholes from a long, hard winter could swallow a small car.

Above her, a solid, arched stone structure loomed against a darkening sky. The Manayunk Bridge, built for trains hauling material for the mills, had an unusual reverse curve as it lined up with Main Street. It stood bleak and abandoned now.

She loped down the wooden stairs and out onto the towpath along the canal. Once used by horses towing canal boats between mills, the three mile path had been refurbished for bikes and runners. This evening the gloom settled down around the bushes and trees.

She leaned against the railing to stretch her calves and tightened the laces on new running shoes. Hitting play for her music, she started off at a swift pace beside the murky canal. Her feet hit the gravel in long, well-practiced strides. She matched her pace to the music in her earphones, sinking down into a melancholy rhythm.

23 years ago

Mac rushed out of the big drafty house, slamming the front door. The old BMW sat low by the curb in the dark, its headlights beaming ahead 20 feet.

She slipped into the passenger side. Tears brimmed in her eyes.

Joe was alarmed. "Are you ok?"

"Yes. Just angry."

He reached out to take her hand. "What happened?"

She recoiled. "Don't. Don't try to play me."

"What?"

"Don't be nice to me right now. I don't want you to play me. I can't handle that right now."

"I would never do that."

"Ok. Forget I said it. Can we just go? Please. Just get me out of here." She bit her lip and squeezed her eyes shut. Tears started to fall.

"You got it." His feet worked magic on the clutch and gas. The BMW exploded down the street, tailpipe roaring, making her smile through the tears.

Later they sat in a dark room on a deep, blue sectional in the quiet mansion. On the television, Duran Duran swayed on the deck of a sailboat slicing through the Mediterranean. A painted model in a loin cloth did a dramatized feline crawl across the deck of the boat, sleek and strikingly out of place.

Joe kissed her neck softly.

Mac whispered, "Why do you like me?"

He eyed her soberly. "You're smart, strong and beautiful."

She was stunned by his sincerity and the speed of his answer.

He shrugged. "It's rare - all together."

Ten minutes later, she choose her words carefully. "I'm strong because I have to be."

He squeezed her hand. "I know."

"I didn't chose it as a a personality trait."

"I know."

"I have to out-maneuver her."

He watched a video, letting her find her voice.

"She smashed down my bedroom door last night."

He didn't look at her, just held her hand.

"She was banging so hard it came off the hinges. Literally. The door is off its hinges. She was screaming that I hadn't walked the dogs yet. I just stood there, saying nothing. It just made her angrier. So she slapped me. Across the face. My head wobbled around. Like really wobbled."

He squeezed her hand again.

"I went cold. All the times she's hit me. I stared right at her. I said to her, 'Did that feel good? Did it work for you? Do it again, Mom."

Her face finally cracked, tears dropped freely. He leaned over and gathered her in his arms.

Later that night, in the darkness of his bedroom, she whispered into his ear, "We agreed, right?"

"It's time to live a little. Away from home. We're young."
"I already miss you."
His hand held her head against his chest. "I know."

Present day

She estimated it was the two-mile mark along the canal when she first smelled the faint metallic scent of paper recycling. On the opposite side of the canal, the darkened silhouette of a huge factory emerged. Below it, a group of geese had found a secluded, dammed part of the canal.

She slowed, then stopped beside the still water. A goose honked, perturbed by the intrusion. Dark green algae blooms rode the pond's gloomy surface. She turned off the music, listening to the noises emanating from the dark shadows.

A metal bridge, corroded and speckled in rust, spanned the pond and touched down between overgrown bushes on the opposite bank; it was a languishing reminder of Manayunk's once proud history of growth, prosperity and optimism.

A strong wave of self-pity ripped through her.

She snapped on her music, turned and trotted back down the towpath toward Main Street.

In the loft, she cooled her body under a lukewarm shower.

Later, she stared at her reflection in the mirror, noticing new creases around her eyes and laugh lines around her lips. Detached, she assessed her face as appropriate for a 45-year-old woman. She understood she should feel resentment or shame, but she had no interest in trying to hide her age or reverse time.

She walked through the loft picking up a t-shirt, shorts, letting dampness evaporate off her body.

In the far corner, she dragged a chair over and stepped up onto the seat. She placed a video camera up in the windowsill, facing it toward the northeast corner of Pretzel Park. She checked the line of sight, turned it on, and jumped off the chair.

A black and white image of the park appeared on her laptop screen. With a few clicks on her touchpad, the view expanded to include the sidewalk leading into the park, past the dog walk, and around to the southwest corner.

She configured the software on her hard drive for the video to run in 20-second intervals.

Outside the sky was a gun metal grey.

Except most guns are black these days.

She lit a cigarette, placed on headphones and logged onto Skype. A phone was picked up in an office in Andorra in the Pyrenees mountains between Spain and France. A Catalan accent answered, "Hallo?"

"Señora Bovary si us plau."

"Who is calling?"

"Tamara de Lempicka."

"One moment, please."

A brusque, cigarette scratched voice picked up. "Ah, my long lost friend Tamara. How are you? It's been far too long since we've heard your voice."

"Yes, but no news is good news for women, no?"

"Indeed. Especially for women like us."

"Checking in, five five zero one."

"Indeed. What can I do for you my dear?"

"Just confirming my latest package has arrived. It would have been post-marked Hong Kong."

"Received. I have already stored it with you other items."

"Efficient as always, my darling. That's it for now."

"Well, let's hope it doesn't need to see the light anytime soon. Your instructions remain the same?"

"Yes. Thank you."

"Of course. Well, you stay safe, my dear Tamara. We look forward to seeing you in Andorra soon, but not too soon."

"Agreed, dear Madame. Ciao."

She noticed something down on Cresson Street. There was a dark lump on the grass near the stop sign. It was dense.

She retrieved lightweight Swarovsk Swarovision binoculars from her courier bag. Many of her male peers got very particular about binocular specs - weight distribution, eye relief, and field of view. To her, these were better than most, worked well, and got the job done.

Through the binoculars, she pulled into focus the image of a fresh goose corpse. She wasn't sure when it had died. She couldn't be sure it hadn't been there when she first moved in to the loft earlier in the week. Pedestrians must have walked by it every day.

From the silent loft, she gazed at the corpose for a long moment through the binoculars.

Thunder cracked in the distance. She began counting slowly to herself. '1 Mississippi, 2 Mississippi.' At the ten count, lightening illuminated Pretzel Park. The weeping willow danced and bobbed in the growing wind. The storm was still a distance off, but it was going to be a big one when it arrived.

TWO WEEKS BEFORE THE SENATE VOTE

It has the features of a specific person, Dora Maar, whom Picasso described as 'always weeping'. She was in fact his close collaborator in the time of his life when he was most involved with politics.
- Jonathan Jones

A strong woman is a woman determined to do something others are determined not be done.
- Marge Piercy

16

Capitol Hill, DC

In the spacious, marble-walled, granite-floored hallway outside Room 226 of the art deco Dirksen Senate Building, Mac stood in a growing line waiting for an early morning hearing of the Judiciary Committee. With oversight for the Departments of Justice, Homeland, FBI, and ATF, it was one of the most influential committees in the Senate. Most Senate Committee Hearings were open to the public. Most, but not all. The Select Committee on Intelligence, for example, often heard from top intelligence officials behind closed doors.

Capitol Hill staff strutted past with an over-preponderance of cardigan sweater-sets, outlet mall sneakers, and badges. When Senator Martha Payne strode down the hall, a reporter called out, "Senator, why introduce legislation now?"

She paused for the cameras. "We believe the sentiment in the Senate is turning. We believe they are listening to their constituents. It's time to take these weapons intended for war craft off our streets."

Inside the hearing room, Mac found a seat in the last row near the aisle. She watched as Senators entered through a private door, stepped onto the raised platform and found their seats. Of the 18 members of the committee, only four were women.

The room hushed and eyes turned as a short, round man with a shock of black hair and full lips, entered from the rear, lumbered down the aisle, and settled at the testimony table in the center of the room. His beady black eyes took in the Senators and he gave a small nod to a few on the right.

Mac followed his movements closely. *Hello, Mr. Charles Osbourne.*

Five men in dark suits filled in the chairs behind him. One of the men was Ichabod Crane-thin and tall, with a shiny, bald head encircled with a closely cropped Caesar hair, coke bottle glasses, and a long chin. He leaned in to Mr. Osbourne's ear and whispered something grave, serious.

Mac squinted, trying to read his lips. *Hello, Mr. Koen.*

Osbourne turned laboriously in his seat and took prepared documents from Koen.

The Senate Chairman opened the hearing. "We continue our series of hearings on Senator Payne's proposed ban on military style, semiautomatic assault weapons. These weapons have been used in mass shootings from Newtown, Connecticut, Aurora, Colorado, to Tucson, Arizona, to Blacksburg, Virginia. Such mass shootings are accelerating. Beyond anything we could have imagined just a few years ago." He solemnly looked around the room. "I don't need to tell this room what is at stake. Such a weighty subject requires hear from all sides." He looked down to the witness table. "Mr. Osbourne, Executive Director of the Society for Guns, this Committee seeks your expert testimony."

Having watched hours of Osbourne online, Mac half-listened as he settled into a monotonous reading of his statement. She wondered what it must be like to be so self-assured, to be so smug. What kind of background bred this sense of infallibility and lack of curiosity?

Thirty minutes later, Osbourne slowed and read the last sentence of his speech. He looked up and said to the Senators, "I welcome questions."

The Chairman nodded to Senator Payne. "Senator?"

Senator Payne sat forward and looked down her nose through her glasses. "Do you, Sir, believe assault weapons should be available for civilian use in the United States?"

Across the room, eyes turned back to the witness table.

"The hyperbole on machine guns..." He stumbled, his lips protruded as he regained his composure. "Let's be clear. What the media says about assault weapons is propaganda. It's misinformation. Many guns are used in sport. Most are used in sport, in hunting --"

Senator Payne interrupted, "—Sir, in this room last week we've heard that in the last twenty years more than half of mass shooters had high capacity magazines, assault weapons or both. These are the guns you are saying are being used in sport. This legislation isn't about sporting guns, Sir."

While she spoke, Mac watched as Osbourne's lips moved rapidly, as if streaming silent mumblings to himself. But Osbourne was undaunted. He responded, "Our members know the truth. They will not believe these lies. They are not victims. Our members stand united and strong. We're talking about liberty for our members."

Senator Payne slowly took off her glasses, impatient in the face of illogic. "I believe, Sir, that you are either mislead or you are purposefully misleading your members. I'm not sure which is worse."

Mac exited the hearing early and positioned herself in the hallway across from the door. When Osbourne appeared thirty minutes later, he was accompanied only by Koen. They passed near where she was leaning against the cold wall, pretending to read email on her cell phone. They both wore finely made, hand-tailored suits and expensive shoes.

Koen said, "You were fine. The written testimony was fine. You handled it fine...."

Putting the phone to her ear as if on a call, she fell in line behind them. She noticed what appeared to be face powder on Osbourne. In the crowd it was easy to stay close.

A journalist raised his camera and Osbourne slowed, looking forward into the lens, lifting his chin slightly to stretch his thick neck. Koen stepped out of the frame long enough for the photo to be taken.

The duo continued down the busy Dirksen Building hallway. Mac let them go.

She had confirmed what she needed.

Later that afternoon, she stood before a townhouse set above street level on 17th St. between P and R Streets. The sidewalks were empty; most residents of this professional neighborhood were at work.

She jogged across the street and up the front stairs. She quickly inserted two thin instruments into the lock and popped it open.

She hustled up the stairs and stood outside the landing of the second floor apartment. There was nothing but silence.

She picked the second lock easily and let herself into the still apartment, pulling the door closed behind her.

The apartment was starkly furnished. The living room was occupied only by a short brown leather sectional sofa, a glass coffee table, and a large, flat screen television on the wall. Across the room, facing the curved, bay window over 17th St. was an outsized antique teak captain's desk. She recognized it as a piece from Indonesia.

Her cell phone vibrated inside her courier bag. She fished it out. "Hello?"

"Hi!" It was Penny. "What are ya doing?"

Mac looked around the foreign apartment. "Not much. What's up?"

"Yeah, not much. Just calling."

Mac reached into her courier bag and pulled out earphones, plugged them in, then slipped the cell phone into her pocket. She pulled out a pair of soft leather gloves and slid them on. "Yeah? How's work?"

"You know, same same. Funny, you probably don't know. You ever work in an office, like 9 to 5?"

By the front window, Mac pulled out the roller chair from under the captain's desk and sat down. It felt like the occupant spent most of his time here. It had a great view down 17th St. She said, "Funny, no, I never really have. I've sometimes been on an op where I had to pretend to work in an office. 9 to 5. But I wasn't really doing much, other than reporting into Langley about an agent."

"How bizarre."

Mac pulled out the desk drawer, riffled through it. "Yeah, I guess it is."

"So, like who knows - other than me and Freda - now? About. You know. You being a spy?"

Mac stood, crossed the living room and walked into the kitchen. "It's not allowed. I mean, for people to know."

The kitchen had the pre-requisite stainless steel appliances and a decent sized table with two chairs. She sat down at the table, taking the measure of the room.

Penny asked, "Your parents?"

"Ha. No way."

"Your sister?"

There didn't seem to be a feminine touch in this room either. There was no floral china, matching dishtowels. There was no rug on the floor.

Mac looked over at the counters. "Nah. She doesn't know. I think she suspects but she knows better than to ask."

A bottle of whiskey sat on one of the counters. She stood up and opened the cabinets. It was the only bottle of alcohol in the kitchen.

Penny mused, "Huh. That must be hard. Not telling your sister."

"It was harder at first keeping it from you guys. To be frank."

"Really?"

"Absolutely." Mac opened the fridge. It was practically empty. There was only a take-out container, two bottles of ketchup and a bottle of mustard. No woman lived here. She closed the barren fridge. "It got easier over the years not telling anyone. You kinda get used to the lie." She stared out the kitchen window into an alley.

"Wow, so nobody knows?"

Mac lied. "Nope, nobody knows."

She headed down a hallway and entered the single bedroom that was dominated by a simple queen mattress on legs, no headboard. Even in the middle of the day, the bedroom was shadowed, dusky.

Penny pondered. "Sometimes I wish I had secrets."

Mac stood in the middle of the bedroom, waiting for Penny. There was a long silence. When Penny didn't speak, she offered, "Well, you do now."

It took a while for that to sink in. "Yeah. I know," Penny said.

Mac opened the closet. It had only male clothes; a few blue suits hung neatly in a row, ties draped a tie rack. Across the closet floor sat a range of men's shoes. She stepped back out. "At least you have a relationship, a family with kids."

Penny sounded distant, her responses slow. "Yeah, my boys are great. But you know what I mean…"

Mac fished in her courier bag, pulled out a tiny camera. She dragged over a chair, stepped up on it, and positioned the camera in the far corner of the bedroom, up near the ceiling. It was almost completely invisible from the floor.

Penny asked, "So what's it like? To be a spy?"

Mac took one last look at the dark room and padded back to the living room. It was a moment before she said, "Lonely."

"Yeah? What do you do most of the time? Do you go to the gym? Get your nails done?"

"The truth?" She stepped up on the sectional in the corner and placed a second camera looking out over the room.

"Of course."

She positioned it so it had a good angle on the desk by the window. "When I have down time I do normal stuff. But when I'm on the job I watch people." She stepped down off the couch and sat on it, leaned back against into it. "Try to figure them out. I spend an inordinate amount of time understanding people. You have to be able to read people. You have to really know your asset or your target, especially their Achilles heel." She let the silence of the apartment settle around her. "You also have to let your gut tell you what to do in any given situation. Instinct is really important. Sometimes you have to back off. If you've pushed too hard, asked for too much. Other times pushing the boundaries of your asset makes them slightly uncomfortable, but nothing they can pin point. That can motivate them, subconsciously."

"Wow. That's kinda creepy. Machiavellian."

"It's certainly not an honest way to get the response you want. The word duplicitous comes to mind. So, yeah, I agree." She rubbed her temples. "But I have to tell you, that my gut has saved me quite a few times."

"Really? What you do is kinda effed up."

"Yup." Mac stood, walked to the door and opened it.

Penny's voice was hushed. "So, when do you start our operation?"

Mac pulled the door behind her, took off the gloves, and pushed them in her courier bag. "You don't need to know that."

17

Capitol Hill, DC

The next morning, Mac stood on a tree-lined street facing a red brick building not far from Capitol Hill. The etched glass on the front door read 'SFG Lobby'. The appointment was in five minutes.

She took a deep breath. A lot was riding on this first meeting with the target; it may be the only shot she got.

With over a hundred similar meets under her belt, she had a well-practiced strategy based on four steps: 'charm,' 'sympathize,' 'incentivize,' then 'retreat'. The target should never know he was being lead along the four dance steps.

She straightened her back, pushed back her shoulders, and stepped to the glass door. Her image was reflected in the glass; she was a blond in an expensive dark suit behind tinted sunglasses. She grinned to herself and practiced Dora's southern accent in a whisper. "Lovely to meet you."

In the lobby, a young woman with a mane of curly, brown hair took Mac's hand in both of hers. She was about ten years younger than Mac, probably 33-years-old. A tomato red dress fit her full figure poorly. " Hi, I'm Amanda. You must be Ms. Maar. We spoke on the phone." Her accent was Southern low-country.

"Lovely to meet you. Yes, I'm Dora Maar. Amanda - sorry, what's your last name?"

Amanda's cheeks colored. She blinked rapidly and repeatedly.

"Oh. Sorry. It's Hughes. Amanda Hughes." Under the mass of brown hair, her oval face was open, friendly and her smile was genuine. But her two-handed shake was hesitant, unpracticed.

Smiling wider, Mac noted, "You sound Southern."

"Yes. Columbia, South Carolina." She led Mac down a long hallway. "I'll take you back to Neil."

Both sets of heels clicked on parquet flooring.

Mac's voice was smooth. "You're a long way from Clemson!"

"I am indeed. That's my Alma Mater."

"Go Tigers! My mother's family is from there. How funny. It's been a very long time since I was back there."

"Wow! What a small world."

"What got you up here?"

"I've been in DC for about 5 years."

"And how did you get to the SFG?"

"Oh, we're long-time supporters of the SFG and my daddy knows some of their folks in Columbia. So here I am!"

"Here you are. Fighting the good fight." Mac grinned at her.

"Ok, here's Neil's office. Can I get you a coffee?"

"That would be lovely, thanks Amanda. Black, no sugar. Any chance ya'll have Splenda?"

"You got it."

Beyond a glass wall, Neil Koen's office was masculine. Black walnut flooring met wall-to-wall bookshelves cluttered with hardcover books, photos of Neil with smiling politicians, and an extensive collection of antique guns. The remaining wall space was scattered with paintings of race horses.

A telephone cord from the desk phone stretched around the back of a large, black leather chair that was slowly turning. As he came into view, Neil Koen noticed her through his Coke bottle glasses. His long, thin arm waved her in.

Ending his call, he stepped around the big desk to shake her hand. His suit was hand-tailored and fit his unusually thin body quite well. His cordovan loafers were expensive and his tie was Armani. His cologne had a hint of leather.

Bony fingers gripped her hand firmly as he smiled. "You must be Dora!"

"Yes, Dora Maar. Nice to meet you, Mr. Koen."

"Please, please call me Neil." He indicated a circle of dark leather chairs around a coffee table where Amanda was setting a coffee.

Mac pretended distraction by the gun collection and walked to one of the bookshelves. "Is this a first generation Colt single action?"

Koen beamed across the office. "Colt Pinch Frame. Serial number 58."

She turned to him, astonished. "What year is that?"

"1873."

"Holy smokes." She crossed the room, sat, smoothed out her skirt. "Well, thanks for meeting with me."

"Of course." He took the chair next to her.

"As you know, I represent Mrs. Bodie out of New Orleans."

"Of course, of course. We're glad to be of service to Mrs. Bodie." He imperceptibly shortened the word 'Mrs.', taking pains to soften a Southern accent.

"Well, again, thanks for meeting with me. Mrs. Bodie is quite pleased about our potential partnership." She looked around the room. "I appreciate your time. I'm sure you're quite busy."

His demeanor was gracious as he leaned back into his chair. "Of course! I've got all the time in the world for VIPs."

She grinned at him but it didn't reach her eyes. He cocked his head, wondering if she had just smirked at him.

She said pleasantly, "If you don't mind, can you tell me about the SFG Lobby? I've done some background reading but I'd love to hear your overview of the type of work you do, and your successes."

Koen grinned widely and began his spiel. "Well, we're the legislative and public policy side of the SFG, as I'm sure you know. We've been fighting the good fight since the 1980s. We follow legislation, we advise where necessary, we maintain strong relations with our elected officials, and of course we offer exceptional transparency on Second Amendment votes through our scorecards. We keep folks up here on Kooky Hill on the straight and narrow when it comes to protecting the rights of our members out in the *real* world."

She encouraged him with a nod.

"Of course, when it's necessary we also get engaged. Sometimes we just have to get involved to make sure the outcome is what America needs."

"Can you explain to me how that works? That engagement part?"

"Certainly. First we keep an eye on legislation. We know what's coming up, what needs to be killed. For example, I'm sure you know the previous Assault Weapons Ban had an expiration date." He dropped his chin and eyed her. "We take pride in our work."

She smiled sweetly. "Was that your idea? The expiration date?"

"My, my, my. As you know, that was written in the legislation that came out of the Senate. That certainly wasn't our language." He winked.

"And what about this new legislation coming up? The new ban?"

"We are certainly letting our elected officials know where the country sits on that particular fence."

Mac feigned innocence. "But isn't a majority of the country in support of a ban?"

He leaned forward with a huge smile and said, "You can not trust the liberal media or those pesky polls, Dora. We run our own polls and can attest to the need for continued sporting guns. No matter what Kooky Hill wants to call them."

Changing the subject, Mac asked, "Mrs. Bodie instructed me to ask you personally, to what do you attest your victories?"

"Well, now I'm glad you asked." He picked up a brochure off the desk corner and handed it to her. "I discovered grassroots mobilization."

The cover of the brochure read "Patriots BEWARE!" in big letters across a dark background. A slug line read, "The Second Amendment is our only protection against the darkest of enemies."

He continued, "Mobilization on a national scale. You see, back in the 1990s we started aggressively tapping into our members. We started explaining to them what was at stake. That if they didn't voice their opinions, their 2nd Amendment freedoms were in danger of being trampled. We have since been on the vanguard of letting law-abiding citizens of the US know what is at stake if they become complacent."

She pretended to review the brochure, nodding at his words. "I see."

"It didn't take much to step up our push for their involvement."

"How?"

"We explained that their support would enable us to run some exceptionally hard hitting, hard charging campaigns."

"Hard hitting?"

"Dora, we call the races like we saw them. As George W was wont to say, you're either with us or against us."

"Yes, yes, of course. And this worked?"

"Our members rallied around the cause closest to home: gun freedoms. We doubled our budget that year alone."

She watched him closely as she said softly, "And those early years of this grassroots mobilization were particularly stellar in fact."

Koen tilted his head, his smile waning.

"We do our homework, Mr. Koen." She set the brochure down. "You haven't been able to come anywhere near your early successes, have you?"

His smile faded altogether as he squinted at her.

She remained silent, watching him. It was a long, awkward moment.

He broke it with a hint of steel. "I'm not sure what you mean, Dora."

She eased her posture, let a small grin appear. "Don't worry, Neil, we'd like to see the SFG Lobby rise again."

"I'm all ears, Dora."

"Mrs. Bodie is particularly impressed with your efforts. Mrs. Bodie is also quite connected. She would like to put her connections - if you will - at your disposal."

"How very intriguing."

"Initially, Mrs. Bodie would make her media companies in the South at your disposal. We understand ads are quite expensive."

"Indeed they are."

"I'll send you a list of the private media companies the Bodie family owns below the Mason Dixon. Private. Not public. Not many folks know about their personal holdings." She gave him a long, knowing look. "The Bodie family also goes way back, within various quiet, private circles. We'd like to utilize the Bodie network to support you."

The corners of his mouth turned up.

"And Mrs. Bodie has instructed me to tell you that we'd like to support you financially."

He broke into a full grin.

She said, "Mrs. Bodie has a private foundation through which to donate directly to the SFG Lobby."

"Well, my, my, my, isn't this a lovely meeting today, Dora?"

She smiled graciously.

"Dora, does Mrs. Bodie express any special interests for her support?"

"There are certain, candidates, shall we say, that are not particularly close friends of the Bodie businesses."

"That you would like us to help consolidate pressure against." He breathed in through his nose, slowing the conversation. "I understand."

"I assure you, our interests are almost entirely in line with your own" Mac tapped on the face of her cell phone. His computer pinged on his desk. "I've just sent you a list of six candidates we'd like to you to support. Through the SFG Lobby of course."

He was startled by her use of technology. He stood quickly and walked around the desk to retrieve the email.

On a shelf behind the desk was a photo of Koen standing next to Chuck Boare. Both men were sporting hats and holding champagne glasses, the ring of the Kentucky Derby stretched out behind them.

The instant he opened the email, the worm she bought from 89 was released, secretly digging its way deep into the bowels of his hard drive, deploying its email forwarding code.

He read through the email. "These are the candidates you'd like us to oppose?"

She nodded.

"It does indeed look like our interests are aligned. Mr. Purdue in Louisiana. Mr. Malcolm in Columbia. Ms. Richter in Montana… "

"Indeed."

He paused on the last name on the list. " You want us to campaign against Congressman Ron Peter?"

"Congressman Peter is not a friend of the Bodie family's corporate interests. His opposition, Zach Hannover, is."

Koen cleared his throat. "Congressman Peter is one of our

staunchest allies."

"Hannover is also an ally of gun rights."

He paused. "Yes, we are aware." He placed two fingers to his lips, contemplating this turn of events.

Surreptitiously she pulled out a small round stone from her jacket pocket and deposited it between the seat cushions before standing. "Mrs. Bodie expected you might hesitate. She asked me to tell you her support will be on-going, year on year. That will involve the media, the personal networks and her corporate networks." She stepped to his desk and set down a Julep Foundation business card. "Through the foundation of course." She reached out and flipped the card over in his hand. On the back was written, "$1M. Every year."

The number startled him.

She looked down, her smugness was genuine. This man would take the money; the incentive was too large.

He feigned hesitation. "Your Mrs. Bodie is quite a business woman."

"Yes, she is. Quite a business partner."

"Quite smart."

"Yes, she is."

"And persuasive."

"Indeed." She paused. "The only real dilemma, Neil, is Congressman Peter. Everything else is very much in-line with your current work."

His bony fingers waggled the business card while he nodded gravely, all in a false, yet dramatic display of deep consideration. Then he stood, smiled and offered his hand. "Please tell Mrs. Bodie we will be delighted to work with her."

She allowed a small breath to escape and smiled. "Superb. I'll tell her this evening."

"Lovely. And lovely to meet you Dora."

"Have a nice day, Mr. Koen."

He opened his door and spoke into the hallway. "I'll leave you in the hands of Amanda here for all our bank information and what not."

Amanda and Mac clicked back down the long hallway. Mac grinned conspiratorially to her. "Well, he seems smart."

"Absolutely. One of the smartest on the Hill."
"Good boss?"
"Absolutely."
"Honest, reliable, all that?"
"Absolutely."
"Great, great. Looks like we'll be able to work together. You, Neil and I."

Amanda beamed.

"It will be nice to have a woman to work with on this. Great to have met you."

"Absolutely." Amanda delivered her to the front door and shook her hand. "You let me know what you need from us."

"I'll be in touch soon."

As she stepped back out onto the street, Mac allowed a small smile. That was easier than she had expected. She had no doubts she would be able to turn Amanda.

Langley, VA

Ten miles from Capitol Hill, Staff Operations Officer (SOO) Frank Odom rifled through a pile of papers in a cluttered inbox. A slight man in his late 60s and a life-long CIA Headquarters Based Officer in Clandestine Services, Odom was wary by nature, timid and hesitant. Those who had seen him in a state of panic, swore that even his breathing was cautious. Once he made a decision, however, he had been known to take bold action, contrasting sharply to his normal demeanor.

The inbox sat on a messy desk that was centered squarely in the middle of a windowless basement office of CIA headquarters. Across the floor was a geometric designed Persian Shiraz his wife had purchased in Iran years earlier and had personally carried - despite his vociferous protests and the embargo - through JFK. It, and the office, were illuminated by a single, green-glass desk lamp hauled home from Marrakesh.

He found the hard copy of an email he had received two weeks earlier. "*CALL LOG. TO: Case Officer Frank Odom. FROM: Operative AD99. Called in via main line. QUOTE: "I've got pen pals. I think in China. I'm going on vacation for two weeks."*

Odom glanced at his desk calendar. It had been three weeks since he had heard from Operative AD99, internally known as Mac Ambrose.

Rumor had it that Mac was not only her Agency name, but was also a nickname for her given name. Odom was not 'need to know' on that. Rumors aside, Mac was one of the CIA's best field operatives. Although she was a risk taker who played a little loose with the Agency rules while on assignment, she stayed on-task and reported in often. Extraordinarily, she had been promoted to personnel grade GS-14 ten years ago at the tender age of 34.

She had grudgingly accepted Odom as her home based office 'manager' for the last eight years. Their operations had produced noteworthy intel; she was the reason he had survived CIA culls and had reached grade GS-13. He knew it. She knew it.

With a gnawing feeling, Odom pulled up an internet chat room on his screen. He typed out an innocent looking message. It was code requesting Mac to report in to him. ASAP.

18

North Capitol Hill, DC

ATF Director George Wilson glanced up from an immaculate desk as Cal stepped into the top floor office in the new ATF building on New York Avenue.

Wilson was a tall, black man with the thick neck and arms of college football that he attempted to disguise with finely tailored suits. Similarly, his bullying personality was never quite hidden behind an affected refinement. He quickly looked back down and barked a sharp, "No."

Cal calmly held a manila folder with both hands in front of his waist, waiting.

Without looking up, Wilson delivered a command. "Go back to Arlington. Whatever it is, my answer is no."

Cal remained silent by the doorframe.

Wilson set down his pen, ran a thumb along his bushy eyebrow and scowled. "What is it Agent Bertrand? It better be uncustomarily good."

Cal stepped forward, pulling the cables from the folder, and slid them across Wilson's desk. "Something you need to see or I wouldn't be here."

Five minutes later Wilson leaned back in his chair, his voice taut. "Let me summarize the essence of what you're presenting here, Agent Bertrand. You have shown me Confidential State Department cables detailing a shipment last year of legitimate DOC licensed M4s to the Pakistani Army."

"Yes."

"Upon arrival in Islamabad, they went missing."

"Yes."

Wilson flipped to the last cable. "They were then spotted going through Peshwar."

"Into Afghanistan."

"From where I sit, this is a standard Blue Lantern investigation. A State Department problem."

"Perhaps not." Cal nodded to the cables. "In the last cable, the Blue Lantern coordinator was able to track down the trucking company that moved the stolen arms. It's one Khan Trucking Company up in Peshawar."

Wilson confirmed this from the third cable.

Cal said, "From the DOC license number mentioned in the cable, I was able to pull the phone records of the US manufacturer."

Wilson's anger flamed.

Cal quickly handed him the phone logs. "It's Scimitar Defense out of Lexington. Sir, I've confirmed two calls made from Scimitar to Kahn Trucking."

Wilson grabbed the logs, his curiosity cooling his temper.

"The evidence points to Scimitar's involvement in the guns running. They called Khan Trucking"

Wilson scanned the phone logs. "Jesus H." He looked up. "Any idea who Maar is?"

"No. Other than someone with either State or CIA 'need to know' clearance."

"Why were they sent to you?"

Cal gave a slight, one shoulder shrug; he had a good idea why.

"Because you've blown whistles." Wilson barreled on, "You've verified these cables?"

"Yes. I have a man inside the CIA. He confirms they are legit. They are in the system."

"Why send these a year later?"

"I believe State dropped the investigation into the missing guns. I believe Maar wants the ATF to finish the investigation into the gun running. And Scimitar's possible connection." Cal crossed his arms. "If Scimitar *is* connected to the guns going missing, we've got a domestic player and it becomes an ATF issue."

Wilson's stare was unflinching. That stare, having unnerved many tough criminals and law enforcement officers alike, had been a significant asset to his career's upward trajectory. Eventually, he conceded, "Maar wants Scimitar nailed."

Cal nodded.

"*If* they're involved."

Cal nodded again.

"So Maar is sending you - a proven whistle blower - the cables," he said. "Ok. Your hypotheses make sense. Two calls to Khan last week aren't an indictment, but they are probable cause. I'm assuming you want a warrant for Scimitar's offices in Lexington?"

"Yes, Sir."

"The case will hang on documentation of Scimitar's involvement in the M4s moving. We'll need tangibles: emails, phone logs, bank statements."

"Understood."

"Get on the plane today. You've got your warrant." Wilson rubbed his eyebrow. "To wit, Bertrand, don't fuck this up. If you find Scimitar is involved, the list of agencies we loop in is going to be extensive. The task force will include DCIS over at DOD, FBI, Immigration and Customs, potentially Homeland and of course State and CIA. There are enormous jurisdictional issues on this one. Especially if State bungled this."

Wilson was politically savvy; releasing evidence to a joint task force across jurisdictions relieved ATF of the political fall-out if it turned out State had screwed this one up.

Wilson eyed Cal. "Bertrand, Maar may have chosen you, so I'll let you lead for now. But if it were up to me I'd keep you out in exile for eternity doing penance for the enormous shit storm you already dropped me in."

"Yes, Sir. I'm aware of that."

"Actually, if it was up to me I'd fire you."

"Yes, Sir. I'm aware of that also."

At the elevator bank on the top floor, two televisions were set to separate news channels. Their broadcasts competed for attention.

An MSNBC newscaster spoke on screen. "The Senate Judiciary Committee completed hearings on new gun control legislation this week. Senators heard from a wide array of experts on the potential impact of legislation affecting ownership, sale and transfer of assault weapons. As expected, two sides of the debate lined up. Representatives of law enforcement spoke compellingly in favor of the ban. In contrast, representatives from the SFG were vociferous in their lambasting of the bill. The Committee now turns to marking up the bill before it heads to the Senate floor in two weeks."

An elevator door opened and a swarm of ATF agents streamed around him. Alone, he stepped into the empty elevator heading down.

19

Capitol Hill, DC

The coffee shop was surprisingly crowded. Mid-morning caffeine needs ran high among Congressional staff. Mac recognized the vibration of the NYC burner phone from deep in her courier bag.

Penny had sent her a text. *"Who was the last person you were with?"*

Mac typed her back. *"An Italian. In Hong Kong. For a few months. Two years ago."*

"Was he a spy?"

"Yes."

"Italians have spies??"

"Everyone has spies."

"Did you like him?"

"Sure."

"Did you love him?"

Mac swirled the latte in its cup. *"No."*

Five minutes later another text arrived. *"Have you ever loved anyone?"*

She hesitated. *"Yes."*

Penny was quick on the response. *"Who???"*

"I'll tell ya later."

"Party pooper. I think my colleague may like me."

"You like him?"

"Yes."

"Uh oh."

"Xactly."

Her regular cell phone pinged with the arrival of a new email.

The worm installed on Neil Koen's desktop had forwarded her a copy of an email he had just sent to Congressman Peter. *"We got a very interesting opportunity here today. A big donor. Could be beneficial to both of us. Can you meet for lunch?"*

An instant later Koen sent another email, this time to Amanda. *"Please do due diligence on Mrs. Bodie out of New Orleans."*

She didn't have to wait long for the next note confirming the noon lunch at a restaurant called Charlie Palmers.

On her way out of the cafe, Mac dropped the rest of her coffee in the trash and texted Penny. *"Gotta run."*

Two hours before the lunch crowd, Charlie Palmers restaurant was quiet. Waiters walked silently through the brightly lit venue, smoothing out table clothes and setting extensive glassware. By the door, the maître d' looked up as Mac entered.

She offered a diminutive wave. "Hi. I'm Amanda Hughes from Neil Koen's office."

"Oh, hi, Amanda. Lovely to meet you in person!"

"I was just on my way to do an errand and I remembered Neil had asked for a private table for his noon meeting with Congressman Peter." She craned her neck, looking down the tables.

He followed her gaze. "Right. How about that one all the way back to the left?"

"Perfect! I'm so sorry, but can I use your bathroom?"

"Of course! Just in the back on the left."

The open hallway passed a commanding glassed-in wine cellar floating above a dramatic water moat.

In the bathroom, she pulled out a one-inch-round container from her purse. Inside, nestled on tissue paper, was a small plastic disk the size of a dime. She positioned the disk on the top of her fingertip and removed the sticky backing.

As she passed the reserved table, she gently stuck the listening device under the wooden, top rail of one of the chairs.

Two hours later, Mac held her left hand against her ear, hiding an earphone, while her right spun a coffee cup on a saucer on the Charlie Palmers bar. Through the earphone, she heard Congressman Peter's twang from the reserved table.

"Now wait a good goddamned minute, Koen. Are you saying she's offering to pay you to support Hannover against me?" he asked.

There was a pause in the conversation as plates were set down on the table by a waiter.

Koen replied, "Unfortunately, one of her political interests is Hannover."

"I am your best supporter in the House, Koen. My record is better than Scott's. I've been rated SFG triple A for my entire elected career. Now you are going to tell me why you would fund Hannover, a Tea Party nut job - over a long-term ally. And it better be a good goddamned explanation."

"She has a huge amount of money to donate. And media support. And a very wide, influential network. It's a sizable package, all up."

"Exactly who is this woman?"

"New Orleans. Just got widowed. They own media. Turns out her late husband was a big gun man."

"I'm listening."

"She's made me a deal."

"There had better be a punch line coming here soon, Koen."

Koen lowered his voice. "I'm going turn around and make you a better deal, Congressman."

"I'm listening."

In her ear, Mac heard them sip from glasses.

Koen explained, "Hannover won't win. You know that. You also know as well as I do that a closer race is better for both of us. It rattles the base." He paused. "So this is how it would shake out. We support Hannover. His numbers rise for a bit. Then our Kentucky brethren see a Tea Party nut job in the position of splitting the Republican vote. You come out strong and explain how this split would sweep in the Democrat. Business is not going to let Hannover win the primary in Kentucky. In the end, more money will actually be funneled to you."

Congressman Peter remained silent.

Koen made the final push. "Crisis and controversy, Congressman, is the name of the game."

Mac heard the sound of knives cutting against plates.

Congressman Peter admonished, "You're playing a very loose

game, Koen."

"It's not a new strategy for us."

"It's also not guaranteed."

"Bigger risk, bigger piece of the pie."

"Talk to me."

Mac set down her coffee and glanced at her cell phone, confirming the recording was on.

Koen said, "She's giving us half a million. I reckon I can get at least 100,000 over to your campaign. An old widow from New Orleans isn't going to be checking our receipts. If she does, I'll make it work."

At the bar, Mac held her breath.

Congressman Peter was quick on the draw, like he'd made corrupt deals a million times before. "Done. How's the steak?"

Mac tapped off the recording app, placed the earphone into her purse, and dropped some dollars on the bar. She worked her way through the crowded restaurant toward the restrooms, careful to keep her face turned. As she passed their table, she snapped three photos on her cell phone of Neil Koen and Congressman Peter eating lunch. She went completely unnoticed; the steaks held their attention.

20

Lexington, KY

Sheriff Soloman, a large man with a commanding presence, spoke in a slow, pleasant Kentucky drawl. "I think he's got about 150 folks working there. Mostly fellas. Manufacturing and all. About half of them live in town. The other half, the lower level guys, live out here in mobile homes, what not. They've never given us any trouble."

Under the mid-day sun, a drop of sweat ran down Cal's calf. He and the sheriff stood at the top of a hill, looking down the rolling green slope to the Scimitar Defense Ltd building in the distance. The air was stifling; even the grass smelled humid.

The sheriff scratched the inside of his ear. "I guess he's been out here going on, what, 15 years? I been by his home in the city. Big, white place. Fences and walls. I'd say some security if you asked me. Lotsa imported cars. Italian, I reckon. No wife. No kids. The city guys say they've seen him out, carousing at the fancy restaurants." He glanced at his freed fingertip, shrugged. "A rich city guy makin' money off of makin' guns out in the country. Not somethin' we usually get involved in."

In the distance, a rooster crowed. Cal stared at the building. "I watched him on an SFG video. He's not a shy guy. He calls himself the Maestro of freedom. Maestro."

The sheriff chuckled. "Ain't that somethin. What's ATF want with him?"

"Possible trafficking of his own product. Pakistan. Afghanistan."

In the reflection of the sheriff's aviator sunglasses, the building remained still even as he shook his head. "There are a lot of folks round here with guns. Most of 'em are not like what ya'll up there would think of. Fine people. Interested in families, their churches, communities, schools. They think gun rights are as American as apple pie." The sheriff paused. "But you ask 'em, most of 'em say regulation - logical regulation - is right."

A mosquito buzzed past Cal's ear.

"Normally I'd be real pissed off 'bout Feds comin' in here on our turf. But when it's international stuff, trafficking and all, I'd actually rather ya'll handle it from start to finish. It's a real screw nut when an early mistake ruins the whole dang case."

A jet stream arced across the blue horizon.

The sheriff warned, "But there may be folks that won't like ya'll comin' in here and hasslin' a local boy."

"Until they find out he's selling to the Taliban." The sweat had built up under Cal's bullet proof vest making his t-shirt damp and heavy.

"You want I should help them know that?"

"I would appreciate you keeping your folks informed, Sheriff."

The mosquito took another dive-bomb pass.

The sheriff shook his head. "It's a complicated issue, regulatin' guns."

"It sure is."

"Real shame the radicals get all the air time."

"Extremists muddy the waters. No doubt about that."

Cal's cell phone ring punctuated the air. He answered with a quick tap.

Wilson barked, "The warrant is signed. In and out. I told the judge this was exploratory."

"Understood."

"You're a go."

The sheriff was already half-way dawn the back of the hill to his men.

Six Lexington police officers stood at attention, circled around the sheriff and Cal, their hands resting on their hips. They were surrounded by four police cruisers and an ATF sedan.

The sheriff took the lead. "Today we're helping out ATF. They have reason to believe this here Chuck Boare may be involved in gun traffickin'. Looks like some shipments to Pakistan have gone a'walkin' into Afghanistan. It may be that Chuck Boare had somethin' to do with those guns gone missin'. That's certainly not gonna help our boys fightin' there." The sheriff nodded to Cal. "Special Agent Bertrand has a warrant to search and seize papers and computers. Pull anythin' that could be holdin' electronic copies. I want professional heads on this one. There will be no sass talk, no chest bumps. Keep your lips locked. I'll give the orders. I hear any of ya'll talkin' and I'll dock your pay a day. We are not gonna screw this up for Agent Bertrand."

The sheriff's car led the caravan, the ATF van pulling up the rear. As they crested the hill, they hit their lights.

The silent vehicles pulled over the top of the hill, wound down the slope of the rural road, and spilled across the Scimitar Defense parking lot, blocking parked cars. The sheriff's car stopped in front of the main door.

In the lobby, the receptionist jolted up out of her chair and grabbed the phone.

21

New York, NY

The evening crowd in the high-end bar felt frenetic. Penny sat back down across from Laura at a small, low cocktail table and gushed, "Oh my. Sorry about that. Didn't mean to abandon you. That was a partner I'm working with on an anti-trust suit." She took a deep sip of her cocktail.

Laura watched Cliff's back as it retreated toward the door. "He's pretty smoking."

Penny slowed her breathing. "I can't believe he found me here. What did you just say?"

"I said he's hot! Trust me, I know when men are hot." She chuckled to herself. "And he clearly stalked you here."

Penny laughed nervously.

"I'm not kidding. He found you, talked to you, and then walked out. You were his only purpose in being in this bar. He had his briefcase thingy so it wasn't like he was planning on staying here."

"Anyway, he just had a work question."

Laura eyed Penny's cell phone on the table. "He can't email you like everyone else in the world?"

"Maybe he did…" Penny scrolled quickly through her inbox, looked up. "Nope, nothing."

"Uh, huh." Laura was all sass. "In my personal opinion that's called stalking with intent to engage. Stalk to talk." She eyed her over her cocktail.

"Stop it."

"Nope."

"Shut the front door."

"I'm not."

"I'm serious. Shut the hell up."

"Didn't say a word. But am thinking all kinds of words. Like, 'he likes you.' Why wouldn't he? You're smart as shit, you're hot, and you've still got killer tits."

"The tits are way better in a bra."

"Don't worry, all of them are. I would know." She grinned widely, her eyes crinkled. "And your career is chugging along to super lawyer stardom."

Penny exclaimed, "Speaking of - thanks for your mandate this week! Another toast to working with the awe-inspiring Laura!" She raised her cocktail again.

Laura sipped, looked back toward the bar door Cliff had just exited. "And so? What's about your boy there?"

"Uh, I work with him."

"Yeah? Problem?"

Penny jogged her head back and forth, emphasizing the point. "I work with him."

"Single?"

"Actually, just divorced."

"Guuurl. A cool lady could really roll with that."

In that instant, Penny imagined a black and white glossy photo that captured the moment she, in a sleek Vera Wang wedding dress, and a tuxedoed Cliff tumbled through the arched doors of a stone church into dazzling sunbeams. In the next instant, the photo became granular and centered in a newspaper, the huge title across the top read, "New York News Weddings".

Back in the moment, Penny looked at Laura. "A cool lady could roll with that. A married lady could not."

"Point." Admitting defeat, Laura changed the subject. "Dare I ask about Mac?"

"I don't talk to her that much actually. Surprisingly."

"How's it going?"

"As far as I know, fine. It's not like she checks in with me."

"I figured as much. Are you concerned?"

"Not yet. I think these things need to run their course. And she sounds confident. But what do we know about covert operations?"

The funky house music drifted over them as they eyed the

crowd, letting their minds wander.

Laura spoke first. "I'm very keen to see what our spy girl delivers."

"You, me and Freda."

Across town, Freda's burner phone pinged with a message. Mac had sent a Youtube link.

Freda turned to her computer screen and pulled up the video. On the screen, the opening still frame showed a young male reporter standing on the top of a green, rolling hill. Behind the reporter was a manufacturing plant with four police cars in the drive.

Freda hit the 'play' button.

The reporter said, "We're here outside Lexington with breaking news that the local police, supporting an ATF investigation, have raided Scimitar Defense Ltd in connection to a gun trafficking case. Anonymous sources inform us that the police have been inside the gun manufacturer's building for over four hours. They are only just now starting to haul out documents and equipment."

Behind the reporter, uniformed officers were carrying out cardboard boxes and placing them in police cruisers.

He continued to the camera. "We understand there are likely to be no arrests made today. But stay tuned. Our source said this may have something to do with US guns going missing from Pakistan. If the ATF finds anything that connects the gun manufacturer to the missing guns, an indictment will very likely follow."

Freda spent the next few minutes researching Scimitar before sending Stacia the link by email.

Five minutes later, Stacia emailed back. "*Hint?*"

"*Act like an investigative reporter and investigate.*"

Ten minutes later, Stacia replied. "*Scimitar is the SFG's largest donor!!*"

"*Start working sources down in KY. I want copy by COB tomorrow.*"

"*I'm on it.*"

Freda sent an email to Jack. "*We've got a lead on a KY local story involving the SFG's largest corporate donor. Perhaps front page? Below the fold?*"

Jack responded, "*Send it through. I'll take a look.*"

Langley, VA

SOO Odom opened up a web chat room and recognized his message from yesterday. It stood alone, unanswered.

In the single light from the green desk lamp, Odom's eyes narrowed. He was now deeply troubled.

He picked up a phone to his secretary. "Get me Ed Wilcox at the Embassy in Hanoi."

Someone in Hanoi picked up. "Ed Wilcox"

"Hi, Ed. This is Frank Odom from Langley. I need one of your men to check in on one of mine - Mac Ambrose. She's gone quiet. Last known locale was your turf - Halong Bay."

"Sure. We saw Mac three weeks ago. Is something wrong?"

"I'm not sure."

"Ok, I'll get one of my guys on it. How quickly do you need it?"

"As quickly as you can."

"I'm just saying it like it is down here in the blank spot of Hanoi, Frank. You know we don't have a full team. Never enough hands on deck."

"Ed, just get it for me. ASAP."

Odom hung up the phone in the dim office.

22

Arlington, VA

Cal sat at the head of a long metal table in a windowless room in the business mall's fourth floor. An air conditioning unit rattled in the corner. He looked at the four agents seated around the table: three were men, one was a woman, none was older than 30, all of them were in crisp, freshly ironed button-downs. This was the tech team for the Scimitar investigation.

He summed up. "So, for the next 48 hours we're going to focus on Scimitar's senior managers and any references to Pakistan and Afghanistan. We'll need to categorize and file everything in one electronic database. I need this database to be painfully - bottom feeder - easy to maneuver."

On tables around the room's perimeter sat ten desk tops, six laptops, a network computer, and two hard drives. Each brandished yellow Lexington Police tags.

"I don't know who is going to be on the joint task force and I don't want to slow them up. I want an IT illiterate to be able to search the database."

A male agent in a light blue shirt noted, "You want a crawler, or a bot, to search content and index it"

Cal grinned. "It pays to get smart people in the room. Yes. That's exactly what I want. What's your name, son?"

"David."

Cal pointed to the chalkboard behind him. "I've listed the categories for the index: landline, cell phone, texts, banking, outgoing emails, incoming emails, Quicken." He asked the team. "Do we have a Quicken expert?"

The young woman raised her hand.
"What's your name, Agent?"
"Sarah."
"How you feel about your Quicken skills?"
"Solid."
"Good, because this devil is going to be in the details. You ready for that?"
"Yes, Sir."
"I'm ok with us chasing down rabbit holes but let's do it quickly. If you see something you don't like, come to me and we can sniff it out together. Otherwise I want you on our key words. This is a straight forward tech search. Got it?"

The four nodded.
"Ok team. Any questions?"
Sarah asked, "What are the odds of us not finding anything?"
"I'd say about 50/50. We acted on an anonymous tip. We've confirmed there were two calls to Kahn. But they were made last week. Which is weird. Overall, it's compelling, but not convincing. We need enough evidence to make this a formal investigation for a multi-agency task force. We need evidence that Scimitar management were aware of and involved in the illegal trafficking of arms last year.

"We've been given 48 hours to get this done. I will be here until the last possible hours. I do not intend to go home until the end. Do not hesitate to involve me in your searches." He exhaled. "This is make or break. If we come up empty handed, I guarantee you these scum bastards will get away from us. They will be far smarter going forward. There won't be a next time. We have to nail them now."

The four agents nodded with a mix of excitement and determination.

Eight hours later, Wilson called. "I just had the FBI Director on the line. He heard about the raid from his Lexington Office."
"Ok?"
"He's hopping mad I didn't loop them in. I told them we're moving quickly."
"We are."
"Good." Wilson's voice was clipped.

"Sir, I'll be real curious how State and CIA react."

"Yeah, me too. Ok, get back to it, Agent. You only have two days. You better find something."

Cal grimaced as the wall clock ticked over to 8 a.m. on day two of the tech team search. The room smelled like stale fast food. A take-out coffee box sat on one of the tables. The four young agents had worked through the night, their fingers flying over keyboards. Now two of them were slumped over their work stations, napping.

From across the room, David waved Cal over. He was hunched over his keyboard. "I've finished the crawler." His eyes gazed blearily at his screen. "We've got really bad news. I set it loose on everything populated in the database - all emails, phone records, hard copy communications, files, reports - everything." His fingers came to rest on the keyboard. "The crawler picked up nothing. I've used all variations of the search words."

Cal's red eyes looked over David's shoulder. "Nothing?"

"Nothing."

"Tell me your gut conclusion."

David considered this. "Guys like these - senior Scimitar guys - are probably worried their communications are not secure. They may not have used real words. They may not have used the key words we're searching for: Pakistan, Afghanistan, shipment. I think they used some kind of secret code. If they did what we think they did."

Looking around the room, Cal stood up. He raised his voice over the rattling AC. "Ok, I need all eyes but Sarah's on emails this morning."

The two napping agents struggled awake.

"We're going to have to do this the old fashioned way. We're going to read through their emails one by one."

Silence greeted his announcement.

"We've got 24 hours left. This is crunch time. Let's take a quick break, slug that coffee and get back to work."

David asked, "What time period emails should we read?"

"Let's start five months before the shipment in August and go into September."

"Whose emails?"

"Boare, the CFO, the COO, and the lawyer."

"That's about 30,000 emails."
"Divvy it up and let's get started."

An hour later, Wilson called. "Morning, Bertrand. How's it going over there?"

Cal looked around at four crumpled shirts, four heads of messed hair, four sets of shoulders slumped over desks. "Getting there."

"I should hope so. Listen, I'm giving you an order. I'm not asking you, I'm ordering you."

"Yes?"

"I've told the FBI - and we're going to tell the task force - that you got an anonymous telephone tip that led us to investigate Scimitar. You will maintain that deception."

"Ok."

"I am not hanging my dick out on some anonymous, disgruntled spook."

"Fine."

"You hear me?"

"Sure. It does nobody any good to know about Maar."

"That sounds suspiciously like you want to protect him."

"No, Sir. I just don't want anyone on a task force going off on a red herring after our tipster. At this point, the task force should focus is Chuck Boare. Not Maar."

"Agreed."

"Ok, so yes, I'm fine with it."

"So, what have you got?" Wilson asked.

Sarah was walking up to Cal, a broad smile on her face. He watched her approach. "We're slogging through the documents."

"Ok, I'll see you tomorrow morning down here."

"Did you get a call from either State or CIA?"

"No. Quiet as a church mice. But they are both sending representatives tomorrow. We've also got FBI, Commerce, DOJ and Homeland. Big reception. It's not every day we investigate one of our own manufacturers. They all want to be on the ground floor when the elevator doors open up. And I'll be damned if I'm not letting them all in on this particular investigation."

"Ok. We'll be ready."

"You better be. This is one hell of a fishing expedition."

Sarah reached his desk as he hung up the phone. She handed

him a printed spreadsheet. "Small - but maybe something."

He looked down at two highlighted entries. His head snapped up. "Go grab the cardboard boxes from the accountant's office. Start searching the hard copies."

He picked up his phone and dialed Sheriff Soloman.

Dupont Circle, DC

The neighborhood by 17th St was dark. A muffled siren from a distant ambulance floated on the city's sticky air. It was 5 a.m. on the second night of the tech search. Cal hadn't slept in 44 hours. The task force briefing was in three hours.

On the stoop of the yellow townhouse, he picked up the morning's *New York News* and let himself in. He lumbered up the stairs to the second floor landing, unfurling the newspaper as he unlocked the door.

Inside the apartment, he took a moment to digest an article on the front page.

He had bought the apartment just after the global financial crisis. The timing had been perfect, a total fluke. He had been a new relocation from the Arizona office. The divorce had just been finalized.

It could have been a simple divorce. They had been the archetypal legal-law enforcement match glamorized in *New York News* bestsellers and Hollywood movies. Both had been career-oriented, working hard at rising the ladders. She had been a smart, sophisticated lawyer with the Tempe DA and a Yale Law degree on her wall. He had been Deputy Station Chief of the local ATF office, a savvy athlete made good from a bad Atlanta neighborhood.

Behind the storybook facade, there had been long hours and intense cases that kept them apart. There had been no kids. They hadn't even had a dog.

After three years, neither one had made an effort to close the emotional distance between them. That distance had sprouted silence. Silence had blossomed complacency. As natural states go, we're either hunting, gathering, or running in terror from dinosaurs. Complacency is not a viable long-term state for humans.

The divorce should have been simple. But that complacency had turned to deep-rooted resentment. Through their lawyers they had fought righteously over CDs, furniture and bank accounts. It had swallowed time and chipped away naiveté. When it was finally over, he had given up most of what he imagined indispensable and asked for a transfer to Washington. He had taken his remaining money and fronted a down payment.

He stumbled through the kitchen, down the hall, into the bedroom, and settled onto the bed. He squeezed his eyes to relieve the strain, then read through the article.

Largest Corporate SFG Donor: Gun Trafficking Investigation
By STACIA DeVRIES
New York News

The Society for Gun's largest corporate donor has come under investigation for international arms trafficking. Two days ago, a local Kentucky news outlet broke the story that the ATF and local authorities had raided Scimitar Defense Ltd in search of evidence that the company had inappropriately moved arms.

Insiders revealed the ATF believes a shipment of military assault weapons purchased and shipped under a bilateral military arrangement went missing from Islamabad, Pakistan soon after its arrival...

His eyes closed and his head fell back. He was fully dressed.

23

Langley, VA

The phone rang in the basement of CIA headquarters and Odom picked up. "Odom."

"Hey Frank. It's Ed Wilcox from Hanoi. Good early morning there."

"You've got some news?"

"As a matter of fact, I'm afraid we don't. We lost her trail as of three weeks ago Monday. Nothing since."

"Damnit."

"I think it's safe to assume she's not in-country."

"Damnit."

"Frank, we do have an unconfirmed sighting."

"Go ahead."

"Some of our pay-roll local guys out at the airport saw a woman Mac's height fly out on Swiss Air. We watched their vids. Grainy. As you can imagine, only the height and color - no other physical characteristics - fit Mac. But it's not like that many 5'8" white women are out here."

"Ok. Thanks Ed."

"Sure," Ed said. "Hey Frank, have you got an issue with Mac?"

"Not sure."

"Shame if you do. I really liked that one. Solid old-school."

Odom hung up without comment.

He scrutinized his options. He could choose to do nothing, for now. It would buy him some time in case Mac was just doing one of her 'oops-failed-to-report-in' routines. Maybe she was diving in the Philippines. However, if it turned out she was 'off the ranch', the longer he failed to report the breach, the worse he looked. The hallway whispers would start. *Odom didn't catch her...it was a cardinal break...on the job too long...lost the respect of his operative.*

The second option was to flag the breach immediately. Run it up to Director Hawkinson now. Get this grenade off his desk. Now. However, Hawkinson would immediately ask, "You didn't see this coming?" Odom would have to admit that no, in fact, he hadn't seen it coming. Whispers hissed in his mind. *Odom's out of touch...lacks authority over his operatives...will cost him his career.*

The third option was to take just enough action to proverbially 'cover his ass'. Such action would have to be swift but mild so that it didn't immediately sound alarm bells. No whispers in the hallway for that third option.

As a deliberate, cautious man, he played out the three scenarios in his mind. He didn't want to pick the obvious third option, only to regret it later.

But in the end, he chose the third option.

He picked up his phone and dialed Security. "We need a trace on Agent AD99. Last known Hanoi."

"Yes, Sir. How far back?"

"Go back two months."

"On it.

He folded his hands together on his desk and dropped his head onto them.

Thirty minutes later, Odom's desk phone rang.

"This is Beam from Security reporting back to you on the trace on Agent AD99."

"Yes, go ahead."

"Sir, we've got no physical leads on Agent AD99. And no electronic vapor trail. She basically... Well, Sir, she's gone off the grid."

"When did we lose her?"

"As you suspected, the last use of any of her assigned Agency ID was in Vietnam. Hanoi to be exact."

"Beam did you say?"

"Yes, Sir, Jim Beam."

In the darkened office, Odom's lips tightened. He stared at a dark corner.

Beam squeaked, "Sir, It's my Agency name."

Odom's voice was ice. "How long have you been in this Agency, *Beam*?

"Three years."

"In that time, have we successfully wiped out your humor?"

"Yes, Sir."

"Good." The clock on his screen read 5:55 a.m. "Run a full electronic trace on her going back 12 months. All files. Report only to me. Understand, *Beam*? Only me."

"Understood."

Capitol Hill, DC

Through the windshield, Mac watched the sun sneak over the horizon, lightening the sky above the rotunda. A very faint smell of gasoline permeated the Alfa. If she decided to keep the car, she would have to fix the gas lines.

The laptop showed the wifi hotspot had found four bars. On the screen was the Wells Fargo home page for the Julep Foundation.

She completed the transaction, transferring $1,000,000 to the SFG Lobby account and sent an email. *"Mr. Koen, we are pleased to inform you that the transfer of USD 1M has been made from the Julep Foundation to the SFG Lobby account. We are thrilled that our donation could help in the work of the SFG Lobby."*

She leaned her head back against the leather headrest.

She remembered sitting in the dark in a different car fifteen years ago, staring at a target's house in a Jakarta neighborhood, the seat sticky with sweat. It had been probably six hours into the watch when a second floor window had lit up. An adrenaline rush had crashed through her. It pulsated through her fingertips, tingled and expanded up along her arms. She had pushed up from the seat, doing something, anything to alleviate the discomfort. Only later did she recognize the extreme intensity for what it is: an adrenaline rush compounding a constant state of fear of discovery.

In the Alfa, her inbox pinged with a copy of an email from Koen to Amanda. *"Forget the due diligence on Bodie. She's fine."*

She turned up the volume on the car radio. A news brief began on NPR. "New gun legislation was reported out of the Judiciary Committee yesterday. The Senate floor will take up the debate in one week. The bill was introduced by Senator Payne. (Senator Payne's voice) 'How long will it take us as a nation to finally say enough - we will no longer allow malls, supermarkets, movie theaters and schools to be sites for massacres? It's time to regulate assault weapons.' This week has seen a significant increase in lobbying efforts from the SFG. Many Senators are keeping their votes close to the chest prompting long time Congressional observers to predict the legislation will fail on the Senate floor."

Mac turned down the volume.

In her mind, it was ten years ago. She had been sitting at a laminate table in the back of a Hong Kong cafe spooning and winnowing a big scoop of Vietnamese noodles, when she looked up and recognized a man walk through the front door; he had been a senior officer from Beijing's secret police and he had been looking directly at her. The adrenaline had swelled like a wave over her skin, cresting down her limbs.

Her spoon had hovered.

The pulse had reached her fingers, her toes. Her heart had clanged in her chest.

She had lowered the utensil.

Her leg muscles had tensed.

She had slid her sunglasses down on her nose, shifted the chair away from the table, stood and inched down the rear hallway past the restroom.

In the back alley, she had surged into a sprint, racing around the corner, down a second alley. She had dived through the door of a karaoke bar and slipped into a private booth, silently gliding shut the booth's door.

It was the first time she had recognized the adrenaline could be harnessed, utilized.

In the Alfa, her inbox pinged.

Koen had emailed again to Amanda. *"Need immediate transfers as follows, keep the remainder in the account:*
PAC for Mr. Purdue, LA ($50,000)
PAC for Mr. Malcolm, SC ($50,000)
PAC for Ms. Richter, MO ($50,000)

PAC for Mr. Rydell, NC ($50,000)
PAC for Mr. Caldwell, AK ($50,000)
PAC for Mr. Ron Peter, KY ($100,000)"

Mac leaned back again. There was one more email she was waiting for.

This time her memory reversed only five years. She had been in a cheap hotel room in Hanoi, watching a video on her laptop of the still, silent room next door. A sheet-draped form slept on a bed. She had been staring at the screen for eight hours. She had contemplated banging on the shared wall or walking out into the hallway and knocking on the target's door, waiting for him to answer. She had imagined she had screamed at him. "The Chinese are coming." It would have blown the operation but it would have relieved the monotony.

That had been the moment of yet another realization. She had become what the old timers called 'hardwired'. She no longer feared - instead she willed - the rush of adrenaline. A red flag, they had said, heralding the time to get out.

The sun was high above the rotunda. A few staffers, the early birds, were heading to their offices.

Her inbox pinged. This time, Koen had emailed the Congressman. *"That donation arrived. My secretary will transfer. Thanks for lunch."*

Mac turned the key in the ignition, starting the old car, and took a last look at the Capitol Hill dome.

After 20 years, there were plenty of reasons to get out.

24

22 years ago - Oakland, CA

The windshield wipers screeched across the slippery glass of the old BMW as it pulled up in front of a dilapidated clapboard house. Joe hefted her duffel bag out of the backseat. Through the drizzle, they sprinted alongside the house. Taking her hand, he hustled her through the basement door into the dark and switched on the overhead light.

The front room was an homage to second-hand. A worn corduroy sofa sat against the far wall. A banged-up 30-inch television rested on the floor. A huge bookshelf of crates sagged under the weight of hundreds of LPs, a turntable and two outsized speakers. The metallic scent of dust mixed with an earthen mildew.

It was exactly what she had imagined.

Two summers before he and his friend had driven out in his BMW, the back seat piled high with bags and records, smoking out the open windows all the way through the green cornfields of Iowa, the endless miles of Wyoming, and the scorching deserts of Nevada. Between the two of them they had $600. They had gotten jobs at Berkley cafes serving authentically acidic espressos and foamed cappuccinos from imported Italian machines. Joe had enrolled at Berkeley.

He was the most independent person she knew. Her pride verged on wonderment.

He carried her duffle bag past the kitchen, the first bedroom, and into the back room. A blue color-washed billboard covered the wall; a buxom model leaned over the side of an old flatbed in the middle of a wheat-field sea, her sad Mona Lisa smile was turned to the camera. Scattered around the room were five laundry baskets filled with crumpled clothes. Next to the bed, a lamp, a candle and an ashtray sat atop a stack of books.

Mac explored the adjoining bathroom. An alcove shower sported a bench seat tucked under a window. A full ashtray rested on the cracked window frame. "Tell me you do not smoke while you're in the shower!"

He poked his head into the bathroom, grinning. "Maybe."

"That's priceless."

His head disappeared. "Saves time."

As she peed, she asked, "Where did you get that poster?"

"Off a billboard."

"Gives your room character." She stepped back into the bedroom. "It definitely was not the blonde that made you bring it home."

He looked genuinely offended.

"Alright, alright, it's the truck, I get it." She nodded toward the hall. "Should we go out and do something?"

They had driven out to Gray Whale Cove beach. White capped waves crashed near the shore, pelting spray into a grey sky. They held hands as they walked along the empty beach, sharing stories, settling into a familiar rhythm that was somehow new. They watched a seagull grab a crab. Their footsteps traced the line between wet and dry sand.

She squeezed his hand. "It's cool out here. California. This weather is totally groovy."

"You get used to the fog."

"How's work, school?"

"Good. Long hours. When I'm not working, I'm studying at the cafe."

"You got enough money?"

"Fine."

"Are you pissed your parents didn't help out?"

"Nah. I don't see the point in sitting around blaming my parents."

She glanced at him. Was that an intentional dig? She ignored it. "What are you studying?"

"Business and engineering."

"You were never the dumb one. How much longer?"

"Two more years."

"Then what?"

"I dunno. Own my own business, maybe." He changed the subject. "So how was last week?"

"Crazy. Big. Huge really. Thousands of kids in black cap and gowns in one section of the basketball arena screaming their heads off. The rest was full of parents. The commencement speaker talked about following your heart. About listening to that quiet voice inside, what you really want to do, not what everybody tells you to do"

"Were your parents there?"

She dropped his hand. "Yeah."

"Did your sister make it?" He picked her hand back up.

"Totally." She grinned. "She stayed with me. Spilled bong water all over my bed. She's moving to Northern California."

He stopped, brought her close, wrapped his arms over her shoulders, pulled her head into his chest. "I'm glad you came. I'm glad you're here."

Tasting salt, they finally kissed.

He stopped in his tracks as they reached the parking lot and the BMW. "The Peace Corps?"

She nodded.

"Where?"

"Indonesia."

He was silent.

She tried to make it light-hearted. "It's my great adventure. To go see the big, wide world. While I'm young and foolhardy and full of excitement and enthusiasm."

"It's kinda the end of the earth, Mac."

She turned toward the crashing waves. "I think that's half the appeal. Living outside your comfort zone. Listening to that little voice inside that's telling you what you want instead of what you should. Stepping into the fear instead of turning away."

He brushed hair out of her eyes. "There are other ways to get out from under your mother's shadow."

"It's not just that. I need to prove to myself I'm a good person."

"Two years working in the jungles should do it."

In the deep night, a candle threw reverse shadows on the walls and the piles of books. They were naked; sheets were tangled at the foot of the mattress.

His chin rested on his hands between her breasts. He inhaled the clammy scent of their first, hurried coupling. "I'm telling you, he slept with his feet out the door."

Her head, nestled in clasped hands, shook in disbelief. "In a motel?"

"Uh huh."

"In the middle of Indiana?"

He grinned. "Uh huh."

"So literally - as in - his bare feet were hanging out the motel room door onto the cement walkway outside?"

"Second floor."

"They were really that stinky?"

He nodded against his hands, watched her small breasts shimmy with laughter. He gently lifted himself up, covered her body with his weight, pressed his forehead against her ear. "Mac, show me how to find you."

She did.

The bedroom's deep shadows were heavy on her back as she sat on the floor watching him sleep. His chest - with more hair than her trip two years ago - rose and fell. His snores resonated in the small room. She smiled in the gloom. Back in his family's mansion, they had discovered together that he snored.

She was safe here. But she was not content.

Her ambitions ensured their separation.

She stared at the buxom blond in the poster, sensing the taunt within the Mona Lisa smile.

He woke slowly, blinking then focusing. He slid up against the wall, clicked the lighter, throwing a second flame into the darkness and inhaled. "So how long do I have you?"

"I leave tomorrow."

He squinted through a stream of errant smoke. "Better make it a memorable weekend then."

She climbed up on him.

* * *

The next day, the drive to the airport through the mist was quiet. The car roared, occasionally belching. His hold on her hand was tight. "So, I'll see you in two years."

"For sure."

They pulled up to the airport drop off. His voice was somber. "Be smart, Mac."

"I'll be fine."

"You don't have to do this."

"I do."

"Come find me when you get back." His aquamarine eyes were strikingly light against the fog outside the window.

Her eyes welled.

"Mac, I don't wait for you. I'm just me and you're just you and who knows what will happen?" He pushed her hair back. "Just take care of you on your big adventure and come back in one piece."

25

North Capitol Hill, DC

Every chair in the top floor ATF New York Avenue building conference room was occupied by a man in either a blue or a grey suit. Another six men leaned against the back wall. All eyes were trained on an email exchange displayed on a large screen.

In a hoarse voice, Cal interpreted for the room. "This initial email is from Scimitar's COO to Chuck Boare dated three months before the July shipment. As you can see, their code isn't complicated." Cal directed a laser pointer to highlight a single line on the screen. *"The A's are begging us for mgs."* He translated the email for the room. "We are confident - given the timing - that the COO means Afghanis when he types 'A's' and machine guns when he types 'mgs' so he's basically saying, the Afghanis are begging for M4s."

On the screen, the laser pointer jumped to Boare's reply. *"What if we transfer P's July package to A?"* Cal interpreted again. "Here, Boare suggests the transfer of the 88088 Pakistani Army shipment to the Afghans. And here —" Cal pointed to the next line. "— the COO responds, with a 'risky'."

Cal's laser pointer moved to Boare's email response. *"Worth twice. :) Blame it on chaos in P."*

The anger in the room grew as the men digested Boare's intent.

Cal stirred their anger when he said, "The smiley face is a particularly nice touch."

He turned to the room. "So, I think we can agree that this is clear intent to resell. Boare follows this note immediately. His next email is quite compelling."

All eyes read the next line quietly to themselves. *"Pre-empt P income that is turning off soon."* Cal again translated. "This is a direct reference to the Pakistani Counterinsurgency Capability Fund that is due to expire next year. Scimitar Defense has gotten $40M in contracts via PCCP since 2009. So Boare is literally referring to when the PCCP will no longer provide them easy funds."

In the heavy pause, chair legs scraped across hard wood flooring. No one spoke.

Cal turned back to the screen, his pointer followed the email conversation when he said, "On the next line the COO asks a question to Boare."

"Who have we got in P?"

"That logistics crew."

"You trust them?"

"Yes. Connected to P Army. They do heavy lifting. Know transporters."

"OK"

Cal said, "And here, in this last line in the email exchange, Boare signs off on the operation."

"Good, let's get this done. Pay dirt. :) Switch to gmail."

An FBI agent whistled from the back of the room. The overhead lights came on.

Cal explained, "We initially ran keyword searches on well over 30,000 emails and thousands of their electronic documents. There were no matches. We found this one email through good old fashioned, slog reading. They were exceptionally cautious. Their code is simple but effective in thwarting a tech search. This is the only exchange from the evidence we pulled that implicates them in the arms trafficking."

The room was still. Jaws were clenched, arms were crossed.

"That being said, we are - I am - fairly confident a trace on their gmails will produce a significant haul for the task force."

Cal switched off the lights. A new document - a spreadsheet - illuminated the screen.

"We've got one more item to show you before we hand this over to the task force. Our team scanned Scimitar's accounting Quicken records starting four months before the shipment and then the two months after. We found something exceptional.

"Two months before the shipment, their receptionist purchased a non-contract cell phone for $25 and a $100 prepaid card. She paid in cash at the local Best Buy. Cash. She was probably instructed to use cash.

"But she then went back to the office...and I can only assume that she didn't want to be out of pocket for about a hundred bucks...so she submitted the receipt to the accountant for reimbursement."

The laser pointer slowly circled two entries under the heading *Q3 Expenses - $25.00 and $100.00.*

"Her hard copy receipt was in the documents we seized. Local police visited the Best Buy. The manager was extremely helpful. Based on the time stamp on the receipts, we were able to confirm her on the store's video."

On the screen, a grainy image showed the Scimitar receptionist at the Best Buy check out counter.

In the crowded conference room, the men were still as statues.

"We tracked down the cellphone's log. Prior to the shipment there are exactly nine calls made to the Khan Trucking Company in Peshawar and three made to an unknown number in Afghanistan."

From the back of the room, someone blurted, "Holy shit."

Cal set down his laser pointer on the long conference table. "They always overlook the little stuff."

Someone called out. "Agent, you said you got an anonymous tip that led to the search warrant. Can you elaborate?"

Wilson shot a glance at Cal. Wilson was inscrutable.

Cal cleared a scratch in the back of his throat. "I received a phone call last week Monday. The unidentified male said only, 'Scimitar Defense stole their own guns in Islamabad last year.' I started digging. I traced their DOC license for Pakistan. Two pieces of evidence emerged that got us the warrant. One: the routine Blue Lantern checks, that are in your packets, indicated there was a problem. Two: we were able to connect Scimitar and Chuck Boare to telephone calls placed again this year to the transport company in Pakistan. It's all there in your packets."

Another question was called out. "Why didn't the Blue Lantern investigation turn up Scimitar's involvement?"

"I think the very simple answer to that is that they didn't have access to domestic phone records."

Wilson stood, crossed to Cal, and thumped his back. "Congratulations, Agent Bertrand. To you and your team. We've got a very strong case against Scimitar Defense for a task force investigation. Fine, fine work."

A soft applause went up around the room.

A blue suited man in the front row asked, "We've all seen the New York News article this morning. Are you angry about the leak and are you concerned that the early press will affect your case?"

Wilson stepped in front of Cal. "I can't say reporters are our best friends." A few in the room chuckled. "But it is what it is and no, I don't think it will affect our case any more than early press has ever affected a case." He looked around the room. "We should know by the end of day how the Task Force is going to shape up. Thanks for coming by this morning. All questions can be directed to my office. We'll let Agent Bertrand get some sleep."

ONE WEEK BEFORE THE SENATE VOTE

A group calling itself Australian Cultural Terrorists and demanding increased government funding for the arts claimed responsibility today for the weekend theft of a $1-million Picasso oil painting.
- *LA Times*, August 4, 1986

It was Dora who continually reminded Picasso of the tragedy.
- James C. Harris, MD

26

10 months earlier - Kabul, Afghanistan

Sometimes she had trouble breathing in Kabul.

It could have been the ever-present dust. It could have been the stench from the stagnant trash along the roads. Or it could have been the ethical maze of working in the world's most primitive nation. Maybe it was a psychological issue; the oppression of the women - the burkhas, the segregation, the slavery - had felt so immediate. Whatever the reason, the city weighed heavy on her chest.

She had been here three times over the last two years to visit her friend Neha Malhotra at the US Embassy. Graceful, thoughtful, smiling Neha had not gotten many friends to visit. But given the huge Agency presence, it wasn't difficult for Mac to drum up excuses for official travel based on a 'critical connection' to an Asian operation. In fact, the Agency approved almost all her travel requests for risk-free, 'internal meetings'; hectic travel schedules made the Agency look busy when HQ reported to Congress.

Mac and Neha walked side by side through the empty Afghan Museum. The Kabul sun beamed through the rebuilt windows. The Hindu Kush mountain range beaconed in the distance. The museum housed only 70% of the collection it had before the Soviet invasion, the US support of the Mujahideen, the 20 years of tribal wars, the Taliban, or the NATO invasion. Looters loved chaos.

Neha stared down into a case of gold coins. "Sometimes I get mad at the mothers. It's the women who suffer here, have suffered here. Why don't they change it? Why don't they rebel? Groom their sons differently? Change their daughters?" She changed her mind. "Ok, ok, 20 years of boys growing up in military camps without education, without women, brainwashed in a personality cult of Islam. All Lord of the Flies shit. I get it."

They wandered down a dusty hall.

Neha grumbled again. "Sometimes I think what I'm doing is ridiculous. Over-ambitious. Arrogant."

Mac had only a dumb, easy answer. "At least you're trying?"

"I guess. But distributing medicine to clinics housed in mud buildings seems so insignificant compared to the history of this country, compared to the current events. Pakistan, the Saudis, Iran, Iraq - they are all still playing chess."

"You have to start somewhere?"

"Does that sound, I don't know - naive - to you?"

Mac conceded, "Yeah. It does."

Neha stared out the window at the mountain range. "They don't want us here. Never have. We're not liberators. We're invaders."

Outside, they sat on a courtyard bench. The dust prickled their sweaty skin. In the near distance, MRAPs (Mine-Resistant Ambush Protected) rumbled past on a side road. Neha fished in her leather courier bag and pulled out a worn Saints baseball hat, worked her ponytail through the back opening, and slid it down on her forehead. She asked, "What are you working on?"

"You know I can't tell you."

"Where are you?"

Mac replied, "Mostly Vietnam, Hong Kong, Indonesia. I do a lot around China, not always in China."

"Huh. Those places sound better than here."

"I get to scuba dive."

"Fuck you."

"Right?"

"Are you helping them?"

"Who? The people in those countries?"

"Yeah."

Mac laughed. "Hell no. I'm helping the Agency. I'm helping the US. In most cases I'm fucking the people in those countries.'

"Does it bother you? That you're not really helping them but you're living there?"

"I'm not living there. I'm visiting. Undercover. I'm not even myself."

"But does it bother you, that in most cases you're fucking them?'

Mac looked out over the scrubby lawn. "We all choose sides. You're the best the US has to offer. I'm probably the worst."

"If I'm the best we have to offer, we're not offering much. I'm pretty sure we're going to leave this place worse than when we got here."

On the road to the Green Zone, Neha steered the Humvee around a goat. Somber, scarfed women gazed from dark doors. Kids caroused in the street as ISAF (International Security Assistance Force) soldiers passed on patrol. A white, UN Range Rover pulled behind them; there was security in numbers.

Neha's voice dropped. "Shit goes on here…shit that's covered up. It's not good, Mac. Night raids. Villages. Killings. A completely hidden war. The Afghans know all about it. Americans back home don't. It's got your Agency's fingerprints all over it." She looked in her review mirror, as if checking for surveillance. "Counterterrorism dominates everything. There are over 1,000 CIA staff here. It's bonkers. You walk into a room and you can't tell where CIA ends and Special Forces begins. I get we're at war, but it's like the CIA are their own paramilitary unit, a killing machine. They find targets, make arrests, and kill suspects. Who holds them accountable? I'm pretty sure the CIA is in charge most of the time. This is far from a traditional war. This whole fucking place is a CIA operation. Don't get me wrong, I'm all about getting those fuckers out of here to help build democracy, but at the end of the day, who is watching over the CIA? At least the military has to report their shit to Congress."

"Yeah, I hear you."

As they near the Green Zone, two hulking MRAPs pulled in front of them, joining the convoy. Red dust enveloped them, the rumble vibrated in their chests.

Neha shifted the Humvee down into first gear. "And do not get me started on the drones. It's all anyone talks about now. I mean, how many drones has the Agency flown over here and dropped on militants? I've heard the number of those killed by the drones is upwards of 2,000 since 2001." She shook her head. "I've met the Agency targeters here. It's weird having a drink with them, talking to them, knowing that all they do is stare at data all day trying to identify their next target. It's all they *want* to do. They get promoted for it."

"They're not like you. They get a bit bent, if you know what I mean. They can't have joined the Agency for this, but this is where they are - in the heart of military operations in Afghanistan. You wouldn't have joined for that, would you have?"

Mac shook her head, staring ahead.

"I'm just saying, Mac, this doesn't sound like the kind of Agency you signed up for."

"It's not."

"Have you been to the Counterterrorism Center in Langley?"

Mac gave a small nod.

"So the build up, the militaristic shit - it's not just here."

"No. It's not just here."

They were sitting over beers in a dark, almost empty restaurant in the Green Zone. A few military types stood quietly around the bar. The small, chipped wood table between them wobbled.

"Please tell me you did NOT just say that." Mac chortled.

Neha twisted her long dark hair into a top knot and clasped her hands behind her neck. "No lie, I just put my head back down on the pillow and I look over at him and I said, 'I gotta leave soon, Honey.'"

"Oh my god. What did he do?"

"He rolls over to me and literally says, 'Can't I get some snuggles?'"

Mac snorted loudly. "What did you do?"

"I said, 'Yeah, not today, Sugar, I'm super busy.' So I got up, pulled on my clothes and bee-lined it out of there." Neha's smile was huge, beaming.

"That's priceless."

"He's like totally after me. He keeps finding me, asking me out."

"Seriously? That's fucking priceless."

"I know, right? Who knew being so hard-to-get would actually pay back in spades? All these years it was us doing the chasing and - boom - in the snap of a finger I've turned the tables." She laughed over the beer bottle. "What a great ego boost! Wait —" the bottle hovered by her lip. "— I have a photo on my camera. Wanna see him?"

"Uh. Duh!"

Neha dug through her bag past head scarves and a toiletry bag. She pulled out a cracked cell phone and flipped through her photo gallery. She handed Mac the phone with a photo of a lean, well-built army officer standing near a military tent.

Mac whistled. "Dude, he's F.I.N.E."

"Right?"

They tapped beer bottles. Mac said, "Here's to something good coming out of Afghanistan."

"Baggage-free, manly sex!" Neha's demeanor changed slowly. She stared directly at Mac. "We just heard SIGAR - Special Inspector General for Afghanistan Reconstruction - estimates $100 Billion has been spent here in non military aid. 100. Billion. All through contractors to State, USAID, DOD. Contractors in Afghanistan are building latrines without plumbing, cafeterias without kitchen facilities and getting paid millions. We've got fuck all to show for it after a decade. 100 Billion. Christ."

"The cost of war and rebuilding?" Another limp answer.

Neha shook her head. "It's more than that. The CIA is literally handing bags of cash over to Karzai."

Mac hushed her. "You're not supposed to know about that."

"Yeah, whatever with the 'I'm not supposed to know that'. You hear a lot of things out here. People forget we're going go back to the real world at some point and it won't be all 'what happens on tour stays on tour'. Guys here were talking about when they were in Iraq and they were moving wrapped cash on pallets between unsecured sites. They were saying stacks of hundred dollar bills often left those pallets and ended up in duffel bags." She took a sip of beer. "And sometimes one of them would just pick up a duffel bag on their way to Kuwait for R and R. That's some crazy shit."

"Yup."

"You see that shit?"

"Yup. It was a cash economy. No other options."

Neha was worked up. "Yeah, but like a cash economy to repair what we did there. It wasn't meant to be a cash economy for our guys to literally just walk off with duffel bags." She calmed herself. "They're saying in Iraq the Coalitional Provisional Authority lost like $20 billion. Poof. Vanished. 20 billion."

"Don't doubt it at all." Mac sipped her beer.

"You think they know this back home?"

"I dunno."

"I know you spooks get close to that cash. You NOCs especially. Officially you're not there." She stared at Mac. "Ethics are what you do in the dark, when no one is looking."

Mac watched her.

Neha said, "This is what I say about ethics. If I'd been that close, if I'd been in Iraq, I'd have gotten some for a nest egg. That would have been my ethics when no one was looking. But little ole me? I'm no NOC. I'm a fucking USAID worker in Afghanistan and all I've got to show for my time out here was some great manly sex, some swell photos of me handing out meds to barely functioning health clinics, a chronic yeast infection and an overinflated sense of patriotic martyrdom. Fuck."

The guys around the bar hooted over a joke. The lopsided fan over their small table creaked as it spun.

Neha whispered, "You ready to talk about Beijing yet?"

Mac blinked, pulled hard on her beer bottle. Her eyes retreated to a distant place and she told the story in a detached voice.

It had been a great cover; her alias had been a mid-level expat banker with a huge American investment bank based in Beijing. It had not been the first time she'd been embedded with a US bank, but it had been the first time in China. She had been meeting the tech start-up kids, the newly emerging rich class. Her list of potential assets wanting to move their money and families to Silicon Valley had been growing every month. Langley's approval to approach hadn't arrived yet, but after 12 months she had been optimistic the green light was coming soon.

Instead, a knock at the door to her high-rise apartment had come in the middle of the night. She had opened it as a mid-level banker would, in a sweatshirt and jeans, blurry eyed.

Six Chinese secret police took her off into the night.

Two months later, she had been released from an off-the-grid work camp fifty pounds lighter, hair falling out, fingernails growing back. They had tried but had not broken her.

Someone back in Langley - most likely Odom - had worked a deal with a senior Chinese Managing Director in the bank who then worked his back room connections.

She had been driven to an airplane, sworn to silence, and blacklisted from Chinese territory.

Langley had given her three-months personal leave. She had chosen a dive resort on a remote Indonesian island where she had spent every day in silent, aquamarine swells, watching fish and sea creatures get on about their lives while the tanks' oxygen cleansed her lungs, veins and memories.

When she emerged, they put her back in the field.

Just not in China.

Under the loopy fan, Mac ran all ten fingernails across her scalp.

Neha placed both hands flat on the table. "Did they rape you?"

Mac whispered very slowly, "You don't want to ask that question."

"Don't I?"

"Of course they did."

"Jesus Christ." Neha reached across the table, squeezing Mac's hands.

A loud laugh from the bar jolted them.

Neha leaned in closer. "No fucking harm in planning an exit from the Agency. You don't owe them shit. You've done your time and then some." Neha's hands were covered in red dust. "Mac, they can't take it *all* away."

27

Capitol Hill, DC

At 8:10 p.m. it was already dark in DC. From the cafe, Mac watched Amanda Hughes step out of the red brick SFG Lobby office wearing another bright, slim summer dress. This time she had paired it with sneakers for the commute home.

Mac followed her and caught her just before the Metro entrance. "Amanda. Hi!"

Amanda turned, unsure but then recognizing the blond bob. "Hi, Dora."

"How's it going?"

"Fine, fine."

"Listen, I was going to try to get in to see Neil about a last minute thing. Darn."

Amanda waited.

"You know, I really would love an invoice or a receipt or something, like on SFG letterhead." Mac nodded back toward the office. "Do you mind? I'm on a plane home later tonight."

Amanda hesitated, but her commitment to the organization combined with the respect for a big donor got the better of her. "Sure, let's just run back up now and I can print and sign something for you."

"Super! That would be great, Amanda." She gave a quick squeeze on Amanda's upper arm.

Amanda unlocked the glass door, stepped inside and punched in the alarm code.

Mac gushed, "I really appreciate your help! Phwew, what a

weight off."

"Sure, sure. I mean, it's not every day we get, you know, such big donations."

They walked in step down the long hallway.

Mac said, "Well, Mrs. Bodie is real serious about her politics."

"That's the way it should be. My father always says 'Good Politics is Passionate Politics'"

"Well said. It must be nice to be so passionate about what you do."

"Sure. Constitutional rights are important."

At her desk, Amanda turned on her computer and printer and sat down to pull up a file.

Mac stepped behind her, looking out the window. It had started to rain. She spoke to the pane. "I've often wondered what I'd do if I found out that the folks I was working for were not all I was led to believe."

Amanda's fingers slowed on her keyboard.

Mac's breath made a small fog circle on the window pane. "Mrs. Bodie is a very careful investor. She asked me to do some homework while I was here."

From behind her, Amanda asked, "You didn't get me up here for a receipt, did you?"

Mac shook her head, watched a car's headlights pass on the street.

Amanda asked, "Then what?"

Mac turned. "I'm not completely convinced…well, how do I say this…that your boss is totally above board."

Amanda gaped at her. "Of course he is. He's the chief strategist for one of the most - if not the - most powerful advocacy organizations in the world."

"Hear me out."

Amanda's voice raised an octave. "I'm not sure I want to, Dora."

"I've got something you need to see." Mac pulled her cell phone out. "I just want to show you something. Two minutes." She pulled up a file. "I think you'll want to hear this."

Mac handed the phone to Amanda. The photo of Koen and the Congressman at lunch was open. "I took this recording while they were at lunch." She hit play on the audio.

Through the cell phone's speaker, Congressman Peter's twang was clear. "Now wait a good goddamned minute, Neil. Are you saying she's offering to pay ya'll to support Hannover's race against me?"

Amanda glanced up in confusion. The audio continued. Mac leaned against the corner of the desk, watching her.

Amanda stared back down at the photo, listening to the recorded conversation.

Very slowly, Mac slipped her hand into a pocket, pulled out the pink barrette, and set it on the window sill. It was being left behind enemy lines but at least it had a view.

When the recording ended, Amanda looked up at Mac. "I don't understand."

"I think you do. In fact, I think you're smarter than they think you are. I think you're a helluva lot smarter than you give yourself credit for."

"This can't be happening. Why are you doing this?"

"My boss is first off smart, second off a good business person, and lastly a woman. She's been burned by husbands. She's been burned by business partners. She checks out her alliances very seriously. Second Amendment rights are something both my boss and I hold dear. We, like you, are true patriots. This partnership is serious for us."

Amanda looked around, searching for an answer.

"It's called fraud, Amanda." Mac's tongue touched her back tooth, opening her mouth slightly. It was a subconscious sign of superiority combined with boredom. "What Neil is doing. Pure and simple. Fraud."

"Shut up! I don't know why you're doing this."

Mac pressed her palm against her mouth, eyeing Amanda for a long moment. When she lifted her hand, she said, "I think you do. I think you knew, somewhere in the back of your mind, that something wasn't right here. Just like we suspected. We - Mrs. Bodie and I - suspected. We just dug in a bit."

"I don't believe you."

"You don't have to believe me. You just heard the recording."

Amanda handed back the cell phone. "Stop it!"

Mac shrugged. She took the cell phone, made to leave, but said a final thought. "There are moments in everyone's life when they get to decide what kind of person they want to be. Amanda Hughes, this is one of those moments. I'll be in touch."

Mac walked back down the long hallway.

Langley, VA

Odom was reviewing documents when Beam knocked lightly on the door. "Sir, I think have something." He sat down and opened a file folder. "You asked me to run a full 12 month trace on Agent AD99."

"Go ahead."

"We found some fairly recent travel plans that may be of interest."

"Go ahead."

"First, Mac was in Kabul ten months back on assignment. Your approval is on her travel documents."

"Correct. She had some intel for our counter terrorism guys there."

"She then returned to Kabul about two months after that. Not assignment related. That trip was unauthorized, to be exact, Sir. Eight months ago."

"What?"

"Unauthorized."

"Then how do you know about it?"

"It was buried in the travel logs. She used an Agency ID."

"She went back?"

Beam nodded.

Odom asked, "What did you find out about the second trip?"

"When she arrived in Kabul she did not check in with Station. Like I said, this was an unauthorized trip. So we talked to Station and one of our guys said he remembered seeing her at the Agency hotel in town."

"And?"

"He said he remembers that specifically because one of his friends - Army - had propositioned her the night before at the hotel bar."

"What?"

"Well, an Army Ranger had…hit on her, Sir."

"And?"

"She, ah, turned him down. So the Army Ranger was on the look out for her in the hotel bar and around Kabul the next few days."

"And?"

"Well, our contact says no one saw her again."

"That's all you've got?"

"Yes. Sir. She has no other unauthorized travel. That we could find. All her official travel was signed off by you."

"You can go."

28

Dupont Circle, DC

Even though the apartment is hot and humid at 9 p.m., the air that rushed Cal's skin as he stepped out of the shower felt chilled. He grabbed a plush, grey robe and swung it on. It had been an anniversary present six years ago from his ex. She had often complained Cal's outlook on life and work was uncompromising, 'too black and white.' They had been in a Tempe department store when she pointed to the robe and mocked him, saying "Look Cal, it's grey. Can you handle it?"

The robe still looked and felt new.

In the kitchen, rain pelted the windowpane. He picked up a mug from the drying rack and stood for a long minute, deep in thought. He poured himself a coffee, walked through to the living room, and settled at his desk. Outside, a street lamp appeared fractured in the heavy rain.

The coffee tasted weak despite the fact that it was the regular Dark Roast from the ACME around the corner he had been buying for two years.

He made a call. "Hi. Ranty. It's Cal here. Have you got a minute?"

"Of course! To what do I owe the honor? Oh, and first things first, I hear through the grapevine you briefed a Joint Task force on Scimitar today. Congrats!"

"You already heard?"

"The Agency is bad at a lot of things. I'm not going to under-represent our failings. But we can spread gossip on the wind my friend. Don't even need smoke signals."

"I was just about to tell you that the briefing went well. Also, that you were an invaluable, anonymous, part of our team. A sincere thank you."

"For you, Cal, of course."

"Ranty, there's something that has been plaguing me."

"Yes?"

"I can't figure out why the third cable - from Peshawar - was the last cable on license 88088. It just doesn't make sense. Why didn't the Blue Lantern Coordinator in Islamabad push any further? Why didn't he investigate beyond that third cable? I overshoot almost everything I investigate. Had it been me, I would have OCD'ed the missing M4s for a long time. Probably months. Maybe years."

There is a long pause. Ranty spoke slowly. "Cal, it's a funny thing you calling me about this. I was actually thinking the same thing earlier this evening."

"Really?"

"Yes. I dislike a conundrum as much as the next man."

"Ok?"

"It occurred to me that the third cable from Singer in Peshawar was classified 'Confidential."

"Yes?"

"Well, here's the potential issue in front of us, my friend. If additional cables on 88088 had been classified Top Secret - instead of just Confidential - well, then only those most senior in State or CIA would have seen them."

Cal instantly recognized the potential gap. "Are *you* able to access Top Secret?"

"Not on this particular topic, no. This is 'need to know' only and severely restricted, even on the network."

On the street below, headlights passed in the rain. Rain hammered down the drain pipe near the bay window.

Cal furthered the thought. "So, if the Blue Lantern investigation did find additional information on the missing guns - and - and sent it up classified as Top Secret, only the Mandarins would have seen it."

"Indeed."

"But, Ranty, if we assume the investigation found that Scimitar - a US gun manufacturer - was involved in the missing M4s there would have been a big scandal. Which would have led to a cross agency task force - like the one we have now."

"Presumably."

Cal leaned back in his chair, the phone was tight against his ear. "So, if there was additional investigation into the missing M4s - it either didn't turn up Scimitar's fingerprints or...they discovered Scimitar resold their own guns and...buried it." The last two words floated on the apartment's humid air like a thick, black cloud. "Ranty, are you thinking what I'm thinking?"

"I believe I am."

"My gut says Blue Lantern did find Scimitar's fingerprints and someone upstairs at State or CIA buried this."

"Your supposition sounds very likely to me."

"Maar isn't mad that the investigation stalled. Maar is pissed off the investigation got buried. I'd have to agree with him. I'm starting to get pissed off too."

"Please be careful, Cal. You're pulling strings that lead right up the food chain. There are a lot of people involved in that industry."

"There are. Lots of people. And a lot of money."

29

Capitol Hill, DC

Across town, Mac was watching the SFG Lobby door when her NYC labeled burner phone rang.

It was Penny. "Whatcha doin?"

"I'm on a stake out."

"No way."

"Way."

"That's awesome."

"Actually, they aren't so great. You sit around just watching crap."

"Like how long do you have to sit around?"

"Tonight is gonna be a long night."

"Wow. Where are you?"

"In a coffee shop."

"It's like a le Carre novel."

"What are you doing?" Mac asked.

"Just wrapping up here at work."

"That's late, no?"

"Pretty normal actually."

"Huh."

Penny asked, "Do they know you're off the ranch?"

"Probably. Right about now. Yes."

"What will they do?"

"Not a lot they can do. They'll try to get me to come in. Then explain to me what I can and cannot do now that I'm no longer Agency. It pretty much boils down to me keeping my mouth shut for eternity."

"Can they direct your future like that?"

"They used to be able to do that. Our parents' generation stayed in for life. I know guys while I was coming up that had their wives and kids with them overseas. They had covers as Political Officers at the Embassies. People like me, we're in the trenches with the garbage flotsam. Anti-narcotics. Counter terrorism. It's not like you can have a personal life when you're deep-cover running a covert op surrounded by Columbian psychopaths or Pakistani mass murderers."

"Good lord. What will they do if you don't go in?"

"Best case scenario: they back off and let me walk, but keep an eye on me. Worst case scenario: they threaten to burn me."

"Seriously?"

"Yup."

"Can you push back on them? Like, maybe…I dunno…do you have stuff to leverage against that kind of pressure?"

"What do you think?"

"I think you're pretty smart."

"I'll take that as a compliment."

They let the conversation idle. There was a growing comfort between them, a rekindled intimacy.

Penny asked, "Do you feel like you've accomplished a lot? I mean, in your life?"

"Yeah. I guess I do. It's all stuff nobody will ever hear about, but it's been pretty impactful I would say. How about you?"

"My boys are awesome."

They fell back into quiet contemplation. Outside the coffee shop, a bus chugged past, its interior brightly lit. Only two commuters were inside. They both sat alone, by windows, looking out into the dark as the neighborhood passed them by.

Penny asked, "Are you sad to be so alone?"

"Yeah."

At 9:15 p.m. Amanda stumbled out and walked slowly toward the Capital South metro. Mac fell in line behind her, keeping surveillance. Fortunately, Amanda was no spy and in all likelihood wouldn't notice.

Down in the station, they both swiped through the turnstiles and headed for the Orange Line metro to Courthouse. Mac kept a 30-

foot distance, stepping into the far side of the car Amanda chose.

When Amanda stepped off the train at Courthouse, Mac did also. Amanda rode the escalator up, distracted, head down. Mac allowed four people to step before her before she also stepped onto the escalator.

Up on the street, Mac kept behind at a decent distance. Amanda was walking slowly through the barren, concrete suburb. She was easy to tail.

Amanda reached a high-rise apartment complex and pushed open the door into a brightly lit lobby. She gazed, immobile and adrift, at the elevator until the door opened and she stepped in.

Out on the street, Mac took stock of her surroundings. There wasn't much but high-rise buildings. She used the bathroom in a McDonalds to change into some sweats and stocked up at the 7-11 with water, nuts, granola bars and energy drink.

Stakeouts were grueling. But when you first recruit an agent, you needed to keep eyes on them.

The next few hours would make or break this operation.

Langley, VA

Odom, holding a manila personnel folder with a small penciled AD99 in the corner, sat in front of the huge desk in the office of the CIA Director of National Clandestine Service. Across from him, Director Benedict Hawkinson, with his sweep of brown hair over grey temples, drooping eyelids behind rimless glasses, and straight lips surrounded by heavy jowls, was a career undercover officer who had risen through the ranks. The halls whispered that his ascent was due to an exceptional ability to cover his own ass.

Hawkinson spoke in a slow, soft style that belied a critical nature. "You think she's off the ranch?"

"I'm afraid I do. She called in from Vietnam four weeks ago going black. She was supposed to check in. I had Security do a trace. They can't find her anywhere. Not even electronic vapor."

Hawkinson's gaze intensified. "Frank, did you see this coming?"

"No, Sir. We didn't. She's had some loose ends over the years - taking off for a week or two. But she checks in again. Mostly it's diving or sailing in Asia. Of course there was the Beijing incident. But no, overall she's been fairly solid. In fact, she's been on counter terrorism for at least 10 years and has brought us our best leads from Indonesia, Malaysia and Vietnam. It helps that she's a woman."

"How long has she been in?"

"20 years."

Hawkinson whistled. "That's quite a run."

"Indeed."

"I don't like to lose them. Especially not this way." He reached out for the personnel folder and skimmed it. "What do you think she's doing?"

"I'm not entirely certain…"

"But?"

"I've got some intel - I'm not sure it's relevant."

"Let's hear it."

"It turns out she was in Kabul unofficially last year."

Hawkinson's eyebrows rose.

"I had sent Mac to Kabul last year to do some exchange with our counterterrorism guys. There was a possible link with another op."

"Ok?"

"Then, oddly, she went back two months later. Off the books. Unauthorized."

"When was that second trip?"

"Six months ago. July."

Hawkinson's eyes widened, almost imperceptibly. He pressed the intercom button on his phone. "Please pull the Scimitar folder." He looked back at Odom. "What I'm about to tell you is 'need to know' only." He waited for Odom to nod then said, "Last year a Blue Lantern investigation found some US guns - manufactured by a shop out of Kentucky - went missing from Pakistan. They were transported into Afghanistan.

"Recently the ATF has discovered that the company had actually trafficked their own guns. A raid last week provided solid evidence. A cross-agency Task Force has been established."

"Did we know they had trafficked their own guns?"

"No."

There was a knock on the office door and the secretary handed

Hawkinson a Top Secret folder. He glanced at the file name and handed it to Odom.

Hawkinson continued, "Here's the coincidence. What only a very few people here and at State *do know* is that one of these missing Scimitar guns killed a US diplomat in Afghanistan. In July last year."

Shocked, Odom asked, "The ATF doesn't know this gun killed one of ours?"

Hawkinson shook his head.

Odom summed up slowly and said, "ATF knows Scimitar ran their own guns. We didn't. We know one of these missing Scimitar gun killed the diplomat. ATF doesn't."

Hawkinson nodded.

"Because we buried this report?" Odom asked, holding up the file.

Hawkinson's face was solid rock.

Odom asked, "Are we going to tell them?"

Hawkinson stared at him.

Odom's mouth opened, but the Hawkinson cut him off, picking up the next subject. "The ATF claim they had an anonymous tipster on Scimitar's involvement. That doesn't sit well with me. Who is this secret tipster? Why now, a year later?" He walked around to his chair. "And just today, here you are in my office, folder in hand, telling me one of your operatives has been missing for the last three weeks *and* she also happened to have traveled to Kabul unofficially in *July* - the same time as the shooting incident. There are too many coincidences."

Odom concluded, "Mac may be involved."

Hawkinson's response was curt. "Find your missing operative, Odom. Now."

30

18 years ago - San Francisco, CA

Sitting on his stoop in the upscale Dogpatch neighborhood of San Francisco, Mac watched the evening fog roll in over the bay, blocking out the weak sunlight. A motorcycle growled around a curve a few blocks away. A few minutes later, a helmeted rider on a 73 Norton Commando 850cc pulled up to the curb. The black visor turned to her for a long moment.

The driver walked the purring motorcycle backward into the curb, turned off the ignition, and lifted off his helmet. His shoulders had filled in and his hair had grown longer, pulled back in a short ponytail.

Joe said, "You're late."

It had been four years.

The third floor apartment had an expansive view of the bay. The modern, black leather furniture was sleek and Italian. Black and white prints hung on tall, grey walls.

He set his helmet on a large, marble island in the open-plan kitchen, pulled out a stool for her, and set to work at a small cappuccino machine, grinding out two pungent espressos.

He handed her a small cup. "I don't want to know how you found me."

"You weren't that hard to find, actually." She sipped. "You look good."

He shrugged.

"You look happy, healthy."

He shrugged again, watching her.

She stared at him. "I don't mean to intrude."
"You're not."
"I always am."
"You never are."
She attempted to be nonchalant. "Especially if there's someone, you know, special."
He finally grinned. "There's not. Not right now."
He led her out to the deck and turned on an outdoor heater. Foghorns bleated from the bay. They sat close to each other on the patio sofa.
She wrapped both hands around the coffee cup. "So you've got your own business."
"You did your homework."
"Not too many of you in San Francisco."
A seagull landed on the deck's wall. Its black eyes watched them.
"Yeah. It's a small firm. We do design for aerospace and big engineering companies. They send us their requirements. We knock it out on software, CAD, stuff. Beats the hell out of having to work for another engineer. I'm hiring two more engineers next week. We're busy. Almost too busy."
"I bet you make a good boss."
"I'm alright. I'm learning. The engineering and design aspects are the most interesting. The management and admin...not so much. And I had to get financing to start up. That wasn't easy."
"You're clearly doing well." She indicated the apartment. "This is not too shabby."
He grinned.
She smiled at him. "I like the hair."
"Keeps my edge obvious. I'd hate anyone to think I'm some dumb everyday 9 to 5 run-of-the-mill engineering dork."
She laughed.
"So tell me. How were the tropics?"

She had been assigned as an English teacher to a rural school near a river along a mountain in Java. The impoverished community had tended livestock.
She had been happy, in the heat, with the kids greeting her every morning in singsong. "Good Morning, Ms. Mac."

God, the kids had been gorgeous, happy, and innocent.

She had planted a lawn and a vegetable garden in her backyard and had meticulously weeded them into a cultured square against the sprawling jungle. The neighborhood children had shown up every day after school to run and tumble on the luscious grass. They would stop to hug her. The very little ones would worm their way into her lap; sometimes they fell asleep. They had trusted her instantly, implicitly.

Half-way through her first year, she had learned the local mission priest - an older, Dutch Catholic missionary - was a monster, forcing himself on the women in the community. Many of them had gotten pregnant.

There had been fair hair kids in the middle of Indonesia with Dutch names like Ernst and Annelein.

She had approached her friend Donna. "Do people like Father?"

"Enough."

"Do the women like Father?"

Donna had shot her a warning look. "We don't talk about that."

She had approached the local mayor. "Is Father well-respected here?"

He had thrown her a warning look. "Father brings in money. Jakarta doesn't. You are an outsider. You will stop asking such questions."

She had been trapped in a jungle version of the Island of Dr. Moreau. She had stayed out of commitment to the students. For a year and a half she had watched powers collude, abuse.

In response, she had studied writings on authoritarian institutions, power dynamics, voices of the masses and the concepts of systemic, sweeping change and revolution.

Their coffees were finished. He showed her the apartment.

In the bedroom, she ran her fingers along his desk, smiling at the piles of quarters and dimes.

"Don't start on me." He mock challenged.

"Glad to see some things don't change."

A shoebox was stuffed with stacked dollar bills. She ran her fingernail along the side like a bank teller.

"I've been fixing old motorcycles for friends. They pay me in cash. If I'd known you were coming, I would have put that away."

"Nah, it's kinda sexy. You've gotta be the only non drug dealer that just has loads of cash lying around in shoeboxes."

She drifted into the bathroom. "You still got a crazy shower?"

He followed. "Not anymore."

She jumped up backwards onto the edge of the sink and held her hands out to him. He stepped between her legs.

Only their first kiss was gentle.

Later, lying in bed, she explained how she had been after another year in the jungle - isolated, pent-up, enraged, saddened.

A white American guy had shown up at a school sporting event. About 30 years old, he had been dressed in khakis and a button-down, had been sweating profusely, and had introduced himself as Felix. At first, she had figured him for a Mormon. But he had told her about his anthropology dissertation and said he'd return in a month.

Every month for six months he had stepped off the bus in the small town center. The word would spread quickly. Eventually one of her students would quietly whisper, "That man is here for you in town, Missy Mac."

They had probably thought he was courting her in some odd, American tradition.

She would get on her bike and peddle in to the lobby bar in the single hotel. They would drink beer and talk politics.

A month shy of her two year Peace Corps graduation, Felix had told her who he really was. He had explained the Agency was interested in talking to her. Just talking. No obligation. Why not go hear them out? He had given her a one-way train ticket and the address of the Jakarta safe house.

At first, they had talked of patriotism. But that hadn't resonated with her. Her parents had protested the Vietnam War. Patriotism equaled protest in her mind. She had no interest in patriotism.

So they had changed tactics. They had talked about protecting the US, protecting those she loved, protecting what they had built at home. She had pushed back explaining that's what the military was for.

Their tactics had changed. They had told her, "We need advocates committed to democracy, to free the world's oppressed." They had explained that her directed, targeted actions as part of the CIA would help millions through regime change.

She, they had told her, could overthrow despots.

She had thought of Donna, the innocent children in the jungle and their voiceless lives.

Joe watched her.

She looked up. "That made sense to me."

He held his breath.

"I told them yes."

Naked, Joe rolled out of bed, grabbed cigarettes and an ashtray, walked silently into the bathroom and closed the door behind him.

She sat up, pulled the sheet around her chest and listened to the silence.

Twenty minutes later, he stepped out in jeans and a t-shirt, his face hard. "Let's go out."

The club was packed, heaving. He led her down into the VIP lounge where the bartender nodded at him and smiled at her, knowing she was special by the way Joe kept her close.

Two hours later, the techno beat thumped louder. At a corner booth, Joe slammed down his drink, his anger peaking. "I think you're wrong. I think this whole thing, this whole fucking thing is just wrong, wrong, wrong. You're a lost idealist, not a fucking secret agent."

She spat, "You can't tell me what to do."

"Somebody should. You're chasing some ridiculous fantasy about changing the world. It's insane." He stabbed a finger to his forehead. "Insane."

"Fuck you, Joe."

She stared out across the packed club, slowing her breathing. "What if I can?"

"Can what?"

"Make some difference in the world?"

"They're just using you."

"Maybe we use each other. They use me to push their agenda. I use them to make a difference."

The anger slipped from him. He saw again the younger Mac taking a bad situation and turning it to her advantage, strong in the face of adversity, not because she wanted it but because she had to.

She hadn't noticed his changed demeanor. "I'm just fucking me, trying to find my way in the world."

His eyes were sad, knowing. "When they finish with you, they'll spit you out."

"Yeah. OK. I don't expect a lifetime commitment."

"So you're pretty much righting the world's wrongs - all on your own? All on your own."

She leaned close, the alcohol astringent on both her breath, and stared into his blurred, blue eyes. "Yes. Right now. Yes. Right now, I need to do this."

31

New York, NY

Colorful 'Day of the Dead' banners hung from the ceiling in the upscale Mexican restaurant in Alphabet City. In the background, a Mexican crooner was accompanied by banjos. The air was thick with cumin and garlic.

Penny and Kenneth sat across the table from another couple with large sangria goblets and 15 half finished tapas plates between them.

Janice gawked at Kenneth. "Leo DiCaprio?"

He nodded vigorously. "Yeah, my agent said he's interested."

Holding a sangria glass in both hands, Penny watched him.

Janice said, "Oh my god."

Kenneth claimed, "He'd be perfect for the role."

Janice looked at Penny. "Wow, not bad!"

Penny shrugged.

"Not bad? That's an understatement." Kenneth gave Penny a sharp look.

Janice asked, "So what happens next?"

Penny sipped slowly.

He said, "Now they pitch him and see what kind of input he wants. You know, how much I'll be working with him on rewrites and what not."

"How long will it take to hear back?"

Penny stared into the distance and mumbled, "If we hear back."

"My guess a few weeks. I've also told them to approach Clooney although…well… he's a bit old for the role…"

Penny excused herself from the table and headed to the

bathroom.

Inside the quiet room, she locked the door. She stared at her image in the mirror. She'd just had her hair done; it was relaxed, shiny and straight. She reached into her purse, pulled out a nice lipstick and brought it to her lip.

In that instant, Beyoncé - the Beyoncé from the "Survivor" video in camouflage with perfect hair and make up - was staring back at her in the Mexican restaurant mirror. Penny smiled at this new mirage. Beyoncé smiled back. Penny placed the waxy tip of the lipstick along the contour of her lip. In the mirror, Beyoncé placed her lipstick against her lips and timelessly stayed within the lines. Penny took out her powder compact, tapped the sponge, and patted her face. In the mirror, Beyoncé patted the powder sponge. Penny flipped her smooth hair off her shoulder and in the mirror, Beyoncé did the same flip. Penny winked. Beyoncé winked back.

Then Beyoncé was gone.

Penny stared back at her from the mirror.

She dipped her hand into her handbag, searching. Her fingers closed around the burner phone.

She typed a text. "*Are you scared?*"

While she waited for Mac's reply, she winked again in the mirror. The bravado was gone. A scared Penny winked back.

The burner phone pinged. Mac had written, "*Nah. Not yet.*"

Penny looked into the mirror and whispered, "I am." She typed, "*Ok.*"

Across town, Charlotte and Stacia made their way through a crowded bar. Up on stage a steam punk band belted loudly. Charlotte leaned over the bar and looked back questioningly.

Stacia said, "A Stella. Thanks."

The bartender placed their drinks on the wide bar. Her beer glass had a round Stella logo.

Charlotte asked, "Dude, where you been all week?"

"My crazy lady-boss has me working on a series."

"On what?"

"The SFG if you believe it."

"Yuck. Really?"

"Yeah. There's this legislation coming up that would ban assault weapons. We're trying to do something in advance."

"Like a series?"

Stacia nodded.

"So are you like the lead reporter on the series?"

"It's looking that way."

"Dude, that's hot!" Charlotte leaned over to the bartender and ordered two shots of Jägermeister.

They held up their shots for a toast. Charlotte said, "Here's to you getting byline my sistah!"

The liquid burned down Stacia's throat.

Charlotte asked, "So how's it going?"

"They're super dodgy and shadowy and shit. Different legal entities, websites, money coming in and going out all under secret. It's some weird shit."

Charlotte was distracted by the lead singer leaning out from the stage, howling into the microphone. Stacia took a long swig from her glass of beer and set it on the bar. Her thumb absently rubbed the gold logo on the beer glass. Something niggled in her brain. She stared at the bassist's fingers plucking strings, but the music sounded distant. She turned and stared at the logo on the beer glass.

She quickly tapped Charlotte's shoulder. "I'll be right back, just gotta make a phone call."

In the alcove outside the bar's door, she fished in her bag for her cell phone and dialed a number. She held the phone tight against her ear to block out the rain.

Freda answered in a worn-out voice. "This better be good. It's Friday night, my daughter is burning down the apartment, and I just can't build it up for you right now."

"It's all about their brand."

"What?"

Stacia raised her voice. "If you don't have a brand, you don't have shit. I'm sitting here drinking a beer - a Stella - and I'm thinking to myself, this beer tastes like every other beer. So how does it get the huge following it does? I mean, does it deserve its very own glass in a bar? With a logo?"

"Ok?"

"Stella's built a reputable brand. People trust it. Whether it's trustworthy or not, Stella has convinced their audience that they're making a superior beer for discerning beer drinkers. People trust the branding."

"Ok."

"Well, I've been thinking about Scimitar. Scimitar is their biggest corporate donor."

"Ok."

"We haven't really chased the corporate angle."

"Ok."

"Well, the SFG's brand is a grassroots membership image, 'we support gun owners of America' kind of thing."

"Ok."

"But what if that's not the truth? What if they really, ultimately, support the gun industry? I mean, to the detriment of their members?"

Freda was silent for a few seconds. "Nice work, kid. Get me something tomorrow."

The following morning, Freda looked up over her morning coffee as Stacia walked into her office. "What have you got for me?"

Stacia checked her notes, squinting in the sunlight. "Background on the gun market."

"Talk to me."

"The US gun and ammo manufacturing industry is a $15 Billion market."

Freda whistled.

"The industry pumps out 6 million guns a year and employs 44,0000 people. Civilians buy 60% of the guns. The military and law enforcement make up most of the rest."

"Wait. Citizens buy more guns than the US military and law enforcement agencies combined?"

"Sadly, yes."

"Go on."

"Manufacturers make a crap load on ammunition. You only buy a gun once. You buy tons of ammo over your lifetime." She looked up. "September 11 and the President's election made a lot of gun owners twitchy. The market has been growing the last five years. I quote, 'His election was the best thing that ever happened to the firearm industry.' Unquote."

"Lovely."

"Also, gun sales spike after mass shootings."

"Double lovely on rocks with a twist."

"Licensed dealerships are on the rise for the first time in 20 years. Get this, Walmart is the biggest seller of firearms and ammunition in the US."

"Really? Christ. Ok, so what did you find? How connected is the gun industry to the SFG?"

"The SFG claim they are not affiliated with any firearm or ammunition manufacturers or with any businesses that deal in guns and ammunition."

"And?"

"They're liars."

Freda sat back.

"First, they take in a ton of 'traditional' donations from gun manufacturers. Because the SFG is registered as a 501c4, we can't be sure how much. Best estimates range between $30 million all the way up to $90 million."

"In 'traditional' donations?"

"Yes." Stacia read from her notes. "Corporate partners who gave $45,000 or more include over 15 firearm manufacturers." She looked up. "I'm talking all the big names here."

"Huh. Big names and big fat checks."

"Yup." Stacia nodded excitedly. "And interestingly, of those corporate donors, 10 manufacture assault weapons and lots of their corporate partners produce high capacity ammunition."

"Huh."

Stacia held up a photo of eleven white men around a campfire.

"What is that?" Freda asked.

"*That* is the Circle of Liberty. If you donate more than $1M you too can be in the inner circle."

They both stared at the photo.

Freda lamented, "None of my charitable contributions gets me a campfire." She looked back to Stacia. "So all these guys have donated $1M or more."

Stacia nodded.

"So the SFG has a lot of corporate donors."

"Exactly."

"What else?"

"Second, aside from donations almost all the gun manufacturers

A Spy Came Home

also 'sponsor' shit. From what's publicly available it looks like corporate sponsorships for SFG events run to the tune of $60 million every year." Stacia started to tick off on her fingers. "One sponsored a fundraising program. Another sponsored an SFG TV show. That ammo company I mentioned, sells ammunition and shooting accessories and are the official sponsor of the SFG Annual Meeting --"

"So they've got corporate donors and then *sponsors*."

"Exactly." Stacia held up a picture of Neil Koen accepting an outsized check for $5M from an older gentleman. "This is Koen and the ammo company founder."

"Not affiliated to gun manufacturers, my ass. They're getting heaps of cash from corporates."

"Correct."

"How about any manufacturers on their board?"

"Funny you should ask. The SFG won't publish it's Board of Directors." She looked up and said, "Which is weird. But, I've uncovered that out of the 80 board members, fifteen are lobbyists who lobby on gun issues - ten of which have gun manufacturers specifically listed as clients - and five of the board members are CEOs of firearms or ammunition companies."

"So the SFG claims to be this big grassroots membership organization but is clearly in bed with gun manufacturers."

"Yes. And another interesting aside: the SFG won't let its grassroots members - you know, the members it purports to represent - elect the Board of Directors. The Board's election is totally rigged."

Freda whistled again. She stood and walked to the window. "Ok, so clearly they're not a membership organization."

"Clearly."

"Let me ask you this: why are gun manufacturers bending over backwards to give them money?"

"Because they lobby on their behalf."

"Explain that."

"There are so many examples. I'll give you just three. 1. The SFG successfully lobbied to end the federal assault weapons ban. Rifle manufacturing went up 38%. 2. SFG's worked to pass the Firearms Owners' Protection Act of 1987 which allowed the biggest ammo producers to ship bullets directly to consumers, dramatically increasing profits. 3. And the SFG successfully lobbied a bill that shields gun makers from liability claims." Stacia looked up. "You can't sue gun makers for damages, say, for a city's health care costs from gunshot wounds."

Freda stood quietly by the window, listening.

"One CEO said that liability shield bill was the only reason the US has a firearms industry."

Freda turned. "If that law had passed, we wouldn't have a firearms industry in America?"

"Correct."

"The gun lobbyists saved the firearms industry."

"Correct."

Freda looked back out the window. "In a nutshell: they've lied all along about not being affiliated to gun manufacturers."

"Correct."

"They're a gun for hire in Washington."

"Check."

"Every year they're taking in 100s of millions in membership fees. And as we've seen, they are then ignoring their grassroots members' interests. They are simply lobbying on behalf of the gun industry and themselves."

"Check."

"It's like me paying for OPEC's lobbyist because I use their oil."

"Check."

"And SFG members are none the wiser."

"Check mate."

"No reputation - I don't care if you're the establishment, the entitled, the rich, or the popular - no reputation is so superior it's above scrutiny. Not here in the US anyway." Freda looked up. "That's it. That's the first article. Get drafting."

32

Dupont Circle, DC

The morning's *New York News* was up on Cal's laptop screen on his desk in the apartment. He sipped his first coffee as he finished reading it.

As an ATF Agent he knew that once every three months the media put out a heated, but despairing, piece on the gun control debate. This article was striking in that it was the second in two days from the *New York News*.

It also had a surprisingly sarcastic tone.

The SFG: Simply A Gun for Hire
By STACIA DeVries
<u>New York News</u>

As the US Senate considers a new bill on assault weapons, one of the country's fiercest and most powerful lobbyist stands ready for a fight. The Society for Guns brands itself as a civil rights group representing millions of the 74 million Americans who own guns. Many are starting to question if this is the case.

The latest polls find a majority of SFG members are in favor of limited gun control. It appears a growing theme is that the SFG has lost sight of their members' interests. Said one member, "Protecting my family isn't just about owning a gun. It's also about keeping the guns from bad guys. I think the SFG has lost sight of this, to my detriment."

The SFG's strategy to fight any infringement on the Second Amendment for the sake of citizens may be a sleight of hand to *cover for a darker agenda. The SFG helps to maintain the very lucrative $15 Billion gun manufacturing industry despite the organizations protestations that it is 'not affiliated to gun companies'.*

Estimates put gun industry charitable donations to the SFG anywhere up to $90 Million. But more importantly, gun manufacturers 'sponsor' many of the SFG's events and programs. Watchdogs estimate corporate sponsorships to the SFG may be as much as $60 million a year, likely a serious under-estimation.

Corporate support frees up the millions the SFG receives in membership dues to pay for staff salaries, including the $1 million-a-year they pay their Executive Director.

The SFG may have chosen a strategy that will eventually fail. An insider at a gun control advocacy group notes, "The SFG has drawn an imaginary line in the sand. Their extremism in the face of logic and reason will eventually exhaust most of their members. Even President George W. Bush cancelled his membership..."

Cal stopped reading and opened a new site. He researched the journalist and realized she was the one that did the piece on the Scimitar raid. He also learned she was quite young and had only been at the paper a year. It was becoming more interesting that the *New York News* had chosen someone so young to lead on two, back-to-back SFG stories.

An email inbox pinged.

It was a fourth email from Maar.

SUBJECT: BLUE LANTERN: POST-SHIPMENT END-USE CHECK ON LICENSE 88088
Origin: Embassy KABUL/AMEMBASSY KABUL
Classification: TOP SECRET

To: SECSTATE WASHDC

Date: 25 July 2013

HIGH PRIORITY

REF: STATE 88088

1. Blue Lantern Coordinator Kabul reports the recovery of a U.S. licensed M4 rifle with E-trace confirmed serial number matching License 88088.

3. The rifle has been confirmed in relation to the September 7 death of Neha Malhotra, US Embassy, by small arms fire attack in Kandahar province.

- JACOBY

Cal whispered, "Jesus Christ."

He stared down R Street letting the revelation sink in. "Jesus Christ."

He quickly pulled up Ranty's contacts and calls him.

"Ranty here."

Cal was almost breathless. "Ranty, it's Cal."

"My friend! What —"

"Listen Ranty, can we meet? Like urgently?"

"Ok, ok, can you make it out to Langley?"

"I'll be there in 30. In the main parking lot."

"I'll be there."

Cal raced back to the bedroom, muttering. "Holy Mother."

In the parking lot of the CIA Headquarters in Langley, Cal canted heavily against the hot hood of his Jeep then righted himself. "Are you kidding me? Not only did someone cover up the Blue Lantern investigation out of Pakistan, but they fucking covered up that one of Scimitar's guns killed a US diplomat!"

Ranty stared down at the cable opened on Cal's cell phone screen. He couldn't hide the stunned look on his face.

Cal pointed his finger at Ranty. "Just exactly like you predicted; this one is Top Secret. This one only went to the top floors of CIA and State. It only went to the Mandarins."

Ranty whispered, "What are we going to do?"

"First, you're going to stay out of this. You have a wife and kids and a job. I'm going to prove there was a cover up."

"Cal, if there was a cover up, it's all the way at the top. Not only in this Agency, but State, and quite possibly other institutions —"

"It doesn't matter. Someone got killed! This Malhotra woman got shot by a fucking Scimitar M4. This has got to get righted."

"Long established institutions in this town. Powerful institutions."

Cal walked all the way around his car to calm himself. He stopped in front of Ranty. "Go back. Go back inside. I'm sorry I called you out here. This is too risky for you."

Ranty paused then handed him back the cell phone and turned toward the lobby door without a word.

33

Courthouse, VA

At 8 a.m., Mac saw Amanda Hughes leave her apartment building. She was wearing a similar summer dress, slim and bright and was carrying her leather briefcase. On her feet were tidy sneakers over pale yellow running socks. Her hair was freshly blown out.

Her stride was even and long. Her chin was up.

This was a woman who was now angry.

Mac threw out a cup of lukewarm coffee and hailed a taxi.

Capitol Hill, DC

Four hours later, Mac watched Amanda exit the SFG Lobby building on her lunch break and started off after her. When they were well out of range of the SFG Lobby, Mac strode up next to her and spoke into her ear. "We need to talk."

Amanda stumbled, glanced over, and recognized Dora. "Jesus."

"We need to talk."

Amanda stopped, turned toward Mac. "I'm totally not ok with this. I have no idea who you are. I'm not getting involved. All I know is you've presented me with a recording and a photo that shows my boss ..."

Mac took her elbow and steered her toward an alley. Amanda reluctantly complied, hissing, "I'm totally not ok with this. I don't know who you are. I am not getting involved."

Mac stopped them near a back door. "I'm from a reputable foundation. I represent very wealthy, very established people. As part of my due diligence on a large donation to the SFG, I discovered your boss was misappropriating funds. That's the language, Amanda. Misappropriating funds. Fraud."

Amanda stared down the alley. Her resistance was palpable.

Mac continued, "I spoke with Mrs. Bodie last night. We strongly believe Neil is tarnishing a valued and respected institution."

"I want no part of this."

"Mrs. Bodie believes it is our patriotic duty to blow the whistle."

Amanda's lips tightened and her head jerked side to side.

"Amanda, we want to clean out the one bad apple so that the SFG Lobby can continue doing the great work you do. We'd like your help."

A door opened and a waiter dropped a trash bag in a dumpster.

Mac asked, "Do you know many wealthy people?"

Amanda wouldn't meet her eyes.

"Mrs. Bodie is extremely wealthy. The bankers call them Ultra High Net Worth individuals. These types of people, Amanda, get things done. They have huge networks, they have serious influence. Mrs. Bodie is going to do this with or without you. If we move forward without you, I don't know what will happen to you."

Amanda hissed, "I'm not ok with this conversation. I want nothing to do with this."

"I hear you. I hear that. Did you hear me?"

Amanda stared off in the distance, her mind spinning.

Mac said, "We are going ahead with or without you. Hear me. You will be left out in the cold."

Amanda's voice, while still angry, was softening, ever so slightly, "I want nothing to do with this. I am not ok with this."

"What you need to understand is that you being ok, is not the point. It stopped being the point when Neil crossed the line into corruption."

Amanda looked away, biting her lip.

Mac hammered her hesitation. "Amanda, you being ok with corruption is also not relevant any more. Your opinion does not in any way change the fact that you are working for one of the biggest civil rights organizations whose key leader is abusing his power. If you do nothing, you are complicit, you are a major part of the problem."

"Me?"

"Yes, Amanda, you. You're part of them and by doing nothing you're condoning their behavior. You're part of the problem."

Amanda's eyes searched the alley for an answer, her mind racing. Eventually she stared down at the ground and her shoulders slumped.

Mac was gentle. "Amanda, we're moving ahead to clean house. You want to be on our side when this hits the fan."

Mac took a step back and let her arms hang loose by her sides.

Amanda looked up. "What do I have to do?"

"Not much. We'll arrange it all. Miss Bodie believes we need to make Chris's actions public in order to ensure that the institution does not cover this up. Your identity will be protected. In fact, you'll be sitting pretty, once Neil is replaced. Amanda, we need something in addition. Something strong. It's not enough that he and the Senator have been caught misappropriating funds. Once. We need to prove there is a culture of fraud. Of defrauding donors and members. Of treating them inappropriately. Of using them." Mac looked directly into Amanda's eyes and softened her voice. "Amanda, Newtown was a turning point. Small kids. Innocent kids. Gunned down." Her voice was barely a whisper as she watched Amanda's face. "Did Neil respond to Newtown in a way that wasn't ok?"

Amanda's eyes rose left as she sifted through her memory, then stopped and looked back at Mac.

There. There it is.

Mac's voice was smoother, stronger. "We need to prove Neil is corrupt. Get me something."

She turned and retreated back down the alley.

Langley, VA

Odom dialed Beam. "Beam here."

"It's Odom. I need anything you can pull on DOC license number 88088. I need everything that's in the State or Agency system."

***

Two hours later, Beam called him back. "There were three cables in the system on license number 88088 for Scimitar Defense Ltd. All classified Confidential. I'm sending them in an email."

Odom looked down at the Top Secret folder Hawkinson had given him. *There are actually four. But the Agency intends to keep this fourth one hidden forever.* "Ok."

"Uhm, I'm not the only one looking into this."

"What do you mean?"

"Last week somebody down in intel ran a search on the Blue Lantern Op cables on license 88088."

Odom's voice lowered. "Who ran the search?"

"We're not sure, Sir."

"Excuse me?"

"I said, we're not sure."

"I heard what you said, Beam. Are you telling me you can't find out who is running a search on our own systems?"

"Apparently not, Sir. The tech guys told me that whoever ran the search hid his identity."

Odom glanced around his office. *Spies in the spy house.* "Ok, Beam, next I need you to track down someone. I need the name and details of an ATF agent who was lead on the initial investigation into Scimitar. When you find him I want you to tail him."

"I'm sorry, Sir, I thought I just heard you say you wanted me to start surveillance on an ATF agent. Here. Domestically."

Odom spoke slowly. "Beam, are we going to have a problem?"

Beam hesitated. "No. Sir. We're not."

"Ok, do it quietly. I'm your only report."

"Yes, Sir."

An hour later, in his dark basement office, Odom picked up his cell phone at the chime of an incoming text. It was a note from Beam. *"ATF agent is named Cal Bertrand. Handed over Scimitar investigation to a task force last week. Is assigned to 'close-out' for Fast & Frenzied. I'll pick him up at his residence tmrw morning."*

Odom looked up Cal Bertrand's address.

34

18 years ago - San Francisco, CA

The hangover was excruciating. Her head throbbed. Acid sloshed in her empty stomach. She squinted at the blank wall, then out over the bay where the morning fog was rolling in. Her thinking was slow, confused.

His body was curled around her back, his arm snaked under her armpit and around her chest. She stared at their two arms lying across the crisp, white sheet. They appeared to be the arms of strangers, of lovers entwined. She looked at the way they slept, these two lovers, these strangers; their bodies were interlocked in a cocoon of serenity. She blinked to capture the image. This is what intimacy and vulnerability will look like one day, she thought.

The fog had rolled in. It must have been hours later. His arm clenched, pulling her back tighter against his chest.

She asked, "Should we talk about it?"

His voice cracked from the sleep. "Nope."

"I should change the subject?"

"Yup."

A moment later she grinned. "So in high school I heard you were Mensa."

Silence.

She wiggled against him. "Go on. Admit it."

His arm tightened. "Ok. Yes."

"What's it like?"

"What?"

"To be that much smarter than everyone else in the room?"

His forehead pushed into her neck. "Really?"

"Yeah, really."

"Remember in middle school we went to the Franklin Institute?"

"Yeah."

"It was really boring for me."

"Really? You mean you knew everything that was there?"

"I could have built the exhibits."

"As a middle schooler?"

"Yup"

"Huh."

"I thought most of our high school teachers were not so smart. Now go back to sleep."

Over coffee she told him the rest of her story.

From Jakarta they had sent her home for training. For the first three months, as part of the recruitment class at the Farm, she had been involved in indoor and field classes in paramilitary operations, getting trained in handguns, machine guns, evasive driving techniques, and explosives. They had also taught them hand-to-hand combat. She had jumped out of a plane and navigated wilderness for days.

It turned out she was a pretty good shot with a handgun.

Then they had learned tradecraft. Classes in clandestine communications included dead drops, one time pads, audio devices, transmitters, and photography. They had practiced techniques to detect and lose surveillance. They had examined personality types, how to convince certain types to divulge intelligence and how to turn them.

Most importantly for Mac, she had learned to trust her intuition.

She sipped her second coffee. "Turns out I'm ok at the interrogation bit. It requires a certain ability to distance your self from the prisoner. They call it 'going cold'. Nice, right? Yeah, it turns out I'm adept at that."

He shook his head and started cooking scrambled eggs and sausages.

In long tedious classes, they had learned about the Agency. The National Clandestine Services was home to all the spies; the

Directorate of Intelligence was where analysts mined the incoming information; and the Directorate of Science and Technology housed all the techies. Out in the field, the Case Officers where part of Clandestine Services, cultivating human assets.

She looked up at him. "Agents are actually the foreigners, the assets. I'm an Operations Officer."

In each station, there was the Station Chief and the Deputy Station Chief, along with the other Officers.

At home, in Langley, the Headquarters Based Officers (HBO) of the Clandestine Services collected and managed intel and staff. On top of this huge bureaucracy were the executives in the Senior Intelligence Service, the Mandarins.

She opened the cabinet and took down plates, then pulled open a drawer and took out utensils. "The Mandarins get away with whatever they want to. It's a secret agency. There is no real oversight. God knows what they get up to on that Top Floor - the secrets they must keep."

"- or manufacture."

She nodded, as she set the dishes on the counter. "At the end of the day, the Agency is a huge bureaucracy with one purpose: gather information. All the levels, the reporting lines, the skills, the Directorates - it's all about feeding and crunching information up the chain till it's cleaned and presented to the president.

"What I'm worried about is how political it all is, at every level. It's like a living organism with thousands of people who all have their own political interests. Lots of maneuvering, covering your ass, lots of turf battles. They spend more time doing that then actually focusing on the intel."

He placed two full plates on the counter. "So I'm assuming you're one of these Clandestine people? Overseas?"

She scooped scrambled eggs on a slice of toast. "Actually, I'm going be a NOC - Non Official Cover. I won't be associated with the Embassy. I'll be out on my own. If a NOC is caught, the US doesn't admit we're Agency officers. They won't come help us."

He threw her a questioning look.

"It's the role that gets the best intel. That's the most effective. Most impactful. No question - it's the most dangerous."

He set down his fork. "So, let me get this straight, if you get arrested, in like, I don't know, Libya, will they come get you out?"

"No."

"So you're on your fucking own. God, why would you do that - work for an organization that doesn't give a shit about you?"

She paused to consider the answer. "I knew that going in. I can't whine about it now. I'm well past naive."

Later that night, she stood by the window, her silhouette illuminated against the thin drapes by a street lamp.

His voice was gravelly, scratched. "You're leaving."

"They're sending me out soon. On my first assignment. I don't know when I'll be back."

He lit a cigarette.

"It could be years."

"Yeah, I figured you would say that."

"They asked me on polygraph tests about boyfriends."

"And?"

"I've always said no. They never asked me if I am in love with someone. I'm glad they didn't. Because I would have had to admit it. Now, they know nothing about you. They can't use you against me."

"That's fucked up."

"I know."

She lit a cigarette, blew out the window. "I've chosen this. Eyes wide open. I have to see it through." After a moment, she said, "I just can't sit around and be a lawyer or an architect."

"Or an engineer."

"That's not what I meant."

"What did you mean?"

"I'm not cut out for normal. Indonesia proved that. This looks like a viable solution." She inhaled deeply. "And it makes me feel worthy."

"Mac, I can't stop you. I wouldn't want to try."

"Joe --"

He interrupted her, "But I want to stop you. I don't agree with this." He shook his head. "But that's not how you and I operate."

"Just promise me --"

"Mac, I don't wait for you." He took a moment to compose his thoughts. "It's like when an object shows up in a totally random, inappropriate situation. A snowflake in the desert. Or when the continuity in a movie is off. You are a dislocated item, a discordant note, in certain scenes of my life. I feel way more than I should, but otherwise my life goes on."

From the window she whispered, "I'm sorry."

"Don't be. I'm not."

She looked over at him through the darkness. "I do love you."

"I know."

"I just feel compelled…to do something. This path makes sense."

"I've always supported you. You know that." He smiled sadly, lifted up the sheet. "Enough talking. Come back to bed. I've got some new moves I want to scorch into your memory."

Hours later, wired with too much nicotine and caffeine and too little sleep, she trembled in the seat as the plane climbed over the leaden San Francisco shoreline. Her fingertips quivered, the blood cells spinning like cups in a tea-pot ride, whipping through her veins.

35

New York, NY

Late in the evening, Freda sat at her desk scrolling through the comments section under Stacia's latest article on the *New York News* website. Of over 500 comments, most were vitriolic rants from the gun rights side:

- *"U.N. is inches away from wiping out our Second Amendment freedoms. They will take away our national sovereignty and our American rule of law."*
- *"Nowhere in the bible does it say we can't defend ourselves. God gave us this freedom. Long live Jesus Christ and the SFG!"*
- *"The communist liberal media spinning tales again. Don't be fooled! SFG represents gun owners across America!"*

There were only a few pro-gun control comments:

- *"We need sensible gun control to keep our children safe. The SFG is the biggest obstacle to common sense in America."*
- *"Background checks protect everyone. It doesn't make sense for the SFG to oppose them."*

She was surprised how few of the comments actually took on the substance of the article. By her count, through weary eyes, only ten comments questioned the SFG's affiliation to gun manufacturers.

- *"It should come as no surprise to anyone that the SFG is a gun for hire."*
- *"I commend the New York News for this investigative reporting. But it should be SFG members who dig into where the organization gets its funds and who it represents."*

She pressed her fingers into her eyelids, then looked out over the bull pen and saw Stacia at her desk. She dialed her extension. "It's me. I'm taking you out."

Not far from the New York News building was a modern bar awash in pale wood and chrome frequented by midtown professionals catching a quick drink with friends. The mid-week Happy Hour special was over and the crowd had thinned.

Freda raised a glass of champagne to Stacia. "Really, well done. You've landed a second front page!"

Stacia clinked her glass and grinned smugly, soaking up the praise.

Freda laughed. "No, no, don't thank me."

"Thanks, Freda."

Freda looked around the bar, already bored with this intense, remote young woman's poor social skills. "So how's your personal life?"

"Huh?"

"I dunno, how is it for you young women today? Dating I mean."

Stacia hesitated. "I date. Pretty low key about it."

"Yeah? You are young. You can be nonchalant."

"I'm definitely not looking for husband material at my age."

"Huh." Freda took a sip.

"I know it was different ten years ago. We saw *Sex and the City*. You all took dating so seriously."

"Well, god knows if there's one thing I'd tell you it would be to wait, wait, wait. Nonchalance is going work for you." She settled into the topic, drinking faster. "You know, I bought the line they sold us that we could be anything we wanted. In the 8th grade, I thought I was going be the President, I was going be a mom, and I was going be happily married for the rest of my life to Prince Charming." She hailed over the waitress and ordered another champagne. "Out of college I moved to LA and got a great gig with the *LA Times*. Then I met Gino. I truly, truly loved him. So we got married. Then Gino and I had M." Her demeanor turned sad. "Then Gino doesn't grow up. I'm growing up. I'm evolving. I've got new priorities. There was a career, a kid, a house, finances. So we're fighting all the time. He wants out. What am I going to say? I can't stop him. So he leaves." Her eyes have become glassy. "All of the sudden, I'm a single mom at 35."

Stacia watched her.

"That story we got fed. About having it all? Reality didn't quite live up to the hype."

Stacia was at a loss. "It's kinda not like that for us."

Shaking her head, Freda talked to herself. "I don't know a single woman over 35 who is happy with who she is dating."

"I'm just not sure you should be telling me all this."

Tipsy, Freda was adamant. "Listen, I'm trying to give you a heads up."

"About what?"

"I'm just telling you like it is for women my age. On Match.com you get a few pings. You go on these shitty dates. You realize all the guys your age are picking younger girls, girls 20 years younger." Freda scanned the room, satisfied she hadn't missed the entrance of an eligible men then held up her empty glass to the waitress. "So you drop off Match. You sign up for the book clubs. You tell all your married friends that they need to set you up. You go out with your other single, age-appropriate friends. You put on make-up, show off your assets."

She tilted the last drops out of her glass. "You go and go and go. You sign up for power yoga. Then they bring out Tinder."

She looked again around the bar. The waitress showed up with the new champagne. Freda took a long sip then continued her saga. "It's all really hard. You lose energy. You start dating younger guys. You know they only like you because you're a cougar." She shook her bangs across her forehead to liven herself up, but her voice had slurred. "You have flings with your ex-boyfriend from college who's married but who flies into NY for work."

"You do?"

"Yup. He's dumb as rocks but can get me off and we have fun. His wife is a total gold digger so he's afraid to divorce her cause she'll take him to the cleaners."

Stacia's discomfort rose. "Uh. Freda…"

"It's what life is like - I'm telling you." Her voice began to calm. "Maybe I should have waited longer."

Stacia was hopeful the rant had ended. "To get married?"

"Yeah. Maybe I would have waited for a man. Not a boy. Maybe at 37, I would have been able to detect boy better. But then, of course, at that age you're starting to get screwed on the kid front."

"I'm telling you, I hear you. Girls today have our eyes wide open. There is no 'having it all.'"

Freda sipped her champagne. Her head swayed. "God it's been fucking years since I've been emotionally intimate with someone --" Suddenly, she latched onto a new subject. "Listen, it was good. The article was good. Jack liked it."

"He did?"

"Let's hope the SFG members read it. They are the ones who should care the most. Yeah. And it's going mean something."

"What do you mean?"

Freda had difficulty setting down her now empty glass. "Just that it's bigger than us, lots of moving parts."

Stacia moved forward, gently prodded. "Huh? What?"

In response, Freda leaned in but slipped on the stool and had to right herself. "Fuck, I gotta go home." She grabbed her bag, threw down some cash, and stumbled off the stool.

Stacia watched her weave through the crowd, reach the bar's glass door, pull it open and walk to the curb, arm outstretched for a cab.

She pulled out her cell phone and texted Charlotte. *"Shiz just got weird up in here with boss lady. The conspiracy theory grows. Must debrief."*

"Grab a bottle of red. LOL"

36

Dupont Circle, DC

At the Dupont Circle townhouse, Cal looked up Neha Malhotra on the internet. There were over 50 articles.

The Washington Post described her as having been a young diplomat posted to Kabul to manage community development projects. A year into her posting, she attended the opening of a clinic in Khandahar Province. She and her entourage had exited their armored vehicles to walk the last few yards, surrounded by a large crowd of excited children. Up ahead, the community had come out in full force; the clinic staff, the parents, and the village elders stood waiting to greet her. Just as the entourage came within sight of the clinic, a lone gunman had emerged from behind a ramshackle house. He had discharged five shots before US military personnel jumped him. Three Americans had been wounded and rushed back to Kabul for medical treatment. Neha Malhotra had died within minutes of reaching the US Army base in Kabul.

At the ceremony marking the arrival of her body back to the US, the Secretary of State had remarked, "Neha Malhotra was the epitome of a Foreign Service Officer. All who knew her, knew of her passion for helping people. She committed her professional career in the service of her country." Ms. Malhotra, a native of New Orleans, was survived by her parents and a younger brother.

Cal stared at a photo of her on the web. She had been a smiling, happy woman.

He placed his fingers back on the keyboard and started a new search on *Blue Lantern*.

It took another twenty minutes, a lot of wrong turns, and a few dead ends before he found what he was looking for. It was a 2010 archived C-Span video on the National Archives website. Cal hoped the video would illuminate who had real authority over Blue Lantern investigations.

The opening still frame was of a Senate committee room with Senator Blake Scott, Vice Chairman (R-KY) sitting alone on the platform in front of a few, bored staffers. He was young for his seniority, about 50 years old but looked 40. He had beautiful light brown hair cut perfectly in a tousled, manly way. In his ads, he always wore a lumberjack shirt and grinned smoothly. In real life, people commented that he was a lot meaner than they had expected for a southern gentleman. Rumor had it his mother couldn't attest that her husband was his father; they bullying had strengthened his mean streak. In the video, he was glaring at a grey-haired man seated at the center table in the middle of the empty room. The video title appeared on Cal's screen. *"Statement of Deputy Secretary General, Edward Thornton, for the US Department of State for the Senate Intelligence Committee"*

Cal hit play. Thornton read from a prepared document, slowly turning the pages. Once in a while, someone walked behind him in the frame, but otherwise the seats remained empty. When the video time stamp reached 1:53, Thornton began a new topic. "Since 1990, the DTC's formal end use checks - known as the Blue Lantern program - have included pre-license and post-shipment checks."

Cal turned up the volume.

"The program verifies end use and end user of US defense exports. It is clear to this management team that the Blue Lantern program requires significant improvements. A key failure of the program is its timeliness of monitoring and completing Blue Lantern requests." On the screen, Thornton paused and looked up at the Senator, who continued to read from a document.

Thornton looked down and read the various responsibilities of the Blue Lantern program.

At the video's 4:01 mark, Thornton's voice raised slightly. "The problems I have outlined today are exclusively an issue of insufficient resources to meet increased responsibilities. This is a significant problem. It is a problem we have raised to this

Committee going on five years."

He looked up again to the Senator, this time waiting for an acknowledgement. "As you know, Senator, we have consistently been denied additional funds in appropriations."

Behind Senator Scott, the staffers were surprised by this unusual boldness.

Senator Scott gave Thornton a withering look.

At the 8:20 time stamp, Thornton completed his statement.

Senator Scott asked, "How many Blue Lantern checks were conducted last year?"

"Last year we conducted 451 'end use' Blue Lantern checks. This in comparison to 44,000 licenses issued. We simply do not have the man power to check more," Thornton said.

"Yes, yes, we hear you."

Thornton sat taller. "Well, Sir, respectfully, I hope the whole Committee hears this. Not just us here today. We're talking about state of the art military hardware that is exported overseas."

"Yes, yes, the Committee is aware of your concerns. Now, of those 451 Blue Lantern checks made, how many were resolved?"

"400 were closed. We have some cases that are still open after an excessive period of time."

"What does your office consider excessive?" asked Scott.

"Our records show we currently have over 29 cases still pending after two years."

"Unresolved cases that have been open for over two years."

"Yes, Sir. We just don't have the man power."

"So you keep suggesting. All government agencies are under budget constraints Mr. Thornton. Yours is no exception."

"Senator, I am not suggesting. I am stating. We cannot do our oversight role with the budget we currently have."

"So you say."

Cal stopped the video, picked up his phone, and dialed a DC number.

A woman answered. "Good morning, Deputy Secretary General Thornton's office."

"Yes, good morning. This is Agent Cal Bertrand over at the ATF. I would very much like to have a moment of Mr. Thornton's time."

"What is this about?"

"I'm just doing a 'close out' on a Blue Lantern check. It's all formality, we just need his approval."

"Ok. How about tomorrow morning at 9:15 here at his office?"

"Any chance we can do it this afternoon?"

She found an opening. "Ok, let's try 3:30 this afternoon."

"Thanks, much appreciated."

As he hung up the phone his inbox pinged. Wilson had sent an email titled "FYI." Cal opened it.

Department of Justice
Office of Public Affairs
FOR IMMEDIATE RELEASE

CEO and COO of Kentucky Company Arrested on Conspiracy to Violate Arms Export Control Act and Related Offenses in International Arms Trafficking

Lexington, KY – The CEO and the COO of Scimitar Defense, a manufacturer of firearms and weapon systems to the United States military, state and local law enforcement, and worldwide commercial markets, have been taken into custody by the FBI at their Lexington headquarters as part of an ongoing investigation into potential criminal misuse of certain firearms.

The Task Force was moving ahead quickly under the direction of the Department of Justice. Cal was surprised by his reaction - he was pleased. He should have felt left out, annoyed.

But the Malhotra cover-up mystery was too compelling.

Foggy Bottom, DC

At exactly 3:25 p.m., Cal was escorted into the US State Department's Deputy Secretary General's office in the State Department Building on C Street. It was a large office with two utilitarian couches centered around a coffee table, a ten-person conference table, and a bank of bright windows.

Edward Thornton, a slight, short man with thinning red hair, stepped around his desk with an outstretched hand. He gave Cal a genuine smile. His bearing was open, friendly.

Cal shook his hand. "Cal Bertrand. Thanks for seeing me, Sir."

"Sure, sure, have a seat. Please call me, Ed. What can I do for you?"

They sat facing each other.

Cal began, "Ed, I'm going to make a calculated assumption that you and I are on the same side of a certain issue."

Thornton was curious. "Please."

"I recently watched your briefing to the Senate Intelligence Committee and Senator Scott on the Blue Lantern programs. I was particularly interested in your request for additional resources."

Thornton nodded slowly.

"And I was curious, off the record, and I'm going to be very frank here, why you think the Senator was so against the idea? Why hasn't the Committee approved a higher budget to a blatantly underfunded program critical to our nation's safety?"

"You said you're with the ATF, Cal?"

Cal nodded.

"Do you mind if I see your badge?"

Cal handed him his wallet, badge side out.

Thornton handed it back, stood, and called out to his secretary. "We're going to go get a coffee downstairs."

They exited into the long hallway.

Thornton asked, "So, tell me again, more specifically, what it is you're looking for?"

"I was curious watching your presentation to the Committee why a certain Senator would be interested in limiting the Blue Lantern budget?"

The florescent ceiling lights in the hallway cast a yellow tint to their skin.

Thornton's steps were slow and deliberate, matching his tone. "I think you may be the first ATF agent to ask me that question, Cal. Which I've always found odd. I've been in my position here for six years. I've been with State my entire career. I've been involved in Blue Lantern for years. And no one from ATF - or the FBI for that matter - has ever asked me about the resistance of the Vice Chairman on the Intelligence Committee to Blue Lantern funding. I've always found that incredibly interesting."

"Yes, that is surprising. Has he consistently voiced his

opposition to increased budgets for the Blue Lantern program?"

"Yes, at least while I've been in this position." Thornton walked on. "I recently read US arms sales have reached $66 billion. I believe I also read that the US controls nearly 80% of the global arms market."

"That's a huge number."

"A lot of money involved in the industry, Cal. Can you guess how many licenses we *denied* last year?"

"I've got no idea."

"And this is public information so I'm not telling you any state secrets."

"Trust me when I say I have absolutely no interest in repeating anything you tell me."

They turn a corner. Ahead of them is another long, yellow-lit hallway.

Thornton shook his head. "1%"

Cal glanced at him, shocked and silent.

Thornton repeated, "1%. We turned down 1% of arms export license requests last year."

"Why is that?"

"We're a hand brake on a huge industry. Nobody likes a hand brake."

"Wait. Are you suggesting the arms industry wants you underfunded?"

Thornton raised an eyebrow. "Why wouldn't they? Fewer limitations equal a freer, more lucrative market."

"Wow."

Thornton stared ahead and lowered his voice. "And arms manufacturers give a lot in campaign contributions."

"So Scott is simply kowtowing to the arms manufacturers?"

"I didn't say that."

"No, you didn't. I did."

"I will say this, Cal. It has not passed me by that the Vice Chairman of the Intelligence Committee not only gets enormous campaign contributions from the defense industry but he is also from a key red state that is very friendly with arms manufacturers."

Cal slowed as they reached yet another turn in the hallway. "Let me ask you one more question and I'll save you the walk to the cafeteria. Has there ever been a Blue Lantern investigation, that you know of, that went...intentionally unresolved? Let's say, guns went missing and no one followed up on it?"

Thornton turned to him with a pained expression. "Cal, I'm hoping that you're investigating a certain situation that has caused me no end of personal grief, so I'll do you one better. I've seen the Vice Chairman bury a Blue Lantern report that identified a lapse in controls that lead to very tragic consequences."

There it was. The cover up. Cal's heart raced. He asked, "Can he do that?"

The agony in Thornton's eyes was real. "He can do lots of things in the name of National Security." Thornton held out his hand. "Good luck, Agent Bertrand."

In his Jeep, Cal jammed his foot to the floor and shot up 20th Street toward Dupont Circle. A single question circled his mind at warp speed: *what would make Senator Blake Scott bury the cable that proved Neha Malhotra was killed by a Scimitar M4?*

By the time he reached Dupont Circle and squealed into the traffic rounding the park, he had a pretty good guess. *The number one motive for any crime is greed.*

He found a parking space right in front of his building, slammed into reverse, and revved into the spot.

There really was only one conclusion. *Scimitar paid Senator Blake Scott to bury the Blue Lantern investigation that proved Neha Malhotra was killed by one of their guns.*

And he most likely had evidence to prove it. All of Scimitar's accounting records were sitting on an Excel spreadsheet on the tech team's USB stick. Upstairs.

He raced up the stairs to his apartment, fumbling with his key ring and the lock. The key jammed.

He cursed, "Damn it." He calmed himself and turned the key slowly, clicking open the lock.

He raced to his desk and pulled up the Top Secret cable to check the date. Malhotra was killed on July 6. The Top Secret cable was dated three weeks later, July 25.

Cal yanked out the desk drawer, grabbed the USB stick, and jammed it into his laptop. He whipped his fingertips across the touchpad, scrolled through the directory, and double tapped the file *Scimitar 3rd Quarter Expenses*.

On the screen, the spreadsheet opened up. He clicked quickly through to July.

His eyes slowed. He read every entry in July.

Nothing.

He moved on to August.

Nothing.

He pushed back into his leather chair, working out a kink in his neck.

This was a roadblock, not a dead end. Just because it wasn't recorded, didn't mean Scimitar didn't pay off Senator Blake Scott.

Cal clicked out of the file and stared at the USB directory complied by the tech team.

Not all roads were clearly signed.

He floated the cursor over the file *Phone Logs* and double clicked. A new spreadsheet opened up on his screen with every phone call made from the Scimitar landline and Boare's cell phone.

His eyes raced to July and started skimming.

There.

A Washington DC number had been called five times in the last week of July. A Northern Virginia number had been called twice.

He would bet money that those calls had been from Boare to Scott's office and cell phone. Cal imagined Boare, with his gleaming smile, making an offer to the Senator.

Cal pulled up his cell phone and called Ruby.

"Ruby here."

"Hi Ruby. It's Cal. How you doing?"

"Fine, Cal. I heard you did a great job with that briefing last week."

"Yeah thanks. Listen, on that note, I've got just a few more telephone numbers I need checked."

"Cal, I think you may be pushing your luck on this. You've handed over the investigation, right?"

"Ruby, you've been a huge help and I know it and appreciate it. I'm really sorry to push. I just need to track down these numbers and hand them over to the Task Force."

She hesitated. "Well. I guess. Ok, shoot."

"Just two numbers. The first is 202 444 5555."

He heard her tapping on her keyboard. "That one's easy. It's the landline over at the SFG Lobby headquarters on Capitol Hill."

The street outside the window went still. Not a single car drove past.

Cal blinked. "Ok, thanks Ruby. Now the second: 703 453 3232"

He heard her tapping.

"That's the private, unlisted number for Charles Osbourne." She took a breath. "Cal, what are you doing with SFG numbers in your logs?"

"I'm not sure."

"You better be damn careful."

"Yeah, I'm starting to get that feeling." He said softly, "Thanks, Ruby."

He gently pressed the 'end call' button.

In Sudoku, as cells filled, your options diminished. There were only so many numbers that could be used in the remaining spaces.

He turned back to the screen. Slowly, he double clicked and re-opened the *Scimitar 3rd Quarter Expenses* file.

He scrolled to the page with the July accounting.

On July 31, Scimitar's accountant had listed the amount of $50,000 as an 'SFG donation'.

The air left Cal's lungs.

Scimitar had used the SFG to pay off Senator Blake Scott.

Apparently, the life of a US diplomat was only worth $50,000.

37

Capitol Hill, DC

She had given Amanda 24 hours to digest her dilemma. That was plenty of time for someone to recognize they didn't have a lot of options. It was more than enough time, actually, when that someone only had one option.

Mac closed in on Amanda as she stepped off the escalator at the Metro station. "Amanda! Great to see you. Can I get you a morning coffee?"

Startled, Amanda turned to Dora. She hesitated, but only for a minute, then tightened her lips and said, "Ok."

"Great. Let's hit the cafe across the street"

Mac watched Amanda over her coffee, waiting.

Amanda took a sip, looked around the cafe. "Ok."

"Ok what?"

"I've decided to help Miss Bodie. To help the SFG Lobby clean house."

"I think that's best for the organization."

Amanda handed her a single paper, folded into quarters. "It's an email from last year. From Neil to Charles." She looked sad, distant. "It's just not ok. It's not right."

"You're doing the right thing."

"So we're done? I'm done."

"If the email is enough. Yes. I hope so."

"What is Miss Bodie going to do?"

"Trust me that whatever she does, your identity will be protected."

"What are you going to do?"

"We're going to loop in an investigative reporter."

Amanda's voice trembled. "A reporter?"

"It's the quickest, most public way, really. Trust me, you'll be fine."

Amanda stared at the ceiling, holding back tears. "He was my boss for four years. He was trying to do right by the SFG. He's not a bad guy."

"Except he is." She reached out to grasp Amanda's wrist. "The SFG is going to need you when this comes out. You did the right thing."

Twenty minutes later, Mac opened up the folder paper. It was an internal SFG email chain.

To: Charles Osbourne
From: Neil Koen
Subject: Response to Newtown
Date: Dec 18, 2012

1. Newtown was a shock to the culture. Key demographics question defense of firearms.

2. Demographic Background: Our base has declined since 1970s.

- *Rural: from 27% to 17% of population*
- *Rural household gun ownership: from 70% to 56%*
- *Montana, New Mex, Wyoming gun ownership: from 65% to under 40%*
- *Northeast gun ownership: from 29% to 22%*

Our base is dangerously homogenous.

- *They are of the lowest income and education levels, based in Southern, Red States (OK, TN, IN, NV, AL, LA, KY, AR, MS, WV)*
- *Older*
- *Republican*

- White
- *Primary Source of News: Fox News*
- *Secondary Source of News: Conservative radio talk shows (Research - significant tendencies toward anger and protectionism.)*

3. SFG research shows key demographic is activated (read donations) through the emotions of fear, anger and pride (e.g. patriotism.)

Recommendation: Refocus strategy on a) increased hyperbole and misinformation and b) on urgent, dramatic fear of gun restrictions.

To Sum: Misinformation > Fear > Increased SFG Donations

Actions:

1. Campaign jargon should utilize key words: steal, affront, infringement, freedom, gun ban, founding fathers, tyranny, government thugs, constitutional rights, break in doors, seize guns, destroy property, common law, natural right, inalienable, fundamental principles, enemies of the constitution, confiscation.
2. Target advertisers/appearances on Fox News and conservative talk shows.
3. Intentional misinformation: spin all national, state and local efforts for gun regulation on government persecution of gun owners and confiscation of guns.

To: Neil Koen
From: Charles Osbourne
Subject: Re: The 2012 elections: New 5 Year Strategy
Date: Dec 19, 2011

Agreed. Approved.

Mac stared out the front window of the Alfa at the top dome of the Capital building in the distance.

Amanda had not only given her Neil's head on a platter, she'd also delivered Charles. Had she known what she was doing? Mac surmised not. Amanda's trust in Dora had blinded her.

It was a huge victory.

But the layers of deception tasted sour, bittersweet. It was the same metallic hint that preceded bile. She closed her eyes and the memories of similar, successful operations flickered past in a parade of lies wrapped in lies. Was there a penultimate deception that would finally cause the bile to erupt?

She reached for her courier bag and pulled out her laptop. She opened an app and began a fast-forward scan through a black-and-white video of Pretzel Park cached on the hard drive in the loft.

Ten minutes later, she slowed the fast-forward. In the grainy background, a shadowy, ghostlike image of a man walked a dog. The date stamp read 8:05 a.m. He started in the northwest corner and followed the dog to the dog park. He let the dog in through the gates and sat on a bench reading a book for ten minutes. Then he whistled for the dog, snapped on the extendable leash, and rambled around the park to the northwest exit.

In her Alfa, Mac released a long-held breath.

38

North Capital, DC

The elevator in the ATF headquarters stopped on every floor, disgorging and ingesting puffed-up, harried agents. When it finally reached the seventh floor, Cal waited for it to clear then pushed off the back wall and stepped toward the open door.

Standing in the elevator lobby, Director Wilson glanced up and saw Cal. He barked, "Goddamnit! No. No. No. The Task Force has taken over. I do not see you here. Because you are out in Arlington closing out Fast and Frenzied."

The elevator doors began to shut. Behind Wilson, three agents stood frozen in place.

Cal slid his toe between the doors.

Wilson breathed in deeply through his nose and glared.

Cal held up a manila folder. "Maar sent another email."

Wilson spun and strode back down the hall, mumbling, "Jesus, Mary and Joseph."

Cal swept between the three immobilized agents and fell in line with Wilson, handing him the folder. "This one is Top Secret."

They reached Wilson's office.

Cal continued, "It connects the missing Scimitar guns to the killing of a US Diplomat in Afghanistan."

Wilson stopped.

Cal added, "But we never heard about that. As ATF, we should have heard about that."

Wilson glanced down at the folder in his hands like it was burning him.

"So I did some digging around."

Wilson's eyes closed and his chest rose and fell in deep breaths.

"There's been a cover up."

Wilson stepped into his office, circled behind his desk and sat down slowly. "Do you have some kind of career death-wish, Agent Bertrand? You successfully handed over a very high-profile trafficking investigation to a cross-agency Task Force. You redeemed yourself in my eyes and in most of senior management here in this building. You made your way back in. Now you come here a week-bloody-later with tales of a cover-up of a diplomatic shooting?"

"A diplomat got shot in Afghanistan six months ago. In July. The M4 in the shooting was under the same Scimitar Pakistan license - 88088"

"Jesus." Wilson slowly opened the folder and read.

Cal summarized the background for the folder's contents. "So first, as we know, the M4s go missing from Pakistan. Blue Lantern investigates but hits a dead end. Here in the US, using domestic phone records, we find out it was actually Scimitar who sold the guns and ran them into Afghanistan." He nodded to the folder. "Then eight months later a separate Blue Lantern investigation - that cable there, Sir - finds one of Scimitar's missing M4s has killed a US diplomat in Khandahar. That cable was seen by the most senior people over at State and CIA. They knew a US-made gun killed one of ours. But they didn't know Scimitar had actually trafficked it." Cal paused. "Either way, they buried that cable."

Wilson was deep in thought.

"So I dug in to it," Cal said. "Who had the motive to bury it? Sir, I believe Scimitar paid off the Vice Chairman of the Senate Intelligence Committee to bury the cable under cover of 'national security'."

Wilson's head snapped up. "Senator Blake Scott?"

Cal nodded.

"Please, for the love of god and his children on this earth, tell me that's some kind of sick, sick joke."

"I'm afraid I can't do that."

"Scott?"

"Yes." Cal indicated the folder. "The most obvious player is Scimitar. They had already gotten away with trafficking these guns. They certainly didn't want anyone finding out one of their guns also killed a US diplomat. So if I'm Chuck Boare, and this cable pops up, what do I do? I call up my friends over at the SFG because I'm their biggest corporate donor and tell them to fix it with one of their most beloved Senators - one Blake Scott, Vice Chairman of the Senate Intelligence Committee - that oversees State Department Blue Lantern Operations and budgets."

A stunned Wilson asked, "Did you just say SFG?"

Cal nodded.

Wilson's eyes drilled into Cal. "You had better have something solid, Agent."

"It was actually not so difficult to connect the dots. We had all of Scimitar's documents from the raid last week." Cal nodded to the folder. "Chuck Boare called Neil Koen at the SFG Lobby office five times and Charles Osbourne's *private cell phone* two times once that cable was sent up."

Wilson flipped through to the phone records and saw the highlighted calls.

Cal continued, "So Scimitar wanted this buried. Obviously. But a scandal is also not in Scott's or the SFG's interest either. Nobody wants the very lax arms export control framework examined. Too many of their constituents - the manufacturers - benefit from the status quo. Scimitar, Scott, and the SFG all have motive." Cal leaned over and pulled up the last paper in the folder, the accounting spreadsheet with one highlighted transfer. "In the same week as the phone calls, Scimitar transferred $50,000 to the SFG."

"Can you connect that $50,000 to Senator Scott?"

"Not yet. But I'll bet a large amount of my salary, Sir, that an amount similar to $50,000 made it from SFG Lobby into Scott's re-election campaign."

Wilson leaned far back in his chair and stared at the ceiling. "Jesus, Mary, Joseph and the mules you rode in on, Bertrand. What you're saying..." he coughed. "What you're saying is that Scimitar, Senator Scott and the SFG covered up the killing of one of our guys by a Scimitar M4 that Scimitar had trafficked. Jesus."

"Actually, Sir, it was one of our gals."

"Excuse me?"

"It wasn't one of our guys. The diplomat was one of our gals."

Wilson watched as Cal dropped a black and white photo from the web of Neha Malhotra onto the center of his desk and whispered, "Fucking hell." He stood, turned to the window, weighing his options.

Cal concluded. "I believe this last cable reveals a lot about Maar. First, I believe this is personal. He must have known Malhotra. So this feels like he's getting justice. Second, I believe he played me. I believe he reeled out the emails like breadcrumbs, just enough to get me to pursue each lead: first he wanted me to find Scimitar's involvement, then he wanted me to find that Scimitar paid off Scott through the SFG. He walked me right to it." Cal paused. "Third, I believe Maar has 'need to know access' which means --"

At the window, Wilson's head dropped in defeat.

Cal finished the thought. "Maar is one of us. Maar is American. CIA, DOD intel somewhere, NSA or maybe State."

"Ok, leave this with me. I need to figure out who's going to lead this." Wilson turned, his anger building. "Agent, it sure as the fucking dawn follows the night is not going to be you."

Cal turned to leave.

"You've done it again, Agent. You've dropped me so far into the shit I may not make it out."

Cal was through the door when Wilson yelled, "If Maar sends you another email, I'm assigning it to a different agent. We'll take care of Maar later."

Cal was halfway down the hall when Wilson yelled louder, "No more chasing Maar, Bertrand. You hear me? That's an order. No more Maar. Get back to Arlington and do your job."

The elevator was slow arriving to the top floor. In the elevator bank, the two warring news stations blared.

CNN played a clip of Senator Martha Payne talking to reporters in the Capital Rotunda. "The influence of the gun lobby is extraordinary. We're watching the votes for next week. This will be a fight to the last vote. I'm confident my colleagues will vote in the interests of the American people."

The elevator arrived and Cal stepped in, his mind racing. The elevator stopped on every floor, letting agents off and on.

It took another ten minutes for him to walk across the ground floor lobby and out onto New York Avenue where he squinted into the glaring sun. His mind replayed the moment he dropped the

black and white photo of Neha Malhotra on the Director's desk.
So this feels like he's getting justice.
Cal's head snapped up.
Maar dropped the Scimitar, Scott and SFG breadcrumbs in the lead up to the vote.

FOUR DAYS BEFORE THE SENATE VOTE

Picasso's "Weeping Woman," stolen 17 days ago…was found undamaged today in a locker at a railway station, the police said.
- *New York Times*, August 20, 1986

With public sentiment, nothing can fail; without it nothing can succeed.
- Doris Kearns Goodwin

39

Philadelphia, PA

"It's weird you wanted to meet here." Penny took in the hushed atrium, the pale walls, and the modern angles of the new Barnes Foundation museum.

"I like museums."

"It's just…this wasn't here when we were kids. I would have thought we would have met at like the Art Museum or something. You know, somewhere we knew."

"Nothing wrong with trying something new. How was the train down?"

"Totally easy. I'm going see my mom for dinner then head back. Nice to get out of the city once in a while."

"How's she doing?"

Penny said, "Fine. You know, same, same."

They wandered into the first room. Modernist paintings in rich gilded frames cluttered the walls. Tourists surrounded them, many listening to audio tours on rented equipment.

Penny said, "You know you never really did tell me what you do. I imagine it isn't all James Bond stuff, right?"

"The James Bond stuff happens like once a year. Those movies are the condensed, edited version of spy work. Walking into a casino and playing cards against a target is so *not* what I do."

"Have you done that?"

Mac laughed. "Played cards against a target? Nah. But I've bluffed a lot."

Penny grinned. "Do you read spy novels?"

"I prefer romance," Mac deadpanned.

"Seriously?"

She grinned wider. "Seriously. You read John Grisham?"

"Hell no! I'm a lawyer." Penny laughed. "So what do you do the rest of the time?"

"Surveillance. Eavesdropping. It can be super boring to build an asset. Lots of high tech. Emails and cell phones are where most people spend their time. So that's where we get most of our intel."

Penny said knowingly, "SIGINT."

"Yeah. Nice word usage. Exactly."

"What's getting HUMNIT like?"

"Nice word usage again." Mac smiled back at Penny. "A lot of it is instinct. One time I was on a meet and the guy was saying all the right things, but I just didn't trust him. I remember checking out his ears. They were flashing pink, then white. Like he had hot flashes or something. It wasn't really obvious. In fact, his eyes were totally trained on me, giving me all the right signals. He wasn't giving me any other indication that he was lying."

"Really?"

"Yeah. But I just couldn't stop fixating on his ears."

"What did you do?"

"I ended the meet early and got out."

"Were you right about him being a bad guy?"

"I don't know. But I never approached him again. There was something about him that just sent up warning signals."

"Wow."

The next room was empty and quiet. They circled the perimeter, careful to keep their voices low.

Penny asked, "We've really gotten ourselves deep into something haven't we?"

"Yup."

"What you're doing, to the SFG, is something big isn't it?"

"Yup."

"I never imagined a world so complicated that I felt compelled to insert myself into something like this." Penny observed the quiet tourists concentrating on the tours, completely tuned in to their earphones. "I never thought I'd see Americans so complacent, so focused on their own small worlds, that they abandoned any kind of responsibility for the wider issues. Lord. I sound like a politician." She fell silent and they continued walking.

In the next room, Mac said, "I found Joe."

"What?" Penny jerked her up up. "Wait. Where?"

"Here. He lives in Manayunk."

"Wait, what? Oh. My. God. In Manayunk? Is that why you're here?"

A slow grin appeared on Mac's face. "He took over his dad's company. He moved back to Philly about five years ago."

"Are you going contact him?"

"I haven't decided."

"Have you seen him?"

"Not in person, no. Not yet."

"Are you ok chasing him while you're, I dunno - running our operation?"

Mac grinned wider. "I'm pretty good at what I do. I'm capable of juggling a few balls at one time."

"But won't that, like, compromise you?"

"I'll be smart." She gave Penny a shrug, trying on indifference, but failing. Instead, she went for realism. "He could be married with kids. Then it's a moot point."

"Or not." Penny's eyes rounded. "God, if he's single the shizizelle is gonna shizizelle."

Mac chuckled. "Ok, Snoop Dog."

"Snoop Lion, dude, Snoop Lion."

"Ok, Mom of two tween boys."

"How'd you find him?"

"I looked up his property."

"You can do that?"

"Totally. When you buy a house, it's public information."

"So you know where he lives." It was a statement.

"I do."

"No shit!"

"No shit."

"That's so insane." The intimacy between them struck Penny. "It's weird to have you home. To be in touch so much. For so long it was like we lost you. For a long while."

"Yeah. I get it."

"Did it bother you? To be so disconnected?"

Mac nodded. "A lot. But it took me a long time to recognize it."

"You lied to us."

"I had to."

"I'm trying to deal with that - that it wasn't a choice, that you had to. I'm trying to reconcile it."

"Yeah, I get it."

They walked into the next room and stopped in front of a Picasso sketch of three women, bathing. Penny glanced over it. "Huh, look at that. It's like you, me and Freda. Except naked. Bathing. Nowadays, that would be kinda weird, but not really. Like when would we be naked together? Maybe a steam room?" She turned to Mac. "You knew this was here."

Mac grinned.

"Always a step ahead, our Mac." They stared at the sketch and Penny lowered her voice. "You know the legislation is coming to the floor?"

"So I've heard."

"We don't have a lot of time."

"I'm on it. Listen, it's going get hot soon. But I want you to know I have your back. I wanted you to hear that from me personally."

Penny nodded.

"If they do come sniffing --"

"Mac, whose going come sniffing?"

"The FBI. ATF. It could happen."

"Ok?" Penny said warily.

"Stay as close to the truth as you can. The more you lie, the more you trip your self up. As the saying goes, 'sail close to the wind'."

"Christ. The Feds? This is bonkers." She paused. "I remember when Smokey and the Bandit were dangerous."

"I'm afraid it comes with the territory."

They stood staring at the sketch, each lost in thought. Next to them, the sun lit a square patch of the shiny floor. A fellow tourist walked through the room.

Penny asked, "Was the job worth it, Mac?"

Mac took time to answer. "I think our country would say it was worth it. I sacrificed for something bigger than me. Every solid piece of intel I sent up the wires probably saved lives. That's a calling. No matter what anyone else wants to say."

Penny watched her.

"A lot of us overseas washed out after one tour. It's hard to not piss someone off at HQ. Or your Station Chief. It makes you really start thinking about why you're in the game and what you're going to do next. But I was good. I stayed overseas a long time." She stared off into the distance. "I was…am…defending the Star Spangled Banner and the Fourth of July. Good luck topping that, right? I don't know. Was it worth it? I just don't know."

"What's the worst part about it?"

Mac pushed her head back, easing the tension in her shoulders. "Now. Now is the worst part. I know I'm getting out, but it scares the ever loving crap out of me."

"Why?"

Mac went still, deep in thought. "Because I don't know who I am without it. I don't know what gets me up in the morning, what lights my fire. I don't know who I am without the Agency."

Penny shook her head, staring down at the bright patch. "I get it."

"In the mirror, I see a face. But I don't see *me*."

Penny heard Mac's fear and looked up. "Are you ok?"

"No. No, I don't think so." She squeezed her eyes shut, admitting for the first time out loud something very painful. "Who am I going to find if I start looking for me?"

Penny stepped in close, put her arms around Mac and gave her a tight embrace. She waited in the moment a long time, knowing as a mother that sometimes you just hold on, letting the tension ease, the stiffness loosen. Then she whispered, "You're a good person and we've always known it. That's what you'll find: a good person. That's who you are. Trust me."

40

Washington, DC

Before sunrise the next morning, something in Cal's subconscious jolted him awake. Closing his eyes, he waded back into the hazy dream, reaching for a clue. Eventually his eyes opened, letting yesterday's reality rush through the cobwebs.

He stumbled into the kitchen and flipped on low lights. His mind was sticky, slow. A half bottle of scotch sat on the counter. An empty glass and a dirty plate rested in the sink.

The ghost of the dream clung to him, hovering just beyond his grasp. He filled the paper basket in the coffee maker with black grinds and started coffee brewing.

A trash truck rumbled into the alley behind his house. Two guys jumped down in the dark and hauled plastic bins to the rear loader where the wheezing compactor chewed loudly. A putrid wave swelled across the alley's still air.

Feeling the first throb of a headache, he swished water in the glass and dusted the plate off, scattering breadcrumbs across the sink.

He stared at the sink for a long time, holding the plate in his hand, the siren song of the dream echoing in his mind. His eyes narrowed. A word whispered in his subconscious. *Breadcrumbs*

Suddenly it all rushed back to him. Adrenaline hit nerve endings as he remembered the conclusion he had reached late last night over his fourth - or was it fifth? - scotch and soda. *Maar was dropping breadcrumbs.*

He was instantly awake, alert.

He sloshed coffee in the mug, gulped down a scalding mouthful and hustled through to the living room.

Under the light of the lamp, his desktop was chaotic. A *New York News* article from yesterday was marked up in red pen with vicious circles and notes. Next to it, the top sheet of a yellow pad had a full column of notes and doodles sneaking up and down the page. 'Maar' was written across the top.

His notes read:
- Personally involved w/ Malhotra
- Top clearances (CIA, DOD, NSA, State?)
- Professional techniques ???

The last line was underlined five times. It was where he had stopped last night, where the line in the sand had been drawn by the scotch.

Cal took a long draw from his coffee mug as he settled down into his chair and let the notes seep back into the slow mechanics spinning in his mind.

He took another sip. An idea emerged.

He opened the desk drawer, grabbed the tech team USB drive and slotted it into his laptop, pulling up the Scimitar phone logs. He scrolled to the fourth page and the call two weeks ago from Boare to the Khan Trucking Company. The spreadsheet listed the GPS coordinates for the cellphone at the time the call was made.

What if Maar wasn't just dropping breadcrumbs before the Senate vote? What if he was actually baking them?

Cal waited though his second coffee before calling Sheriff Soloman.

"Morning Sheriff. This is Cal. Sorry to call so early."

"No, no problem. What can I do for ya, Agent?"

"I've got a GPS coordinate from a cell phone. When I punch it into Google it spits out the address 9861 Harrodsburg Road, Wilmore, Kentucky."

"Harrodsburg Road. That's out by the turn in the river. Sure, sure, I know it. That's the Red Light Bar out on the Kentucky River. It's an ok spot, not as bad as it sounds. Not too country either, if you know what I mean."

"I think I do." The thought of anything related to alcohol made him queasy. "Sheriff, can I ask you a favor?"

"Shoot."

"Is there any way you can you ask at the bar if they happen to have security cam?" Cal read off the date and time of Boare's cellphone call.

"Not a problem at all. I'll ring ya if we get a hit."

"Sheriff, I'm looking for whoever was with Boare at that time."

"Hmm. Well. That makes it easier. This just keeps getting more interesting." Down the phone line, Cal heard the sheriff sipping his own coffee. "I'm not going to lie to you, the folks round here ain't too happy with Boare selling guns to the Taliban. That's very unpatriotic."

"I agree with you."

"That there is a moral issue. He damn well should have known better."

Cal pulled his hand down across his face. "Frankly, Sheriff, Boare makes guns. That's his product. At some point, some of these guys may not actually care who uses them. They just want to sell their product. Like cigarettes, I guess."

The sheriff chuckled. "That's an awfully liberal, elite, northern thing to say for a law enforcement type. But you may be right. Anyway, I'm just sayin' that guys round here, some of them, can be a slight bit unhinged."

Cal looked out over the street. The sun was starting to rise.

"No telling who thinks of themselves as a vigilante these parts. Many of them are excellent marksmen."

"I suspect he won't be walking the streets of Lexington anytime soon, Sheriff."

"Let's hope for his sake he doesn't. We do read newspapers here."

"I appreciate you calling me as soon as you get anything."

"Will do."

Cal clicked on CNN while he sipped the last of his second coffee and turned up the volume.

The pretty newscaster spoke into the camera. "In a spectacularly timed set of events, the *New York News* is reporting that one of the SFG's largest corporate donors has been indicted for international firearms trafficking just as the new assault weapons ban bill comes to the Senate this week."

Cal set down his coffee and read the marked up *New York News* article on his desk for the eighth time.

SFG's Biggest Corporate Donor Indicted for Gun Running
By STACIA DeVRIES
New York News

Chuck Boare and Scimitar Defense, a federally licensed manufacturer, distributor, and exporter of firearms and firearms components, was arrested and indicted today by a federal grand jury on charges of international firearms and trafficking violations. The Defendants were indicted on ten counts involving Conspiracy to Violate Arms Export Control Act, ITAR, Defraud the United States, False Statements, Mail Fraud, Wire Fraud and the Smuggling of Goods.

The ATF's Director Wilson commented at yesterday's press briefing, "The indictment closes the door on an excellent example of how the United States Attorney's Office, ATF, CIA and international law enforcement agencies are working together." Further, Wilson explained, "The import and export of firearms, firearm parts, and technical data is tightly controlled to prevent these items to be used to harm America or its allies overseas."

Manayunk, PA

Mac stood by the loft window. The rising sun threw light under the railroad tracks and across Cresson Street. She tried not to look, but like a magnet the goose carcass pulled her eyes. She focused the binoculars for a closer look. Even though it had deflated, it still resembled the original animal. The feathers were distinctly black, white and grey but were starting to fray around the edges.

Everything had a beginning and an end. She was quite comfortable with that. But this goose had died on a fairly busy street running under a train line, far from its likely home on the canal. It felt ignominious, unnatural.

A week ago, when she had first seen it, she had called the Philadelphia Animal hotline. She had spoken to a very nice man who asked her a few questions about the location of the dead goose. She had been very explicit and he had assured her they'd be out to take care of it.

Around the eye rim of the binoculars, something caught her eye in the northwest corner of Pretzel Park.

She tilted the binoculars away from her face and watched as Joe stepped down the park stairs.

The wind was knocked from her.

He was sipping a coffee and walking a black and white, medium-sized mutt on an extended leash.

She slammed the binoculars back over her eyes and twirled him into focus.

He was as she expected. He was not anything she could have expected.

He had a new edge about him. His head was bald, clean shaven and he sported a tightly trimmed goatee. His nose looked like it might have been broken at some point: it added to the appeal. His shoulders were broader, stronger.

She followed his walk. His gait was light, almost playful; he walked on the front of his feet like a soccer player. It was incredibly familiar.

He looked up.

Her breath stopped.

She had only seen the hue of his eyes a few times. Once, while scuba diving in Sarawak, Malaysia, in the moment before breaking the surface, the sunlight had refracted through a thin strata of water and cast a color of blue that was at once radiant and pale.

On the end of the leash, the dog was bossy, pulling feverishly in his quest for squirrels. In contrast, Joe's movements were gentle, almost thoughtful.

In the loft, Mac's stomach tightened and her pulse raced.

Joe and the dog crossed the park in front of the warehouse. She zoomed in with her binoculars. His t-shirt was bright white. The hair on his arm had been bleached in the summer sun. He wasn't wearing a wedding ring.

She exhaled.

In the park, the weeping willow swayed in a soft breeze.

She watched him circle the park, round back toward his house. He stepped back into his yard and closed the fence.

Her grip relaxed on the binoculars. She swallowed through the

thickness in her throat.
She had never felt so alone.

Twenty minutes later, Mac pulled on soft, museum gloves. She plugged a USB drive into her laptop and copied three files: a photograph of the SFG Lobby Response to Newtown email, three color photos of Neil Koen and Congressman Peter from the restaurant, and a copy of the audio recording from the restaurant. She sliced open the plastic wrap on a pile of small Tyvek envelopes and slipped the USB drive inside. She labeled the envelope to Ms. Stacia DeVries, New York News. She placed the envelope into a paper shopping bag.

An hour later, she stepped outside of 30th Street Station into a brewing storm. A biker approached rapidly down Market Street through the traffic.
She stepped to the curb.
He pulled up in front of her. "You got a package for the New York News?"
"Here you go." She opened the shopping bag and held it out to him. He grabbed the Tyvek envelope and from his clipboard, slapped on a routing sticker, scanned the bar code, and dropped the envelope into his courier bag. He tore off her receipt from the clipboard and handed it to her.
"Thanks," she said.
Throwing the clipboard and scanner into his courier bag, he pushed down on a bike pedal, and wove back into the traffic.
A single, cold rain drop landed on her hand.

Langley, VA

Odom stepped into the large office of the Director of National Clandestine Service. "Sir, we have been unable to locate her."
Hawkinson asked, "So you've lost your operative?"
"It appears so."
"Off the ranch."
Odom nodded.
"No hints of this in her personnel files?"

Odom had prepared an answer. "She's been top of her class in terms of testing. She's consistently received top marks in terms of risk appetite. Her tactical instincts are almost flawless. She has strong conceptual thinking. She thinks in big pictures. She does, however, push boundaries and has been off the ranch before, but accounted for after."

"What are her weaknesses?"

"That's the thing. I have read and re-read her personnel file and frankly, nothing stands out."

"And no romance?"

"She's been loosely involved with various men. They are all listed there. But none of them were serious. On the polygraph every year we ask her. Not a blip."

"Everybody has a weak point."

"I'm sure you're right, Sir. I'm sure there's something. But she's done an exceptional job of concealing it. We don't have a clue."

Hawkinson asked, "And no residual resentment from the Beijing affair?"

"Not that we know of, no."

Hawkinson pointed to a *New York News* folded in the far corner of his large desk. "Did you see the *New York News*? Scimitar has been indicted."

Odom nodded.

"You need to stop her."

"Understood."

"What have we got to hold over her? What can we use against her?"

Odom saw this coming. He felt neither shame nor guilt. This came with the territory. He wondered if Mac had seen this coming. He answered, "Her parents have passed. She has a sole sister living out in Northern California with a kid and a husband."

"Use them."

41

New York, NY

That afternoon, Stacia sliced open a white Tyvek envelope that appeared to be empty. She felt something loose in the bottom and poured out a single USB thumb drive. She inserted the USB into her port. She opened the first file and read the email between Neil Koen and Charles Osbourne.

"Holy, holy, holy shit."

She read it again.

"Holy crap!"

She rapidly clicked back to the USB drive menu and opened up the second file. Three photos appeared on the screen. They were photos of Neil Koen having lunch at a restaurant with an older man who looked vaguely familiar.

She closed this and clicked on the third file. It opened as an audio and she fumbled in her purse for her earphones, plugged them in, and hit play.

As the conversation between Neil Koen and the Congressman played out she clicked back over to the photos. She held her breath through to the end of the conversation.

She sat up, looked around the bull pen at the other journalists. All of them were hunched over keyboards. No one had seen what had been on her screen.

She sunk back into her chair and mumbled, "Holy, holy, holy s..h…i…t."

Ten minutes later Freda, Jack Diamonte and three New York News lawyers were crowded around Freda's desk, heads down, listening to the final seconds of the taped conversation. The photos were splashed across Freda's screen.

From a perch on the windowsill Stacia broke the stunned silence. "Can we publish it?"

Freda peeked over Jack's shoulder and winked at her, grinning widely.

Jack said, "Yes. We can. Bartnicki v. Vopper protects media for publishing information on public issues when they know it was obtained unlawfully put they did not encourage it."

All three lawyers nodded.

Stacia snapped both hands shut in victory punches. "Yes!"

"But whoever sent you this could go straight to jail. Private electronic recording of conversations and electronic surveillance of emails is illegal and prosecutable. Look at Bradley Manning and Snowden."

The most senior lawyer looked at Stacia. "Let me confirm: you don't know who sent this to you? This was an anonymous tip."

"Absolutely. Yes. A blank white courier envelope."

The second lawyer asked, "You don't know the source."

"No. I have no idea who the source is."

Freda looked to Jack. "I think we run two stories out of this. The first on Koen and Congressmen Peter defrauding a donor. The second on the SFG's fear-mongering strategy. Two in quick succession. Tomorrow the first. The second 24 hours later."

Jack was thoughtful for a moment, staring absently past Stacia. Finally he said, "Yes, agreed."

The lead lawyer said, "When we drop the first story tomorrow, the Attorney General may come after us."

"Won't be the first time." Jack looked to Freda. "You sure you want to give this to a junior reporter?"

Stacia sat up, ready to intervene, but Freda held up her hand. "The source clearly intended it for Stacia. The source wants her to write it, given her last article. I'll shepherd it."

Jack spoke to Stacia, "Ok kid. You've got a huge scoop. Make this paper proud. Get started."

Stacia jumped off the sill, grabbed the USB from Freda, and rushed back to her cubicle. The lawyers followed her out.

Alone with Freda, Jack said quietly, "It's all a little too clean."

"It's fine."

"It makes me nervous."
"There are absolutely zero fingerprints on any of this."
"There better not be."

From the bull pen, Stacia watched Jack and Freda whispering.
She fished out her cell phone and texted Charlotte. "*Holy Crap! Another huge bomb just dropped. I'm going be mega. But my conspiracy theory builds.*"
"*Keep your head down. Just do your job for now.*"

Across town, Cliff sat across from Penny in a small conference room. Stacks of folders were piled at the bottom of one long wall. She was reading from notes out loud, prepping for the next day's presentation. "We can't let them establish conspiracy in violation of Section 1. There is no present direct or circumstantial evidence they can use to prove our side had a conscious commitment to a common scheme. I think we make a preemptive move and ask the judge to move past this and immediately on to the price fixing."
"That's ballsy," Cliff said.
"No reason not to take the risk."
"I agree. It's just a bit of a bold move for you, that's all. Unusual. I like it."
"To be fair, their side's evidence on the price fixing is a lot stronger. I'd rather head right into that. They've presented a lot in discovery." She looked up when she realized he had gone still and silent. "You want me to back up here?"
His tone was unusually personal, soft. "No. I was just thinking."
She tilted her head. "Which part threw you off?"
"The risk."
"Really? But it's the right move. We need to pincer around them on the price fixing, get that sewn up --"
"I was wondering how things were at home for you."
The question jarred her. "What?"
"How are things at home? Kenneth still writing scripts?"
She responded very slowly. "Yes."
"Any selling?"
She shook her head. "Not really. His latest just got turned down yesterday."
"It can't be easy."

She hesitated. "It's not."

"Must be hard on a marriage."

She was silent, stunned.

He looked past her and out the window at the city's skyline. He spoke to the glass. "Do you ever think about changing your circumstances?"

It took her a moment to respond. "Not anything I would discuss with a colleague."

He turned back to her. "What if I wasn't just your colleague?"

Her heart clanged. Her brain jumped into hyperdrive, suddenly noticing details in colorful magnification. Cliff's eyes were hooded, hazel. His lips were crooked. The stubble on his upper lip was just starting to shadow his skin. His hair was full and without any grey. How could he not have any grey?

Her mind blew up an image in mega pixel of them naked, spent from sex, lying on 1000 thread count sheets at the Four Seasons at lunch time. She was pulling up the sheet to cover her boobs in the harsh light of the day. He was leaning back against the pillows, smiling at her. She was running her hand up and down his large, erect penis.

In an instant, she was back in the conference room. She made a decision and looked at him. "I can't say I haven't thought about it."

He was surprised by her frankness. "What did you conclude?"

"I've concluded that I haven't concluded yet."

"Of course. Take your time," he said, taking it in stride. "I'll wait." His intention was clear.

She laid her hands on the table, blinked three times. When she finally spoke, her voice was once again neutral, professional. "So you agree on stepping into the price fixing issue early? I'm sure they'll be coming at us hard on the 'horizontal agreements among competitors' angle'."

Those hazel eyes. "Of course. Anything you need." His cadence was intentionally slow, the statement was full of nuance. A tiny thrill raced up her spine. She couldn't contain the small grin so she quickly looked down, back to her notes.

Later in her office, Penny pulled out the burner phone and texted Mac. *"My colleague just hit on me."*

"Is this good or bad?"
"I don't know. I feel like I'm in high school."
"What did you say?"
"I told him I hadn't made up my mind."

Washington, DC

Cal's phone vibrated. Sheriff Soloman was calling. "Hi Sheriff."

"Cal. We got lucky." The sheriff's voice was as slow as molasses. "There was a stranger chatting up Boare at the bar before and after that exact time."

Maar baked breadcrumbs.

"Get this, it was a woman with Boare. They got her on the video."

Cal paused. "Hold on. Did you say a woman?"

"Yup. I suspect that's not what you expected?"

"Uh, no. I'll be damned." Cal was astounded. "But this is really solid stuff. Thanks Sheriff."

"She's not very big."

"Pardon?

"She's quite lean. She looks to be about 5'8", blond, fit - from what I can tell. She did some flirting with Boare, went to the ladies, then headed out. Wasn't in there very long."

"Hmmm"

"I'm sending you the best photo we got of her."

"Sheriff, I really appreciate your help on this."

"Ain't no thang. We aim to please round here."

"Would you mind doing one more thing for me?"

"Shoot. No pun intended." The sheriff chuckled.

"Could you have someone take that same photo round to Scimitar's receptionist and ask her if she recognizes her?"

"Of course. And Cal, I don't mean to put my nose in your all business, but if this gal did indeed break open the biggest gun running case in years, are you sure you want to chase her for it?"

As he hung up, the sheriff's email popped in on his phone. Cal pulled up the black-and-white photo. She was partially turned from the camera but he could make out an angular chin, a trim nose, and a razor sharp blond bob. She was indeed on the slender side.

She had also kept her face turned away from the camera.

Clever, clever Maar.

42

Manayunk, PA

Through the open windows, Mac heard the 'twenty-somethings' milling around the bars on Main Street. It must be happy hour.

She remembered being in her twenties in crowded bars. It had been nothing for her to lean on the bar, give the bartender a smile, order a Cosmo, and scope out the crowd as she sipped her pink drink. She had done exactly that in bars across the world, what, a 100 times? Possibly more.

Tonight she sat crossed legged on the architect's desk, staring out across Pretzel Park, waiting.

At 7:15 p.m. he entered the far northwest corner. His dog led the way.

Her stomach tightened. She raised the Swarovsk, rolled her finger over the knob and Joe emerged in focus. She steadied her breathing and tracked him as he crossed to the dog run and let the mutt off the leash. He sat on a bench, crossed one leg over his knee and started a book: Tolkien's *The Twin Towers*.

There was movement in the left of her field of vision. Mac sighted on a blonde woman walking a pug who was just reaching the dog park. The blonde waved at Joe with a big smile as she let herself and the pug into the dog-run.

On the desk, Mac's back straightened.

The blonde walked over and sat down next to Joe, flipping her hair over her shoulder.

The binoculars were riveted on the pair.

Joe gave the blonde a small but genuine smile.

Mac was paralyzed. Butterflies swarmed her stomach.

The blonde began chatting with Joe, her hands flapping about in the air. Joe watched her but every few moments he eyed his mutt.

Mac noticed the pug was crazed, bounding from dog to dog, deliriously barking, shoving his flat face into dog butts. She gripped the binoculars tighter.

The blonde started laughing at a joke Joe made.

Mac held her breath.

The blonde reached out and placed her hand on Joe's forearm, laughing so hard she needed support, strength to keep from falling over.

Mac bolted to her feet. The binoculars trained on the park bench.

Joe tilted his head shyly, grinning at the blonde.

Invisible hands twisted Mac's intestines.

The blonde's laughing subsided. Joe reached for the leash, unconsciously moving his arm out from under her hand. The blonde pushed a strand of hair behind her ear.

Joe whistled for his mutt.

The pug barked maniacally.

Mac's eyes began to water from lack of blinking.

The mutt ambled over. Joe hooked the leash on its collar and stood, nodding to the blonde.

Mac fumbled with the focus, following Joe to the gate.

Joe looked back once and nodded goodbye to the blond. She waved goodbye with a huge white grin, calling out something.

Joe walked through the park and existed the northwest entrance.

Standing on the architect's desk, Mac dropped her head from side to side, working out the stiffness.

She jumped down from the desk, walked over to the sink, leaned down on both hands, and hung her head.

An hour later, she sat at the desk with a cold glass of Sauvignon Blanc. She swatted away a fly, noticing for the first time that the windows had no screens, then opened up a chat room.

Odom had left a message. *"We know you're off the ranch. We know about Scimitar."*

She typed back. *"Ok?"*

He responded instantly. *"Cease and desist. Or Northern California will be used."*

She shook her head at the Agency's predictability. She pulled up Skype and called Andorra, who picked up on the second ring. "Hallo?"

"Señora Bovary si us plau."

"Who is calling?"

"Tamara de Lempicka"

Señora Bovary came on the line. "Hello my darling, Tamara. What can we do for you today?"

"Señora, please forward the first package to FOdom@cia.gov."

"My pleasure, my darling." They disconnected.

Mac watched the clock on her computer for 15 minutes then left another message in the chat room. *"That's the first of 20 CYA packages of my operations and targets, including your stand down orders to save your own hides."* Her fingers were flying on the keyboard. *"Those stand down orders, in particular, make great reading. Odom, we could have saved 100,000s - even millions - of Americans if some of those operations had been approved by Langley. I will make these packages public if you go anywhere near my sister."*

She leaned back to take a sip of her wine but changed her mind and added one more line, just to screw with them. *"The Agency has made mistakes. Wikileaks proved that. Those mistakes are coming home to roost."*

She looked out over the darkening park.

Ten minutes later a ping announced a new message in the chat room. *"Let me take this higher."*

She responded, *"You do that."*

43

Washington, DC

The next morning, Cal walked into his living room in his grey robe, drinking his coffee, leisurely pulled out his desk chair, and sat down. He clicked on his inbox and scanned his new emails. Nothing was urgent.

He clicked open the *New York News* website. The first article on the front page grabbed his attention. He set down his coffee and read the first few paragraphs quickly.

SFG Defrauds Donor: Caught on Tape
By STACIA DeVRIES
<u>New York News</u>

Only three days before a Senate vote to nationally ban assault weapons, The New York News is releasing evidence that Mr. Neil Koen, the SFG's Chief of Strategy, and Congressman Rand Peter (R-KY) colluded to misappropriate donations.

In a recorded conversation, Neil Koen, who controls tens of millions in SFG lobbying funds, and Congressman Peter are heard intentionally agreeing to siphon funds from a wealthy donor. Mr. Koen handily convinces Congressman Peter that SFG financial support of his opponent in the Republican primary is good for the gun cause in that "crisis and controversy...(are)...the name of the game" and that "no one will be the wiser." Koen sweetens the deal with the offer of a campaign contribution.

Senator Martha Payne, a ranking member of the Justice Committee responded swiftly. "If it walks like fraud and talks like fraud, then it certainly opens itself up to investigation into criminal wrong doing. Shocking. Truly shocking."

Cal stopped reading. His hand remained still on the laptop.
I'll be damned. Maar's baking breadcrumbs on a whole other game.
His mind clicked over to a new thought.
This is how I find her.
He checked the name of the article's author, pushed back his chair, took a last slug of his coffee, and strode into the bathroom. Twenty minutes later he hailed a cab out on 17th St. Climbing in, he said, "Union Station."

Langley, VA

Hawkinson threw the *New York News* on Odom's desk in the dark, basement office. "Did you see this?"
Odom quickly scanned the Stacia DeVries article.
Hawkinson seethed, "I'm starting to think your Mac is involved in a full scale domestic operation around this new gun legislation."
Odom blinked.
"Did you warn her?"
Odom handed Hawkinson a folder. "She sent it last night. I was just on my way up to you."
Hawkinson read Mac's email. "Are you sure this is from Mac?"
"Yes."
"You got this last night?"
Odom nodded and said, "She sent it from an anonymous email."
"You can't trace it?"
"No, Sir. Tech tried. She's using the latest electronic evasions." He handed him a print out. "Here's our web chat."
Hawkinson read the back and forth between Odom and Mac. "Jesus Christ."
"She's apparently got a full dossier on every op she's ever done."
"I can read, Odom." Hawkinson stared into the light from the

green lamp, his head shaking as he thought through a plan. "We leave her alone."

"Sir?"

"We only have three options. If we burn her sister, Mac releases her blackmail dossiers. Not an option. If we report a rogue CIA officer is running a multi-faceted, domestic operation to the Task Force - or, frankly, anyone - we all go down. Not an option. But if we leave her alone, she may finish out her operation and no one will be the wiser about Agency involvement. This may blow over. That's our best option. We leave her alone." Hawkinson leaned over into Odom's face and pointed his finger at his nose. "In the meantime, Odom, you find your missing operative and you follow her. I don't care how."

Ten minutes later, Odom pulled up the private chat room. *"Ok. You win this round. Wildfires in CA are off the table."*

She had been waiting for him. The Agency was so predictable, even down to their hours in the office. *"I thought so."*

"Take some time off. Come in when you're ready."

He waited a full hour, but she never replied.

He picked up his phone and dialed Beam. "Where are you?"

"I'm on a train to New York"

"Talk to me."

"The ATF agent took a taxi to Union Station first thing this morning. It's not clear where he's going."

Odom glanced down at the *New York News* on his desk. "Stay on him."

44

New York, NY

On the 7th floor of the New York News building, the sun streaked through the shutters of three-story-high glass windows, casting horizontal stripes across the cafeteria's pale, wood floor. Outside, the city's westside stretched for miles.

A frowning Stacia found Cal by the window. "Agent Bertrand?"

He turned. "Stacia DeVries?"

"Sorry to keep you waiting. Did you get a coffee?"

"I'm fine."

"So what can I do for you?" She sat at a table, putting a laptop between them, and crossed her arms over her chest.

He sat and pulled out a notepad and pen. "I'd like to ask you a few questions in reference to your article this morning on the SFG."

"The FBI was already here."

Cal was surprised but didn't let on.

She asked, "How is this an ATF thing?"

"I'm afraid I can't get into that."

She watched him, letting him lead the discussion. She didn't appear to have an ounce of fear.

He asked, "Is it fair to assume you won't name your source?"

"Agent, it's fair to assume I don't know my source."

"A deep throat?"

"Something like that."

"How did you get the evidence?"

"It came in a white courier bag from Philadelphia"

"Addressed to you?"

"Yes. We're assuming it's because of the articles that went out earlier."

He nodded. "I would have concluded the same thing. You've been writing quite a lot about the SFG. A bit controversial, actually."

"The new legislation requires we examine the issue. And the players."

"And when you say 'we', you mean the New York News?"

"Of course."

He read from his notebook. "What came in the package, actually?"

"A thumb drive."

"What was on the thumb drive?"

She opened the laptop and started up a program. "I figured you'd ask that." She turned the laptop toward him.

The audio of Neil Koen and Congressman Peter played while the slideshow lapped the three photos of the two men in the restaurant. Cal leaned in, listening. He jotted down a few notes.

When the audio finished, he asked, "Can we play it again?"

She hit play.

When it finished a second time he asked, "Who do you think the donor is?"

"We don't know."

"And the donor's assistant that went to see Koen?"

"Again, we didn't look into that."

"A million bucks is a lot of money."

She shrugged.

"So. That's it, just the audio and the photos?"

Stacia turned the laptop toward her, clicked on the keyboard, and turned the laptop back toward Cal. "This was also on the USB stick."

On the screen he read the email from Neil Koen to Charles Osbourne and whistled. "Wow. That's going to be quite a scoop."

"I'm writing a piece for tomorrow's front page."

"You're really on a roll."

She shrugged again, genuinely nonchalant.

He said, "It's quite something that someone is leaking all this to the New York News. You ever wonder why?"

"We have to assume they want the SFG's influence diminished

in the lead up to the Congressional vote on the new gun legislation."

"Exactly." He watched her. She stared at him, unflinching. "Don't you think all these revelations and these leaks - Scimitar investigation and indictment, Congressman Peter and Koen colluding, this SFG internal email - coming out now is a bit too convenient?"

Cal realized, when her face cracked for just an instant, that this Stacia had come to the same conclusion but she would jeopardize her position at the newspaper if she expressed this. He changed the subject. "Do you have the envelope from the courier service?"

She stood. "Sure. And just so you know, I've been instructed by my superiors to cooperate with the authorities." She turned on her heel. "I'll be right back."

Ten minutes later, she handed him the white Tyvek envelope. It was wrinkled from having been balled into the trash. He took out his cell phone and snapped a photo of the mailing label, making sure he had a good image of the bar code. "I'm going to assume there are no fingerprints." He handed it back to her. "And you really aren't naming your source?"

"I'm telling you, I don't know who it is."

"But, with that email you were sent - it's gotta be someone in Neil Koen's office."

She held his gaze.

He conceded. "Ok. No need to answer. One last question. Who gave you the instructions to write the first article on the SFG two weeks ago? The one about them kowtowing to the gun industry?"

"My boss, Freda Browne. She's a managing editor."

"Right." He wrote down the name then handed her his card. "Ok, well that's all I need. If you think of anything, give me call."

"Probably not, under the First Amendment."

He smiled wryly. "I appreciate the sentiment. Stand up for what you believe. Well, keep my card handy anyway. You never know."

Back at her desk, Stacia breathed in deeply. Looking down, she flipped the ATF agent's business card through her fingers. Cal Bertrand. Agent. Bureau of Alcohol, Tobacco, Firearms, and Explosives.

She set it gently, face up by her keyboard, and turned back

toward her screen, returning to the draft of tomorrow's front page article.

She felt someone standing over her and turned, glancing up. Jack Diamonte was looking down at her. He reached down and picked up the business card and said softly, "You're a rising star at this paper. Let's keep it that way."

He walked off.

Across town, the summer sun beamed down on Penny's head from a cloudless sky as she walked along 7th Street toward Central Park. The return trip - 12 blocks up and then back - would take about an hour, but she liked to clear her head during lunch.

Halfway to Central Park, she started to feel damp from the heat and decided to circle back.

Walking down 53rd Street, a one-way street, she noticed how unusually quiet it had become. There were no people out on lunch breaks. There were no cars. Only her footfalls on the sidewalk made noise. In fact, it was so quiet that up ahead a lone squirrel had decided to sit in the middle of the street.

As she got closer, she became increasingly curious about the squirrel. He was still as a statue. When she was within ten feet of the squirrel, she noticed his features with clarity. He faced her, sitting on his back haunches with his two front paws curled tight up against his chest. His fur was a mix of brown and grey except his belly which was stark white. The hair all traveled in one direction. His black eyes stared straight ahead. His tail, with it's slightly tattered edges, stood erect behind his back.

From behind her at the beginning of the block, she heard a car approaching. The squirrel did not move.

She continued to close in on him; she was now only six feet away. He remained motionless. From behind her, the car was getting closer.

The car, a taxi, rushed past her. She stopped. A strand of her hair whispered against her cheek in the taxi's slipstream.

The squirrel did not move.

The taxi rushed on.

Time slowed. She was mesmerized.

The taxi, at full speed, was now a foot from the squirrel. Penny held her breath.

Suddenly, the squirrel jumped to the sidewalk, shimming out of view.

45

Washington, DC

Late in the afternoon, Odom noiselessly slipped through the front door of Cal's apartment. A humid heat pressed against his face and he let his eyes adjust to the interior darkness. He gently shut the door with his gloved hands.

He inhaled deeply through his nostrils, taking in the measure of the home. There were no pets, no recent cooking, no smoking. There was an undercurrent of pine. The ATF agent must have a cleaner; few professionals clean their homes mid-week.

He concentrated next on noises. Cars passed in the front and a cat's howl echoed from an open window in the rear. There were no human sounds inside the apartment.

He surveyed the spacious living room. His line of sight led directly to the desk by the front window. An old, high-back leather office chair, its tan leather wearing thin, rested a few feet from the desk as if the owner, getting up quickly, had set it rolling on its five casters. The ATF agent spent considerable time here.

Odom settled into the warm, worn leather. Feeling a powerful, yet fleeting sense of sexual invasion, the corners of his mouth turned up.

His feet tugged the chair up to the desk as he studied the montage.

The two clipped *New York News* articles by Stacia DeVries were intentionally placed next to each other. Odom's heart sunk; the ATF agent had connected the two operations within a larger plot.

Next to them was a yellow pad. The top page had been doodled

243

on endlessly, hundreds of blue ink loops haphazardly filled the margins. In the center of the page was a list:
 - Personally involved w/ Malhotra
 - Top clearances (CIA, DOD, DNI, NSA, State?)
 - Professional techniques ??? This last line had been underlined five times.

It appeared the ATF agent later had added two items to the list - afterthoughts perhaps - that appeared to be hastily written, in red:
 - A woman!
 - Acting alone?

Odom blinked. It was the last line that was an interesting twist; Odom had not considered that Mac may be working with others. She had always been such a loner. Who could she possibly be working with?

The cat in the back alley howled again as Odom entered the kitchen. Noticing the half empty bottle of scotch on the kitchen counter, he lifted the highball glass from the drying rack and sniffed its contents. Nothing. He systematically opened and closed cabinets.

Heavy drinkers had reserves. The ATF agent had no other bottles anywhere in the kitchen.

Through the screened window, the faintest smell of rot road a warm breeze, prickling his nose.

In the bathroom, mismatched towels dangled from the shower rod. The toilet rim stood upright.

Odom unzipped his khakis and relieved himself, looking around. One gloved hand flushed while the other reached toward the medicine cabinet. Ibuprofen. Non-prescription sleeping pills. Colgate. Men's deodorant. Shaving cream.

An expensive grey robe hung on a hook on the back of the door. With both hands he folded the soft robe around his face, breathing deeply, smelling dryer sheets and ivory soap. Its terrycloth did not harbor the perfumed scent of a woman. He rubbed its softness against his five o'clock shadow.

In the darkened bedroom, he laid down on the unmade bed. With crossed ankles and gloved hands behind his head, he slowly surveyed the room. There were no frames on the walls or pictures. There wasn't a television. In the dark closet, blue suits hung evenly across a pole below a bare light bulb. A chain dangled from the bulb.

He closed his eyes, hearing only the street noises. The sheets smelled of male sweat; there was no hint of sexual musk.

This was a solitary, quiet man with nothing obvious to lose.

A few minutes later, Odom was scowling as he silently let himself out.

Manayunk, PA

The blades whirled with a soft buzz as the fan slowly oscillated left and right. Every ten-count the fan dispatched a brief breeze on her face, sending hair dancing across her forehead. She sat with her back up against the cement loft wall, her legs stretched out before her on the white sheets. Her bare unpolished toes pointed toward the ceiling.

A bright green Ipod Shuffle rested next to her. The song ended and she hit repeat for the fifth time.

Her lips began silently mouthing the song's words. Through the wires and the earphones, the music released long buried memories.

It reminded her of a moment with Joe. They were on his balcony overlooking a dark San Francisco Bay. She remembered the salt air, the seagulls' culls, and his bright blue eyes as he laughed. The moment was the strongest memory she owned.

She wiped tears from her cheeks as she took the earplugs out and rolled down onto her back. She stretched her calves and thighs. She let her mind creep back into the present.

She held her hands to her face, examining them. They looked different to her today, not old exactly, just aged and unrecognizable. They reminded her of her mother's hands.

Through the window, the layer of rippled cloud-cover resembled the underside of an ocean's surface. She felt safe, hidden far below the imaginary whitecaps and for a moment, wanted to stay on this bed forever, gazing up at a sky turning pink.

She sat up and took stock of the loft. Everything of value was arranged on the architect's desk: her laptop, the hard drive, her burner phones, her leather case of alias documents. In the corner, by the bed, her few clothes were folded on a cardboard box. Her

Dora alias clothes were in a travel bag in the Alfa down the street in the garage. On the kitchen counter was a box of cereal and some V8 juice boxes. The cleaning products were in a supermarket box on the floor.

She stood, walked to the kitchen, and grabbed a disinfectant spray and a sponge.

She started at the sink. She sprayed and scrubbed, then repeated.

In the bathroom, she threw cleaner across all the porcelain and scrubbed in small rotations, creating green, sandy circles. After, the stream from the shower washed everything down the drains.

Across the wooden floor, she leaned into forceful strokes, her biceps burning as the sponge swept the splintered planks.

An hour later, she dropped down into a sitting position on the mattress, her legs stretched out before her. The breeze from the fan hit her sweat-soaked face. She felt the dry roughness of her hands.

46

Manayunk, PA

A vivid nightmare jarred Mac awake before 5 a.m.

In the dream, she had been hauling luggage through a Chinese park, finally on her way home. She had needed a toilet before her flight and was searching for a luggage locker for the wheelie bag full of precious documents. Time was running out.

Desperate, she had set the wheelie in a sea of other bags and had run toward the toilet. A crowd of Chinese tourists had surged around the bathroom entrance and she had found herself behind 100 prattling women. Their voices had aggravated her, building her anxiety about the flight leaving in ten minutes and the wheelie bag sitting vulnerable among hundreds on the other side of the park. Her need for the toilet had been extreme, but instead, she had turned, ran through the park to the bag making mental contingency plans if the passport, the plane ticket were stolen.

Racing around the last corner, she had woken up in a panic.

The loft was dark and humid. The only noise was the whirring fan.

There was depth in the surrounding silence, as if the loft was connected to the Chinese park.

On cobblestone below, the wheels of a lone truck thudded past and pulled to a stop at the corner. There was a loud thump as a block of plastic wrapped newspapers hit the pavement.

She stood, pulled on sweats, and stumbled down the three flights of stairs.

SFG Manipulates Members, Stokes Fear After Newtown

A Spy Came Home

By STACIA DeVries
<u>New York News</u>

Three days before a Senate vote to nationally ban assault weapons, the New York News is releasing evidence today of a second scandal rocking the Society for Guns. A leaked internal email between the SFG's chief strategist, Neil Koen, and CEO, Charles Osbourne, outlines a strategy in response to the Newtown massacre that purposefully manipulates members' fear.

In the email, Neil Koen clearly sets out the points for an initiative to increase falling membership and donations based on systematic fear-mongering and misinformation. Koen lays out willfully misleading tactics that dramatize and inflate potential 'threats' to the right to bear arms under the Second Amendment. Koen writes, "Our research shows that our key demographic is activated (read donations) through the emotions of fear, anger and pride (read patriotism.)" In short hand, Koen summarizes the new strategy: "To Sum: Misinformation > Fear > Increased SFG Donations." Charles Osbourne replied to Koen's suggested strategy with two words: "Agreed. Approved."

Senator Martha Payne, the author of the assault weapons ban legislation, responded swiftly. "At the very least, the SFG's top two leaders reek of contempt for their own members. How anyone still gives them a cent is a complete mystery to me."

Gun rights activists and SFG stalwarts have been hit hard by this latest scandal. Many long-term SFG members have tried to discount the brewing investigation into arms trafficking by a top SFG corporate sponsor. One SFG lifetime member commented, "We joined the SFG because we believe in our constitutional rights. To learn that our most revered leaders literally tread on us - well - the irony is rich."

Many both within and outside one of the largest nonprofits in America, are beginning to question how much the SFG Board of Directors knew about this calculated approach.

New York, NY

Cal was standing in the morning sun at the same bank of

windows in the New York News building when his cell phone vibrated. Checking his phone, he ignored the five missed calls from headquarters and opened the text from Sheriff Soloman. *"Scimitar receptionist ID'ed your gal immediately. Turns out she stopped up the office toilet. They had to call a plumber."*

A striking woman in her early 40s with a pretty face, shoulder length hair, slim jeans, and heels walked toward him across the cafeteria floor.

Her hand was outstretched. "Freda Browne."

"Agent Cal Bertrand. Thanks for seeing me on such short notice. I'm grateful you could make the time before I head back to DC."

She motioned him to sit, looking him over. "I know you, don't I, Agent?"

"I had some notoriety last year."

She examined his face with alluring eyes. "Ahhh yes. Fast and Frenzied. You're the whistleblower that gave shit to Congress. And caught some heat in the Bureau. Tough to be such a baller, am I right?"

He grinned but gave nothing away.

She said, "I would have thought you'd be staying away from guns these days. As I understand from Stacia DeVries that you're interested in our SFG scoop."

"I'm with the ATF. Guns come with the job."

She mocked chagrin. "Of course. So, I understand you'd like some information on our confidential source."

Opening up his notebook, Cal told her, "Well, I've seen a few stories on the SFG in the last few weeks. And two-in-a-row just this morning."

"Right. Exactly. As Stacia informed you yesterday, we're not going to give that source up. This paper has withstood many an official attempt to divulge the identity of sources. We're certainly not going to start now over a very clear criminal case involving leadership at the SFG"

"Stacia implied that you may not even know your source."

"Maybe." She tilted her head at him. "I'm surprised. You're the first person from the ATF we've heard from. Usually we hear from your legal department. Is this an official investigation?"

"I'm actually chasing early leads related to an ongoing

investigation. Just chasing possible connections."

"Really?" Serious men didn't intimidate her. "Chasing leads from articles in the *New York News?* You appreciate the First Amendment, right?"

"Of course."

"So shouldn't you be chasing leads with the SFG? Strong arming a newspaper isn't exactly… highbrow investigative work."

"So, you don't know your source?"

She stood. "Want some coffee?"

"Excuse me?"

"I'm going to go get a coffee." She tapped her inner elbow like a junkie. "Can I get you something?"

"No, no, I'm fine."

He watched her walk off. Her tight jeans accentuated how fit she was.

His phone vibrated with a second text from Sheriff Soloman. *"She also said she thinks your gal probably 40+ y.o. But couldn't describe her in physical detail: seemed nice but distant."*

He watched Freda as she returned across the hardwood floor, blowing on the rim of her paper coffee cup. As she sat down she asked, "Do you think it's a bad thing that the SFG has been caught out for their bad behavior?"

Cal considered this. "My job is to make sure we follow the law."

"That seems…a bit too simple in this case. Surely you have an opinion about the SFG?"

"I do."

"Is that coloring your investigation?"

"I should think not. I try to stay professional."

"That must be difficult. Because I would imagine in your shoes, this case would be complicated by the players. They've been caught-out for their own, very questionable, unethical, behavior. It all seems a bit grey to me."

He released a small chuckle accompanied by a self-depreciating grin.

"What's that for?"

"Nothing."

"I'm just trying to get a sense of how serious you are about investigating our journalism."

"Well, I saw Stacia did a piece on the SFG a few weeks back."

Freda nodded. From around the rim of the cup she said, "We were going to do a series actually. But it got canned. All she got was the one front page story."

"Why is that?"

"The Chief thinks it's an old story." She wobbled her head and slipped into heavy sarcasm as she imitated someone, finger-quoting. "'Old News. SFG. Guns. Our legislative failures. Kids shot in schools. We need something new.' I paraphrase there of course. From higher-ups. I'm sure you know all about that cynicism around guns, being ATF and all."

Her attempts to befriend, possibly flirt with him, were intriguing. Was she trying to deflect his inquiry? "Was it your idea to run the series?"

"It had been percolating for a while."

He noticed she hadn't answered the question.

Her eyes narrowed. "I know the other reason I recognize you. You were the agent on-site down at the Scimitar raid in Lexington."

"You've got a good eye." Before she could distract him again, he changed tack, smiling and dropping into a personal tone. "Freda, I'm an investigator. When I'm on an investigation, I tend to notice coincidences. I noticed that Stacia's first article —" He flipped through his notebook. "was published just a week before the Scimitar raid and just two weeks before these latest articles."

She maintained a look of innocence. "And?"

"The focus for the article on the SFG seemed particularly well-timed, given the gun control legislation."

She sipped from her coffee and without missing a beat said, "We're no dummies here, Agent. And we're all on the same side I believe. We are a liberal media outlet - according to Fox News - that wants to see some smart gun regulations passed. Nothing nefarious here."

He watched her closely. She didn't look away.

Quietly, he asked, "So no connection between Stacia's first article and the latest on Neil Koen?"

"What do you mean?"

"No way you knew the Koen scandal was coming?"

She feigned surprise, contemplated his question, and said, "We were handed the Koen scandal by a courier. If I had that kind of ability to see into the future I would not be living in a 900-square-foot apartment in the East Village."

He nodded, closed his notebook, and slipped it into his back jeans pocket. "Gotcha. Ok, well, I can see you're quite a stickler for the law."

"Yes. The First Amendment is pretty important around here, Agent."

"Right. Ok, well, I'll show myself out. If you change your mind --" He stood and handed her his card. "You grow up in New York? You have a slight accent."

It was Freda's turn to be intrigued: was he flirting? "I went to school in Michigan."

"Ann Arbor?"

"Yup."

He noticed that, again, she hadn't answered the question. He reached out to shake her hand. "Ok, well, thanks again."

Freda watched him walk toward the elevator bank.

In the elevator ride down he listened to the latest voicemail from Wilson. "Where are you?" he asked, clearly seething. "Ruby says she hasn't heard from you since you asked for phone logs last week. She says the GAO guy out in Arlington says you weren't in the office yesterday. I will not have you on the loose this week. Not. This. Week. Check in. Now."

Standing at the window, Freda watched Cal step out onto the sidewalk below. Into the cell phone at her ear she said, "*And* the ATF was just here."

Penny asked, "What? What did he want?"

"He thinks there may be a coincidence with all the heat coming on the SFG right now, but he doesn't know anything about us. It was fine. We chatted. I played nice, got him chatting. He's a good guy. I'm telling you, I'm tits. I played him like a fine-tuned, bluegrass fiddle." She watched him head down Broadway. "He's hot. No wedding band."

"What?"

"The ATF agent is super hot."

"Fuck off."

"I think he flirted with me."

"Seriously. Fuck off. Are you kidding?"

"Nope. We had serious vibes. I'm talking scorching. He's like 6'3" and built. I bet he played serious sports in college - like on scholarship. I'm telling you, Benjamin Franklin could have lit up a light bulb with our sparks." Her eyes followed him in the crowd.

Penny growled, "I'm hanging up."

Back in her office, Freda dialed Jack's extension.

He answered gruffly, "Jack Diamonte."

"Just so you know, both the FBI earlier and now this ATF agent for a second time are chasing the source from our stories. No connection to us."

"Keep it that way."

"And Jack, thanks."

He hung up.

47

New York, NY

After leaving the New York News building, Cal started walking without a destination, just to clear his head. His stride was purposeful, chewing up whole blocks, but his mind churned randomly.
- Maar was some kind of intelligence operative, a woman in her 40s.
- She chose him because he was a whistleblower.
- She left breadcrumbs.
- She first piqued his interest with the Blue Lantern cables then revealed Scimitar's gun trafficking, then the cover up of the Malhotra killing.
- And she planted evidence. She had to be involved in the Koen scandal.
- It looked exceptionally likely she was discrediting the SFG in the lead up to the Senate vote.
- The New York News was serving as well coordinated publicity tool.

Forty minutes later, he found himself looking up at the entrance to Grand Central Terminal on 42nd and Park Ave with a singular, pounding thought.

I have no idea who Maar is.

The only thing he had to go on was that Maar was a woman about 40 years old. So was Freda.

Cal searched for an internet cafe but stumbled on a public

library on 46th and 3rd. The branch was remarkably small, but bright and airy. The overhead air conditioner belt whirled steadily. Aluminum lights hung from cross bars under a ratty looking dropped ceiling. Busy professionals popped in and out of the clean, modern space, dropping off books, scanning the computer catalogues.

Along the front window, Cal banged on a laptop checked out from the front desk. He was researching Freda Browne.

In a professional photo on the New York News website, she was wearing a stylish business suit below a cheeky smile. He deliberately scrutinized the photograph out of the corner of his eye, trying a different perspective. There was definitely a mischievous and knowing look about her.

According to her bio, she had joined the LA Times in 1990 as an investigative reporter after graduating from the University of Michigan. In 1995, she had become a special projects editor for the business desk. In 2000 she had become the Managing Editor.

Seven years later, she had moved to the New York News to take over as one of three Managing Editors. Her list of work accolades was long, including a Pulitzer Prize for investigative reporting on corruption in LA's social services.

His internet search delivered 50 pages of links to articles she had written on varied subjects. There was no unifying theme. This must be true for all journalists. Methodically, he scanned each link, often clicking through.

He almost missed an outlier. It was an article, "Local Reporter Loses Brother to Santa Monica Shooter', in which she was mentioned in the content, not as the author. He clicked through. Just after she had moved to LA, Freda's brother was shot by a random man who had opened fire with a semiautomatic weapon on a pedestrian mall in Santa Monica. Michael Browne had been dead on arrival at UCLA emergency room.

Outside the library window, men and women hustled through their day. A telephone rang. He heard the front desk librarian answer. He wondered where Freda had been when she had gotten the call. He rubbed his eyes. This was a tragic bit of information.

But it also was not a coincidence.

He resumed his search.

A Spy Came Home

Freda Browne sat on the PTA of the New York Lab School for Consolidated Studies. The school was for 8th and 9th grades. He located the school on a map of New York City near the West Village. He wondered how Freda got her kid to the school each morning. To stay as fit as she was, she must have an established routine of walking her child, hitting the gym, then heading to work. She was organized, not afraid to be driven.

After a few more clicks on the touchpad of the borrowed laptop, he stopped. He leaned back, lifting his hands off the keyboard. Freda Browne was listed on the Board of the non-profit Citizens Against Illegal Guns.

It was a significant, intentional omission on her part to not have mentioned this. It was one of the nation's largest gun control advocacy group.

On the organization's site, he discovered the photos from their last gala. The photographer had captured a large hall, white linens, and silver bedecked tables, candles, flower arrangements and bottles of wine. It was a very tony setting for the very tony of New York City.

On stage, the 50 smiling faces grinned out to the photographer, hands raised in a toast. Freda, in a slim, blue dress, stood on the left, toward the end of the row between a tall, bearded man and an attractive, petite black woman. She wore a wide smile and held up a glass of champagne.

He wondered if the bearded man was her date.

Under the photo, a caption listed the names of the board members. Cal leaned in close to the screen, then realizing his mistake, expanded the font. He looked around the library, embarrassed, before pulling out his cell phone and snapping a photo of the list of names.

The coincidences were piling up.

After another twenty minutes of searching, he found that Freda had graduated in 1986 from the Germantown Friends High School in the Chestnut Hill area of Philadelphia.

He sat back.

The courier for Stacia DeVries' informant had come from Philadelphia.

Freda had omitted that she was from Philadelphia.

He scanned through the photos on his phone, pulling up the image of the label for the courier company, and dialed their main number. He lied easily. "Yes, hi, this is the New York News. We received a package two days ago that originated in Philadelphia. I have the tracking number here for you. Can you please tell me the street address where it was picked up?" He read out the tracking number.

The courier company secretary said, "Sure, give me sec." There was a pause as she tapped on her keyboard. "Yeah, looks like we picked it up at 30th and Market. That's 30th Street, the train station."

"Nothing more definitive?"

"Nope, looks like the directions were to pick up literally at the corner outside."

"Ok, thanks."

He pulled up a map of Philadelphia's SEPTA suburban commuter trains. It was extensive.

Chestnut Hill sat the end of a tentacle that spread northwest from the city, roughly following a river, called the Norristown Line. The Chestnut Hill station looked to be about 30 minutes from 30th Street and the tenth stop: 30th Street, North Philadelphia, Allegheny, East Falls, Wissahickon, Manayunk, Carpenter, Allen Lane, St. Martins and Chestnut Hill West

Did Maar and Freda know each other from high school? Could it be that simple?

If Cal was right, it meant Maar had come back to her roots and was hunkered down in Chestnut Hill to run an op. When she needed to, Maar sent her results via courier to Stacia DeVries - Freda's front man at the New York News - to run an article.

If Cal was right, there would be records of Maar attending the high school.

The website for the Germantown Friends High School displayed historic buildings spread across a rolling green campus littered with sports fields. For a kid from a working class neighborhood in Atlanta, the school looked like an Ivy League college. It touted 100% of graduates attended four-year colleges. There were 850 students enrolled and 85 full-time teachers.

He called the principal's office. "Good afternoon. I'm with the

Bureau of Alcohol, Tobacco, and Firearms here in DC. I wonder if I couldn't ask you a favor."

"Oh?" The secretary hesitated. "Yes? How can I help you?"

"We believe one of your alumni may be able to help us out in a federal investigation."

"You say an alumni is involved? How is that?"

"I'm afraid I can't say."

"Oh. Ok. What do you need?"

"Would you be able to send me a copy of the school's yearbook from 1986? Perhaps an electronic copy?"

There was another long pause. "Well, they are publicly available so I suppose that's fine. Let me have your details. I'll need to verify who you say you are, then I'll send you a photocopy by email."

He gave her his name, Ruby's number, and his email. "Thanks so much."

Ruby called his cell phone ten minutes later. Her voice was harsh. "You had better know what you're doing. I just vouched for you for some school in Philadelphia."

"Thanks, Ruby."

"You know the Director has been looking for you. He found out you're not in Arlington."

"Yeah, I meant to call him. I'll try him in the morning."

"Cal, you're on thinner and thinner ice around here. I'm not sure I can keep helping you. It may get me in trouble."

"I know. I appreciate everything you do for me, Ruby. I promise to not call you again."

She whispered, "I heard your name mentioned today. The DA was in there two hours ago."

"Oh yeah?"

"Something about a Senator covering up some State Department report. Seemed like they were all in a big hurry to meet. The Director came out during that meeting, asking me where you were. I couldn't find you. You're not answering your cell."

"Sorry, I've been occupied."

"You're supposed to be out in Arlington doing menial, non-occupied work."

"Yeah, I know. I'm heading back there ASAP."
"Where are you? What are you doing?"
"Nothing, nothing, Ruby."
"Listen, call in the morning and appease him, will ya?"

Manayunk, PA

The burner phone pinged on the architect's desk with a text from Penny. *"ATF interviewed Freda."*

Mac texted back, *"As expected."* She sat back and lit a cigarette, blowing her smoke toward the open loft window.

Penny pinged again. *"I can't stop thinking about that squirrel."*

Mac took another drag.

"If he hadn't moved, the cab would have plowed him. I would have watched guts splatter all over street."

Mac stared at the burner phone. The pine from the cleaner was strong in her nose. *"Yup."*

"I just stood there. I should have shooed it."

"It was a squirrel."

"Yeah. I get that. But what's weird: where was my own self-preservation?"

Mac didn't know what to say to this.

"I could have been splattered in guts."

Mac texted, *"Are you at work?"*

"Of course."

"There aren't always answers. Find a distraction."

The burner phone went silent.

Mac fixed herself a cup of coffee and lit another cigarette as she stared at the weeping willow in the park.

Twenty minutes later Penny texted again. *"Aaargh!!! Still can't figure out why I just stood there."*

Very slowly, Mac pecked out, *"XO"*

New York, NY

It was late but the newsroom was still packed and rowdy. Stacia leaned back in her chair and stared up at the bright ceiling lights. She reached across her desk and picked up her cell phone, texting

Charlotte, *"We agreed I should do something right?"*
"Yes. It's not ok for a newspaper to put finger in news."
"Right. Ok. Will discuss tonight what I should do."
"Agreed. Bring wine."

Stacia smiled weakly. Her apprehension was growing. She turned back to her screen and checked her inbox. There were fifty new messages that had arrived in the last five minutes.

She sat up, startled. She opened the first. It was from an obviously illegitimate user, 'gothhand2210' and read, *"We know where you live Stacia. With your roommate. Pretty girl Charlotte. PS we like our guns. You shouldn't be treading on us."*

She closed it quickly, staring at the newly full inbox. Another three emails arrived. All the new emails looked to be from illegitimate users.

With a trembling hand she picked up the desk phone and dialed the tech team.

48

New York, NY

The next morning, Stacia read through the mounting comments to her latest article. The IT guys had called earlier, told her they couldn't do much about tracing the anonymous emails that had hit her inbox. "The trolls kinda come with the territory."

They were trying to remove the threatening comments from the website, but she was seeing them before they were scrubbed.

- *Stacia you are a toadie of the liberal media elites. Use your brain!*
- *Another twisting of the facts. The SFG protects our freedoms.*
- *You need to be more careful, dumb bitch. The SFG has put you on their hit list. (Link)*

She clicked the link on the last comment, her brow furrowing. It directed her to sub-page of the SFG Lobby site titled 'SFG Traitors List.' She scanned down the 100s of names starting with celebrities, corporations, and foundations. Her fear hit a new level.

Manayunk, PA

Mac's eyes snapped open from a sound sleep. She rolled over and yanked up her cell phone. It read 7:30 a.m. as she knew it would.

If she got up now she could be dressed and outside when Joe passed on his morning walk around the park with the mutt. She stared at the ceiling and imagined herself waving, his eyes widening as his face cracked into a huge, tender smile. It was an unconvincing image.

She glanced at the few folded clothes perched on the cardboard box. She rolled easily off the mattress and picked up jeans and a black t-shirt, glancing at a pair of dark shorts, weighing her choices. She pulled on the jeans.

She leaned into the mirror over the bathroom sink as she brushed her teeth. She turned her head left and right, looking for any new wrinkles. She brushed out her hair while digging into her courier bag for mascara. She hurriedly stroked a few wipes on her lashes. She backed out of the bathroom nook, trying to see her full length in the small mirror.

At the loft door, she sized up the meager collection of running shoes, flip-flops and Dora's pumps. She slipped on the flip-flops.

She grasped the doorknob.

Her eyes gravitated to her hand. There it was again, unrecognizable.

The thought immobilized her. Time slowed.

Her heart began to race. Her chest felt heavier and heavier. She began to pant in short bursts. Sweat stormed her armpits and around her neck. She glowered at her hand, forcing it to release the knob. It held fast.

With a concerted effort, she spun herself around.

She leaned back against the door and slowly slid to the floor.

She raised both hands, fingers splayed in front of her face, and stared at them.

The chill began at her feet and swelled up through her legs. An icy undercurrent dragged down on her hips. The cold rolled up over her chest, forcing her to gasp rapidly, hyperventilating.

Finally, her mouth stretched wide around a silent scream as the frigid wave of panic crashed over her.

New York, NY

The next morning, inside an internet cafe, Cal checked the headlines on the *Huffingtonpost*.

SFG Board "Had No Idea" - Too little too late?

Early this morning, after a hastily called meeting, the Society for Guns' Board released a statement. "The Board of Directors of the SFG is deeply outraged and saddened by what appears to be an ill-informed strategy undertaken by the Executive Director and Chief Strategist. To be clear, the Board is hearing of these emails for the first time and deem them inappropriate and unacceptable. We will take all necessary actions to rectify this situation."

As well they should. According to IRS rules governing non-profits, a Board of Directors has fiduciary responsibility for the organization.

The Virginia State's Attorney commented, "Both my office and the IRS take non-profit governance issues very seriously. Board members are charged to ensure that the organization pursues its mission, that it not waste assets, and that it not involve itself in what the law calls self-dealing."

Senator Payne, the author of the assault weapons ban up for vote tomorrow fired off a quick statement. "If they didn't know about this egregious strategy then they were duped. If they did know about it, they are liars. Either way, the SFG has systematically defrauded their members in a wholly premeditated manner."

The SFG communications office did not respond to inquiries.

Cal opened the email from Germantown Friends High School. The school secretary had sent him a PDF of the entire yearbook and the cafe attendant informed him that he could print it for $.50 a page.

The printed 1986 yearbook was 100 pages of photos: professional photos with captions, group photos, sports photos, photos of the campus and buildings. He found Freda's formal, senior class photo. She was a young, innocent teenager with big hair curled back off a fresh face. In her caption, she had quoted The Who. The yearbook listed her activities as field hockey, lacrosse, student newspaper, and Student Government.

He slowly flipped through the rest of the yearbook looking for her image. In one photo, she was jumping, her legs kicked up behind her with a hockey stick raised in the air, on a lush, green hockey field. In another, she was hunched over a paper-strewn desk. The caption read, "Newspaper journalists hard at work."

A Spy Came Home

The last photo in the yearbook was landscaped across two pages. Twenty students stood in formation on risers on a high school stage, a red theatrical curtain hung in the background. The caption read, "Senior Class Student Government." Freda was front and center in the first row, her arm thrown around a striking, petite black girl.

His eyes narrowed on the petite girl. From the caption he read her name, Penny Navarro.

On his cellphone he pulled up the photo of the Board of Citizens Against Illegal Guns and skimmed through the names. There. There it was: Penny Navarro stood next to Freda Browne.

In the yearbook photo, Penny Navarro was smiling shyly, her hair pulled back off her face in a ponytail. She had pearl earrings and a pearl necklace. Cal squinted trying to decipher more, but she revealed nothing. Perhaps she was still inscrutable in real life.

He flipped to her formal, senior class photo. She quoted Virginia Wolf and was listed in swimming, debate team, and Student Government.

An internet search of Penny Navarro revealed she was a partner in the litigation are of Ruben, Walters, Thompson and Arrpen. It was a top tier, 'white shoe' law firm with blue chip clients and offices on Times Square. A second search revealed their offices were near the internet cafe.

Out on the street, he got his bearings in the crush of commuters and headed toward Times Square.

A block later he realized his oversight; once he had identified Penny Navarro he stopped cross-checking the Citizens Against Illegal Guns board members with the Germantown Friends. What if there is another high school friend?

He stepped into a diner and ordered a coffee. Using the Yearbook and the photo of the Board members on his phone, he continued to cross check the rest of the 1986 student body.

He came up empty handed.

He returned to the list of board members for Citizens Against Illegal Guns and began, laboriously, checking each member's biography on the internet.

He found her twenty minutes later. Ms. Laura Franklin was also from the Philadelphia area. In the gala photo she stood in the back row, a heavyset black woman with a dazzling smile.

She had attended a rival school in the Chestnut Hill area. It turned out she was a self-made billionaire. Billionaire. Having built a very successful online gambling site, she was part of the 32 self-made billionaire women who made up the 1.9% of all the world's billionaires. Her address was listed on the Upper East Side overlooking Central Park.

Within five minutes, he was back out in the swarm of people heading toward Times Square.

Behind him, Beam followed at ten paces. He was blending in well with the morning commuter crowd. His suit was blue, nondescript. His sunglasses weren't out of place.

He texted Odom. *"Doing searches on computers. Appears to be heading to Times Square."*

49

New York, NY

Penny's assistant looked around the wall. "There's a G man in the big conference room, waiting for you."

Penny flinched. "A G man?"

"Yeah, like FBI or something."

"How do you know what the FBI look like?"

"I dunno. Maybe the movies? For sure he's a Fed."

"Can you let Cliff know I need him in there? Probably something to do with our case." Really, she just wanted a friendly witness to whatever was about to transpire.

She headed down the hallway, smoothing back her hair. Stepping into the conference room, she saw a tall man in a blue suit sitting opposite the door at the long table. She stepped around the table, her hand held out. "Penny Navarro."

"Agent Cal Bertrand with the ATF." Cal shook her hand as Cliff stepped into the room.

She introduced the two men. "I've asked Cliff as a partner in litigation to sit in with us."

"Sure, sure." The three sat and Cal began. "I'm investigating a case that I believe may involve you, Ms. Navarro."

Her heart began a mild but consistent beat inside her chest. "I'm not sure I understand."

"We have reason to believe you might be able to shed some light on a current line if inquiry."

She squinted at him and adopted her professionally neutral 'lawyer-in-a-confrontational-meeting' tone. "Please, proceed."

"It has come to our attention that a certain high-net-worth

individual in New York is quite heavily involved on the issue of gun control."

Penny raised her eyebrows, said nothing. Beside her Cliff perked up.

"Turns out this individual also has ties to the Citizens Against Illegal Guns."

"As do I. Who are you talking about?"

"Laura Franklin."

"Laura?"

"You know her?"

"Of course, we're from the same area in Philadelphia. Our families were friends, you could say. Are you investigating Laura?"

"No, no, nothing like that. It's just a hunch I'm chasing down."

"A hunch?"

"Have you been reading the *New York News* articles about the SFG?"

Penny nodded.

"It appears someone has provided the SFG with a million dollar donation that landed them in pretty hot water. I'd even go so far as to say it looks incredibly like a set-up."

Penny glanced at Cliff. He was stock straight in his chair, his lips pinched, holding his mouth closed. She turned back to Cal. "I'm sorry, Agent, I'm not following you."

"I believe the donor intended to entrap the SFG."

"Well from what I've been reading they stepped right into it. I would have thought the ATF would have found that admirable? No? Wait --" Her tone darkened. "Are you suggesting Laura is this secret donor?"

Cliff sat forward. "Penny --"

She cut Cliff off by asking Cal, "That's what you're implying, right?"

"We're working on a hunch."

"Speaking of hunches, isn't fraud an FBI issue? Why is the ATF on this?"

Cliff tried to smooth her. "Penny, perhaps we should be here to help out the ATF?"

Cal spoke over him, "It's cross-bureau cooperation."

"How convenient," she said. "But I'm not sure how I can help you."

"Have you been in touch with Laura recently?"

It took a long, slow moment before the sweat condensed below her arms. A mild pressure built in her ears. She crossed her legs and clasped her hands in her lap. *Sail close to the wind.* Her tone remained perfectly neutral and professional. "Yes, in fact, we had lunch about a month ago."

"Where?"

"A lovely place across town. Jean Gorges."

"Did she mention anything unusual?"

Penny's response was quick, tinged with a mild sarcastic. "About funding a sting operation against the SFG?"

Cliff jumped in again. "Penny, let's see where this is going —"

She faced Cal. "Absolutely not did we discuss anything of the sort. " She threw Cliff a questioning look. "Cliff, of course." Like a litigator in a courtroom, she smoothly turned back to Cal. "Just so we're all on the same page, Agent. Laura and I had a personal lunch. We didn't speak about any work. We didn't speak about donations. We didn't speak about the SFG. What you're suggesting is actually absurd to me. That being said, my personal opinion on gun control is public record. I abhor the level of gun violence in this country and am proud to sit on the Board of Citizens Against Illegal Guns." She glanced at Cliff. "This firm and its partners are proud to have me sit on that board." Then she turned back to Cal. "Have I been watching the news about the SFG's fumbles? Yes. Am I glad the SFG is finally crumbling under the weight of their own shady practices? Of course. Am I glad the *Times* is throwing public grenades about how hideous and manipulative and fraudulent and fear-mongering the SFG truly is? Absolutely." She took a breath. "But I'm afraid I'm not one who can shed light on Laura for you. We were loose friends growing up. We stay in touch mostly around Board meetings. We meet up once very six months. She's not what I would call a close friend."

Cal jotted down notes and closed his small notebook. "Well, Ms. Navarro, I appreciate your time this morning. If you think of anything, please call me."

His abruptness surprise her.

All three stood. Cal moved around the table, paused in front of her with his card. As she took it, he leaned in slightly, making her

crane back and spoke one word. "Germantown."
"Excuse me?"
"You grew up in Germantown. In Philadelphia."
"Yes." She noticed Cliff stood apart, a non-partisan observer.
"So did Freda Browne over at the Times."
Her heart somersaulted but her voice was strong. "Yes. Freda and I went to high school together."
"And from what I understand she's the one managing the SFG pieces over at the Times."
"Ok?"
"Convenient, that."
"I'm sorry?"
"It's just convenient that all three of you sit on the Citizen's Board and that there appears to have been a set up at the SFG involving a very large donation and that got reported almost immediately by the *Times*."
She squinted at him, her resolve steely. "Agent, we are all involved on the gun issue here in New York. That doesn't mean we're connected to the various incidents happening now."
"Hmmm. Just interesting." He stepped back, then thought of a further point. "Still friends to this day. That's nice. That kind of long-term friendship."
"I'm sorry, Agent, I'm not following you."
"You, Freda Brown, Laura Franklin."
"Yes?"
"You must have had other friends, growing up."
She tilted her head, furrowed her brows. She said nothing.
"Maybe a fourth friend?" He let the question hover.
Her mouth dropped slightly and she stood immobile. Was that a tiny, smug grin on the Agent's face?
As if her reaction confirmed his suspicion, Cal shrugged, glanced at Cliff. "Well, thank you. Both of you. I'll see myself out." As he turned to Penny his face was inscrutable. "That kind of friendship is good for kids growing up. That kind of life-long friendship. You've got two kids, right?"
"Pardon me?"
"You've got two sons."
In that instant, her suppressed fear and tension finally won over reason. She stepped forward, her voice ice. "There are civil rights

in this country, Agent. This is a country of rule of law. Threats against my family, whether explicit or implied, from law enforcement, without cause - just on 'a hunch' - are definitively crossing a line that could very well get you in trouble. You would do well to stay within your remit."

Cliff finally moved in. But it wasn't in her defense. "Penny, Penny, I'm not sure that's necessary."

She was ramrod still, staring at Cal. "I will not have a law officer threaten my family."

Cliff broke the momentary silence. "I'm sure the ATF is just doing its job. Agent, why don't you let me show you out."

Cliff returned, closing the door behind him. "What's gotten into you? Penny, for god's sakes you're not supposed to get uppity on the Feds. They better not hear about this upstairs."

"Uppity?" Her look of disbelief was genuine. "Is that a sexist thing? As in a woman who protects her children is uppity? As in a woman who questions the mandate of a law enforcement officer who has stepped beyond his boundaries is suddenly uppity? Or is that a racist thing? I'm uppity because as a person of color I shouldn't be questioning authority? Either way, really, really poor word choice, Cliff." She stomped to the door, her legs finally trembling. "And, just for the record: thanks for coming to my defense. If an ATF agent used your family as part of his strong arming, I would have…as someone with a…vested interest …I would have stepped in." She jerked the door open with a parting shot. "Now I know better."

The diner was loud, the tempo of the lunch crowd rapid. Full plates landed on linoleum tables and empty ones clattered into the bins by the kitchen door. The waitress cleared their two dishes and poured two new coffees in one simultaneous move.

Charlotte looked over at Stacia. "Ok, lay out your options for me."

Stacia rubbed her face with two hands, pulling lower eyelids down as her hands slid down to her chin. "I walk. I just walk."

"Is that an option?"

"I mean it kinda is. But I'm already in danger. The nutters already know my name. Where we live. So yes, but it's not the best option."

"Ok, so what else?"

"I take it lying down."

"Not really a great option either."

"Yeah, no. Not a great option. They get away with it, without any consequences."

Charlotte was thoughtful. "To be honest, Stacia, I don't really disagree with what they did. I mean, if they were involved in some huge conspiracy to take down the SFG - that's kinda cool."

Stacia rebuffed her. "We're the most rarefied news outlet in the country, arguably the world. We're not supposed to *make* news. We're supposed to report it. Getting involved is absolutely not ok. Not as newsmen."

"I guess." Charlotte shook her head, unconvinced.

"There is a third option."

"Go ahead."

"I threaten them with something."

"What have you got to threaten them with?"

Stacia looked around the coffee shop. "Really, the only thing I've got is my sense that they are involved in this. Deeply involved. It may be enough to start, I dunno, an investigation or something."

"But you've got no proof." It was a statement, not a question.

"No. I've got no proof."

Charlotte dropped her chin, stared over her glasses. "So you kinda bluff it. You go in, to Jack, and you tell him you're going to go to the ATF if they don't give you what you want. See what he says. Worst case scenario is he says no and fires you."

Stacia looked out the window. "It's an option."

Charlotte grinned widely. "Now we're talking."

Five minutes later, Penny was out on the sidewalk in front of her office, hissing into her burner phone. "What were your words? I believe they were: 'you didn't tell the ATF guy anything?' Or was it: 'I'm good at what I do, missy?' Wait, I think you said you were 'tits.'"

Freda was calm. "What are you talking about?"

Penny's voice was pitched high. "That ATF agent was just here in our office. He interrogated me. He found me via you.

Goddamnit."

"Ok, calm down. What did you let on?"

"Nothing." She replayed the meeting. "Nothing. Freda, I *am* good. I got all lawyerly up on his ass. Oh my god. I'm so angry and scared right now." She took a deep long breath, her palm over her eyes. "My colleague is a total douche."

"It's going to be fine. Fine."

"How do we know that? I am not going to jail, Freda. I have two boys at home."

"We are not going to jail."

"We're harboring and abetting a spy working on US soil. That's got to be related to aiding and abetting a traitor which is punishable by death. That's written in the constitution for god's sake. Jesus Christ."

"There's no way they'll ever prove that. Think about it, Penny. If she gets caught, she's a friend of ours. We never fess up that we knew what she was going to do."

"Is that your Plan B? Are you kidding me? We'll just say 'We're her friends'?"

"Actually. It's Mac's Plan B. Has been all along. Think about it. Has she ever told us what she's doing?"

There was a long silence.

Penny asked, "Do you think she planned that? Do you think she planned that we would never know so we could never be implicated?"

"I think she's planned this whole thing down to the finest detail. You know who that ATF agent was, is, right?"

"Who?"

"He's the dude that blew the lid off Fast and Frenzied."

Penny noticed the crowds of people bustling around her.

Freda continued, "He's not exactly the most trusted source right now in the ATF. Our girl has got this shit covered."

"Wow." Penny said, "Also, he knew about Laura. What if they connect Laura's money to Mac?"

"No way. How? Via a Swiss bank? Nevah."

"That's what Laura keeps saying. Ok, I'm calling Mac."

"Use the burner phone."

"No shit, Sherlock."

* * *

Langley, VA

Odom's cell phone pinged with a message from Beam. *"He went into a building in Times Square about 2 hours ago. I wasn't able to follow - card swipe turnstiles."*

"Keep an eye on him."

Odom dialed Hawkinson's office. "The ATF agent is in New York. He went to the New York News building twice and then into a Times Square building."

Hawkinson responded, "He's chasing the lead through the reporter. Smart. Can you get close?"

"I don't think so."

"Ok. Stay on him. Keep your distance."

"Sir, I think the ATF agent has concluded that Mac is not working alone."

"What?"

"I think he may be right."

"Talk to me."

"I think Mac has someone inside the New York News that has a vested interest in the gun legislation and who is fanning the flames of public sentiment."

"You're suggesting Mac may be part of a domestic…cartel… of some sort. That's quite a conspiracy theory, Odom."

"I'm not sure what the conclusion is, but it seems suspicious that the SFG stories are getting such high profile coverage."

"Look into it."

Odom hung up and turned up the volume on his computer. On the screen was MSNBC. Rachel Maddow sat at her desk in front of the camera, with a smirk. She began the segment in her typical informal style, speaking directly to the viewers, her friends. "Let me start today with a quote. It's an unattributed quote of a long-time Capitol Hill staffer working for a Democrat. He made the off-record quote to me last week when I called him on background about the assault weapons ban."

She looked down to her cue card and air quoted. "'I can't stand that we pander to the SFG. All the other issues, all the other topics that I deal with support either our constituents and interests back home or the larger country and our citizens. But when it comes to guns, I just bend over and say, 'Yes, Sir, may I have another?'" She looked up at the camera. "What kind of failure in our democracy, what kind of failure in our constitutional checks and balances have allowed one organization to become so all-powerful that they can 'call all the shots' on a single issue?"

She held up three *New York News*. "Thankfully, the SFG took some pretty serious hits this month. First, their biggest corporate donor was arrested for gun running. Then some fairly solid investigative reporting revealed the SFG is really just a hired lobbyist for the gun manufacturers. Then, just this week, their chief strategist Neil Koen is implicated in an egregious embezzlement scheme. And yesterday —" She held up yesterday's paper. "It came out that the SFG had a very intentional strategy to mislead and defraud their members after the Newtown massacre. And just today we hear the their board is circling the wagons, undoubtedly with their lawyers, discussing how liable they might be.

"I spoke to that same Hill staffer earlier today. You know what he said? 'Free at last, free at last, thank God Almighty we are free at last.'"

She set the papers down, slowed her tempo. "I think he speaks for many of us who have been supporters of sensible gun regulation for years. By some miracle we have been handed an opportunity in this country to finally push through reform. Tonight, I have one thing to say to Congress: 'Your move.'"

50

Manayunk, PA

Penny called as the sun was setting. "There was an ATF agent here to see me today."

Mac looked out over Pretzel Park. It was empty. "Smart. He's faster than I expected."

"You expected him to find me?"

"Tell me about him."

"He asked about my boys. He insinuated that my boys were a weakness somehow. That if I were involved in some crazy plot to bring down the SFG, he knew I had kids. I lost my shit."

"Huh. He played it a little heavy handed. He must not have much."

"Are you kidding me? Heavy handed? We're talking about my kids, Mac."

"We're going to make it through this, Penny. It's going to be all right."

"It better be."

"What else did he say?"

"He knows about Germantown Friends. That's how he found me. And the Board of Citizens Against Illegal Guns."

"Impressive."

"Seriously? You knew this was coming?"

"You plan for the worst. You know your weaknesses. I imagined it would happen so it doesn't surprise me."

"I can't believe they found us."

"First of all *they* haven't found *you*. The ATF agent is a lone player without official backing. And he suspects you. He's got no

A Spy Came Home

evidence. That's an entirely different thing."

"Was he the whistleblower for the Fast and Frenzied?"

"Yup."

"Did you set him up?"

"The less you know the better."

"You did, you totally did. Are you going to bring him down?"

"Nah. That's the kind of shit the CIA does. I wouldn't do that to a law enforcement officer. We're on the same side."

"He knows Laura was the bank roll."

"He suspects. He's got no evidence. But you should send her a warning. Do it over your normal cell phone. Act normal. They could be intercepting your calls. Act like you would if you were innocent and some random ATF agent started prying into your life and then mentioned Laura. Remember, you're the lynchpin to Laura. If he can't make that connect stick, he's got nothing." Mac let the advice sink in. "We're fine. This will be done soon. Then you can go back to your normal life."

"I don't know how you do this for a living."

Darkness was settling in the park.

Mac said, "When you apply to the Peace Corps they ask you what you are going to get out of it. They know two years in some third world country is a tough thing to take. They want to know you've got some skin in the game, that you're going to stick it out. They want to know what your selfish reasons are."

In a hushed voice Penny said, "My boys. I don't want them to be shot in a movie theater."

"Remember that. Remember why you're doing this. Only one more day."

"Ok."

"And trust me. I'm good at what I do."

"What is it with you girls?" She hung up.

Mac clicked into the chatroom. There was a note from 89 waiting for her, *"Your Hushmail is compromised."*

"Roger that. Who?"

"Looks like Agency. But it's behind walls so I'm not totally certain."

"Roger that. Am finished with it anyway."

"Good timing. Live long and prosper. Chat soon. :) "

She laughed to herself and logged out.

She used her burner phone to call Amanda.

"Amanda Hughes."

"It's Dora."

Amanda's whisper was hissed, "I can't believe they are blaming Charles!"

"What did you expect? The bad apples go all the way to the top."

"It wasn't what we agreed. You were supposed to take down Neil. That's it."

Mac's voice was calm, in control. "Amanda, we didn't agree on anything. I showed you proof of corruption, you supplied me with ammunition to clean house. Your actions, by the way, have set you up very nicely." She let the complicity sink in. "It's going to be fine."

Amanda remained silent.

"How are you?"

When it returned, Amanda's voice was tired. "Ok, I guess. I feel dirty, like I'm hiding an enormous, dirty secret. It's awful."

"Just stay the course. Mrs. Bodie is pleased. We're all pleased. The storm will pass soon."

"They're going to promote me since I'm the only one who really knew about Neil's work."

"Because you're clean, Amanda, despite your recent actions. Focus on that."

Amanda remained silent.

Mac said, "Mrs. Bodie wanted me to relay some advice to you. We think it would be wise to take down the Traitors List. As it stands, with the article out about Messieurs Koen and Osbourne's strategy, well, it's really just salt on an open wound."

"Uhmmm."

"Amanda, to get the job you want, you have act like you already have it."

"Yeah. Ok."

"We're keeping an eye on you. We're proud of you. You'll be fine."

New York, NY

* * *

Cal stared at an Upper East Side, four-story Georgian townhouse set against a dark sky. He was debating how to smooth-talk Laura Franklin's butler or maid when his phone rang.

A very smooth, deep voice said, "Agent Bertrand, I believe you've been trying to contact Ms. Laura Franklin. I'm Larry Klein, Ms. Franklin's attorney. Can I help you?"

A garage door opened down the block throwing light onto the street. The nose of a Bentley emerged.

Cal spoke calmly. "Yes. Thank you for calling. I'm leading an investigation that I believe Ms. Franklin may have some information about." The Bentley, with a white hatted chauffeur, slipped past him. "Purely informational."

Larry Klein was direct. "Well, that's quite interesting. Because just moments ago I was speaking with Director Wilson —" Cal's mouth dropped open. "And he informed me quite emphatically that you were, and I quote here, 'in Arlington on a close-out.' He informed me that you were indeed not running an investigation. At all."

Cal swallowed and responded with as much confidence as he could gather. "I see."

"In fact, he asked me to tell you that you should, how did he put it? Ah, yes, you should call in. But he added some quite colorful words."

"I see. Well, thank you Mr. Klein. Message received loud and clear."

"Yes, I hope so, Agent. Have a good night."

Cal contemplated the abrupt dead-end to this line of inquiry. He had hoped to tease out more clues to Maar's identity from her high school friends but they had proven quite adept at thwarting him. They were good. Almost as if they had been briefed.

He turned from the Georgian and was walking back toward the intersection when his phone rang a second time.

In his ear, Wilson spoke very deliberately. "Agent Bertrand, ask yourself what you're going to do when you're not working with the Bureau anymore. Ask yourself who you'll be when you're not an ATF agent. Now ask yourself, is it worth it? Whatever hard-on you have for Maar, whatever witch-hunt you're on - ask yourself - is it worth it? This is the last time I call you off this. End this now. Tonight. Not tomorrow. Tonight." The line went dead.

Time was running out. But he was within striking distance of uncovering Maar. Despite himself, he thought of Suduku.

When the lines present no more options, turn your attention to the squares.

Manayunk, PA

This time she had worn jeans, a white t-shirt, and a baseball hat. Her hair was clean, pulled back in a ponytail. This time she had made it out of the loft and was sitting on a bench along Pretzel Park, reading a newspaper under a street lamp.

In the distance to the right, she saw him coming through the park. He was walking gently, absently. The mutt was far out in front, the leash fully extended.

She held the paper close to her face, watched him approach from around its side. She tilted her chin down, sloping the bill of the baseball hat down also, across face.

The mutt ignored her as he passed.

The leash was taut as it passed.

She held her breath.

She raised the newspaper higher.

Then Joe was there, in front of her, walking past her, unaware.

He passed.

She exhaled.

She watched him recede around the park.

A bird chirped overhead. It sounded like a megaphone.

She lowered the newspaper, leaned down on her knees, and breathed deeply. The spinning in her head increased. She lowered her head further between her knees, started counting backwards 10, 9, 8…

The pressure against her scalp began to fade.

A breeze tickled the grass by her feet.

The leaves on the weeping willow rustled behind her.

It was 11 p.m. when Freda sent her a text. *"It's on CNN."*

Mac pulled up CNN on her laptop. Across the bottom of the screen the ticker tap read, " ** BREAKING NEWS ** "

The newscaster was almost breathless with false excitement.

"In breaking news, we've just learned that Senator Jack McCaster, Chairman of the US Select Committee on Ethics, is looking into allegations that Senator Blake Scott, Chairman of the Senate Intelligence Committee, orchestrated a cover up of national security intelligence. It appears Senator Scott may have prevented an official investigation into how a US-manufactured assault rifle killed a US diplomat in Afghanistan. No official investigation into the incident was ever initiated. A State Department source confirmed, 'anytime questions arose about the incident, Senator Scott squashed further inquiry.'

"If Senator Scott acted intentionally on behalf of the manufacturer of the gun, this would be a clear violation of Senate ethics guiding outside influence on official actions. One Senator commented, 'All I've heard is that he's hired a very prominent lawyer versed in Congressional investigations. He's in trouble and he knows it.'

"The timing is remarkable. Gun rights groups are concerned the normally confident Senator - one of the SFG's highest ranked members - is shaken, just as the new assault weapons ban bill comes to Senate vote tomorrow."

Mac's phone pinged with another text from Freda. *"This has got to be it! Over. Done. Cooked. Finished. Delivered. We're running it bold headlines in the morning."*

Her phone pinged again, this time with a text from Penny. *"OMG. This has to be it. Tmrw is going to be huge!!! Xxx"*

Mac set down the phone and closed her laptop.

She grabbed a garbage bag and an outsized serving spoon from the kitchen and headed out into darkness. She paced down the block, scanning the grass, and stopped at the decomposing goose corpse.

She bent down, breathing through her mouth, positioned the bag around the carcass, and using the spoon, gently slid it into the bag. She didn't know exactly why she was doing this, but it lightened her mood immediately.

Birds called softly from Pretzel Park as she headed toward Main Street, the black garbage bag held awkwardly ahead of her with straight arms.

She passed in and out of the light of street lamps, past the cafes, the restaurants, and Starbucks. No one noticed her.

She walked reverently along the canal. The package was only about 5 pounds - much lighter than she had anticipated - but her biceps were burning. Ducks swam lazily by the first underpass. Not a single person was on the towpath at this time of night.

The moon was bright and round. She imagined a face on the surface, peering sideways down at earth, a glum disappointment in his eyes.

It took her 30 minutes to reach the corroded bridge that spanned the pond; it cast a moon shadow across the murky canal. She stepped off the path and picked her way through the roots and brush down to the spongy bank. A surprised turtle splashed from a log into the still, dark water.

With the spoon, she slowly, diligently dug a hole about a foot round, then gently upturned the bag and slid the goose into the grave. Using the spoon, she shoveled the dirt back over the body.

With the bag and the spoon, she headed back toward Main St.

51

Washington, DC

At 8 a.m. the next morning, Cal barged through the front door of SFG Lobby office and flashed his badge at the receptionist. "Neil Koen's office."

Startled, she pointed down a hall to the right. "But he's not there --"

Cal charged down the hallway. "I know."

The long, silent hallway ended at an empty executive office behind a glass wall partition. On this side of the glass was a young woman at an assistant's desk. She glanced up.

He held out his badge and slowly set down the photo of Maar he received from Sheriff Soloman. The young woman's eyes widened. She looked up to Cal, afraid.

His voice was calm, authoritative but gentle. "What's. Her. Name?"

The young woman swallowed. "Dora Maar."

"Do you have contacts for her?"

She shook her head.

"Did you ever speak to her on the phone?"

She glanced left and lied. "No."

He looked into Neil Koen's huge office. It looked like a men's club. Cal took comfort in the fact that Koen didn't even see it coming. "And the money? The $1 million your boss mentions on the video."

She was confused.

He explained patiently. "How did you get the money?"

"A wire transfer."

"Do you have the record?"

She turned to her computer, clicked through icons, pulled up a bank statement, and scrolled a finger down the screen. "Here. From a Wells Fargo, in New Orleans."

"Give me the account number and the branch number."

She wrote out a ten-digit number and a seven-digit number on a sticky note and handed it to him.

He turned, doubled back down the long, silent hallway.

Langley, VA

Odom stepped into Hawkinson's office. "Last night he stood outside a house on the Upper East Side. Then he got a phone call which prompted him to return to DC via Amtrak. This morning he went to the SFG Lobby office."

"How long was he in there?"

"About 10 minutes."

"What's your assessment?"

"He's closing in on Mac."

"Does she have help?"

"The ATF Agent believes she does. Otherwise he wouldn't be pursuing these other avenues. It's all he's got."

"What do we have?"

Odom shook his head. He was running out of answers.

Hawkinson's eyes narrowed. "So the Intelligence Agency of the United States of America has no leads on a missing operative but an ATF agent is closing in on her in lightening speed."

"That's about right, Sir."

Hawkinson's sarcasm was thick. "Impressive. You may lose your job after all, Odom. Now go follow your ATF agent."

Manayunk, PA

She held a perfectly pink, ripe grapefruit at the kitchen counter, her mouth watering. As she pressed down with the knife for the first cut, it slipped off the fruit and sliced through the skin of her finger.

She didn't feel anything for a moment. Then the burn hit and the blood streamed out.

She reached for a dish towel, wrapping it tightly. The burn was turning to a throb. She leaned her forearms on the counter and closed her eyes. There was a tingle behind her eyelids. She squeezed them tight.

A moment later, she found her strength, stood, and wrapped two Band-aids tightly around the cut.

At the desk, she stepped up onto its green surface, sat cross legged and pulled up her binoculars.

He appeared as always in the corner of the park, the mutt pulling on his leash. She placed the wrapped finger up to her neck, took her heartbeat. It was strong and steady.

She followed him all the way around the park. Her hand was steady.

Next to her, the NYC burner phone pinged.

Penny texts. *"Today is the day!! Women rule the world and all that shit!!"*

Mac grinned to herself and typed back. *"And all that shit."*

New York, NY

Stacia was bleary eyed at her desk. She and Charlotte had spent hours last night perfecting the tactics for the impending confrontation. She sipped her coffee gently, the acid on her tongue making her stomach flip. She reread the Op Ed on the back page of the front section.

A Shattered Mystique: New Hits on the SFG
THE EDITORIAL BOARD
<u>New York News</u>
What happens when an opaque, zealous nonprofit, a top industry manufacturer and crooked politicians join forces to prevent regulation in one, specific industry? Unfettered bad behavior. What happens when their behavior is uncovered? It tears apart the social contract the nonprofit has with its members. It reveals that the wizard behind the curtain is simply a mean-spirited, money-chasing lobbyist.

The gun rights side appears to be toppling under the weight of

four scandals involving the bad behavior of a Senator, a Congressman, a CEO, a Chief Strategist, and a gun manufacturer.
The first involves gun running.
The second involves embezzlement and fraud.
The third involves manipulation.
The fourth involves government cover-up.
Criminal, civil and congressional investigations are underway. It is unlikely any house of cards could survive just one of these scandals. It is extremely unlikely the SFG will survive all four.

Stacia took one last look at the Op Ed and stood slowly. Down the length of the newsroom and past the water fountain, her confidence grew with every stride. She stepped into Jack Diamonte's office.

He looked up and dismissed her. "You need to talk to Freda. I'm not your boss."

"They're coming after me."

"I heard. And what did IT say?"

"They've given me a new email spam filter."

He nodded.

"They are threatening me."

"I'm sorry to hear this. But I'm also sorry to say it doesn't surprise me. Our articles have been scathing. Why are you bringing this to me instead of to Freda?"

Stacia looked around his office. He had Pulitzer Prizes and pictures of himself getting Pulitzer Prizes. The strength in her voice surprised her. "Is Freda compromised?"

He rolled his chair backwards, placed his feet on the desk, and took a long time to respond. "Compromised?"

"Is she somehow involved, like maybe actively involved, in the SFG scandals that are unfolding?"

"I'm sure that's absurd."

"Is it?"

"How could Freda have pulled those kinds of strings?"

She shrugged, but held her ground. "I don't know."

"I'm not sure what you want me to say."

"Tell me if you know anything."

He shook his head, remained silent.

"Because if she is, then she's responsible for them coming after me."

He clutched his hands behind his neck. "Stacia DeVries. New to New York. New to the *Times*. Already trying to maneuver around her boss. Bringing in crazy conspiracy theories to my office."

She didn't say a word.

It was his turn to shrug. "Let's for the sake of argument assume Freda is somehow involved in the SFG stuff. If she is, what is there to be done about it?"

"I thought our job was to report the news. Not make it."

"The question remains the same. What if she is involved?"

"We would need to report it to the authorities."

"Stacia DeVries. Let me explain something very fundamental to you. If the SFG nutters decide to come after you for your articles —"

She interrupted, "*Our* articles. Freda assigned me to do these."

"If the SFG nutters come after you for the articles, this paper will protect you. We protect our own." His statement landed in the ether, not as a threat, more as a fact. "And in protecting our own we do not go to the authorities. Even with absurd conspiracy theories."

She faced him, felt her chest expand with bravado. "I want the female Millenials beat."

He dropped his feet, stared at her.

She pressed on. "In exchange for not calling that ATF guy."

He chuckled at her guts. "You've got some moxie."

"I want the female Millenials beat or I'll take the story - the story of *your* involvement - somewhere else. Plenty of other, more modern, news outlets."

He reared back in a half-mocking display of surprise. "Woah. No need to play your hand too heavy, kid. I already told you I liked your guts."

In that instant, she knew he wasn't firing her. She took a small step toward him, her mind clear. "Forget moxie. I've got skin in the game now and I want to be rewarded. Properly. Not this once-in-a-blue-moon-hand-me-a-great-story crap. Not this 'we take care of our own' platitude. I want proper, regular, beat coverage. Of the stuff I care about. And frankly, of the issues this paper should be more concerned about considering the old white guys in this county are very soon going to be outnumbered."

She watched as he actually smiled and leaned back again into his chair. Her heart raced a million beats a second but she felt relief and elation building.

"I like your style, kid. Ok."

She squinted at him, feeling the emotions expand further through her. She took advantage of the momentary confidence. "And don't call me kid. My ambition works just fine without you trying to needle me with condescension."

He nodded, his smile growing.

She turned without a word and walked out of his office.

52

New Orleans, LA

Inside the cold Wells Fargo branch, Cal sat across from a confused bank manager. He explained, "The Bureau is looking into a trafficking case."

The older black woman wrinkled her brow.

He took a more serious tone. "Guns. Trafficking."

"Trafficking?"

He nodded to the sticky note on her desk. "That wire transfer has been involved. I'd even go so far as to say, it's been nearly responsible."

"I'm just not sure on the rules on this one." She looked around at the empty branch. "But I will tell you that since 9/11 we have been told to help out law enforcement."

"I won't tell a soul."

Making up her mind, she tapped the number into her computer. "Ah, yes, Julep Foundation. I remember that. Nice girl opened it just a few weeks ago."

"Do you remember anything about her?"

"Well, says here her name was Dora Maar. That's right. I think blond. I remember she had a nice, clean cut."

"How did she open the account? Do you remember anything about that?

"Let's see." She clicked on the account records. "Ah yes, deposited one million. Anything that large would have had to have been with a check."

His heart picked up a beat. "Can you track down who wrote that check?"

"Well, that's highly unusual, Agent."

"I'd get a warrant but we're under a very strict timeline here."

She wavered.

He leaned in. "The timeline pertains to a drug deal. And we have agents involved. Who may get hurt."

"This gal Dora was involved in that?"

"I'm afraid so."

She whispered, "Let me go see what I can find."

She sat down a long 20 minutes later, empty handed. "My, my, what a trial that was. So first I found that Ms. Maar opened the Julep Foundation account with a cashier's check from Credit Suisse in Zurich. We had a copy of that on file. So I called Credit Suisse and got a bit of an old fashioned run around."

He waited.

"Well, it turns out, a Swiss national picked that check up. And according to Swiss rules unless it's a foreigner they can't get involved. They can't tell us anything. Cold case or whatever you call it."

"Dead end." He settled back into the chair.

Clever, clever Maar.

An unusually strong disappointment swelled through him. He sighed and looked up at the bank manager. She was watching him intently, with a slight grin.

He asked, "Any chance you found something else?"

"I thought you'd never ask." She handed him her own sticky note with a telephone number. "That was on the original paperwork. She left a contact number."

His lungs emptied. "Thank you."

"You go get those gun runners now, ya hear?"

Outside in the heat, he punched in Ruby's telephone number. "Ruby, just one more. Just one more GPS check."

Her voice was strident. "Did you get my text? Do you have any idea how much trouble you're in?"

"Ruby, I shouldn't, I wouldn't ask - but I'm literally hours away from closing this thing."

"No." She hung up.

He dialed her back and groveled. "Ruby, how many years have

we worked together?"

"You're going to lose your job."

"Not if he doesn't hear about this. Please, Ruby, I'm begging you. I can not let this one slip through my fingers."

She took a deep breath. "Give me the number. I'm going to look it up now. I am *not* logging this in the system." She put him on hold. When she came back she was whispering. "Most of the calls from that number were made from a neighborhood in Philly called Manayunk."

"Manayunk. You got the street address?"

"135 Cresson Street, Philly, 19127"

"Ruby, that's the last favor I'll ask, till I'm right with the Director again."

"If you get right with the Director, Cal. If he asks about who was feeding you GPS, it was not me."

He immediately looked for a cab. Jumping in he practically yelled, "The airport, and there's 50 bucks in it if you do it fast."

The taxi squealed into the light afternoon traffic.

New York, NY

Freda and Stacia sat in Freda's office with the television turned on to C-Span and a view of the US Senate floor. A vote was in progress.

Freda looked over the desk at Stacia. "You wanna go get a drink after the vote?"

"Uh, no thanks. I'm meeting a friend."

"A guy? A date?"

"Uh, no. Just my friend Charlotte."

"Oh. Ok. Well, listen, well done on your articles."

"Yeah, thanks."

"We'll need a piece for tomorrow," she said nodding to the C-Span image on the screen. "You want it?"

Stacia stood quickly. "Absolutely."

"You deserve it. Ok, you better go get started."

Stacia was half-way out the door. "On it."

Freda stared out the window and listened to the reporters' camaraderie on the other side of the glass wall. Some joked, others laughed, and still others responded loudly. On the desk was the ATF agent's card. The phone number had a DC area code. DC wasn't so far from New York.

In her office in Times Square, Penny also watched C-Span. She picked up her phone and dialed Laura.

Laura's voice was hushed. "Hey. I'm watching it right now."

"It's crazy, right? It seems to be falling our way."

Laura almost whispered, stunned. "Crazy."

Penny glanced out the window. "I wanted to thank you —"

"No need. It was worth every penny."

Penny grinned before she turned serious. "I'm waiting to hear from Mac. But I'm pretty sure this won't come back on us."

"Penny, it was worth the risks. All the risks each of us took. You, Freda, Mac, me. It was worth the risks."

"I hope you're right. God, I hope you're right."

Langley, VA

Odom sat at his desk staring at the green lamp. His hands rested heavily on the armrests of his chair.

A text from Beam arrived. *"We're leaving New Orleans. Flight to Philly."*

Odom jumped up and ran down the hallway, typing a response. *"DO NOT LOSE HIM"*

He rushed into the Hawkinson's office. "Philly. The ATF agent is headed to Philly. I know Mac is originally from Philly. She's gotta be camped out there."

Hawkinson recovered quickly. "If he finds her, I want our guy to engage"

"How?"

"I don't care. I want our guy to interfere somehow. I do not want her talking to the ATF agent. Odom, do you understand?"

"Yes." Odom backed out through the door.

"This is career make or break time Odom."

Out in the hallway, Odom punched in Beam's cell phone. "Beam, listen to me. If the ATF agent finds Mac, I want you to engage him."

Beam's voice pitched high. "What?"

"She cannot spend time with the ATF agent."

"How am I supposed to *engage* him?"

"Do what seems as natural as possible in the situation. Do not let Mac spend time with the ATF agent alone. He is a loose canon with nothing to lose - we cannot allow him to ask her questions."

"Sir, how do I do that?"

"Just do it, Beam. Your career depends on this."

53

Manayunk, PA

Joe ambled along the sidewalk below the loft. Mac leaned over, eyeing down three floors of warehouse wall, watching his bald head bobbing slightly.

Her burner phone pinged with a text from Penny, "*You watching the news?*"

Mac watched Joe to the end of the block. He had a book under his arm.

When he turned the corner, Mac responded. "*Nope.*"

"*We should know in 30 minutes!*"

Mac counted to five then hustled down the loft stairs.

She poked her head out the street door. The street was empty.

She raced to the corner, slowed. She looked around the building's corner.

He was sauntering along Roxborough Avenue toward Main St.

She remained by the corner, watching him.

On Main Street, he turned left and headed up the small hill.

She hustled along to the next corner, peeking around onto Main Street behind him.

He was in her line of sight.

She let him advance 100 feet, then followed.

Two blocks down he stepped into a bar with an open, large front window topped with a red awning. Bright red umbrellas were stretched over sidewalk tables.

She entered a women's boutique and pretended to browse, giving him ten minutes lead time. In between racks, she opened the burner phone and typed a response to Penny. "*You can stop worrying. ATF agent not after you anymore."*

She exited the boutique, ambled toward the bar's open window, and peeked in

He sat alone at the end of the bar, his back to the window. He had a beer in front of him and a book open in his hand. His head was bowed, reading.

She passed. When she reached the next corner, she stood for a moment, killing time. She felt her pulse with her injured finger. It was normal. Strong.

Penny had texted. *"Are you sure?"*

Mac typed back. *"Yes."*

She slipped the burner phone down into her courier bag, crossed at the corner, and meandered back on the opposite side of the street.

Minutes behind her, Cal stood at the door to the loft. The lock had been jimmied and it stood ajar.

A naked mattress rested, tilted length-wise against the far wall next to an old fan. Otherwise the loft was barren. Only the sterility of the space, the absence of dust, suggested someone lived here.

Through the window, a street lamp blinked on.

Cal shook his head once, twice. A small smile formed.

Clever, clever Maar, you saw me coming a long time ago.

He slipped his Glock inside his belt at the small of his back.

He walked the loft's perimeter slowly, noncommittally opening empty drawers and the bare, warm refrigerator. She must have had an arsenal of cleaning products; the place was spotless. Even the waste basket was empty.

There was a noise in the hallway.

Cal pulled his Glock as he turned on the open door. A tall, dark-haired man walked by and glancing in saw Cal with his gun drawn. The man jumped out of sight, yelling, "Holy shit, man. Just making my rounds. I'm the building manager!"

Cal called around the doorway. "ATF. Sorry. Come on in."

The man peeked around the doorframe, hands raised by his head. "Just making sure everything is ok up here."

Cal holstered his gun and flashed his badge. "Sorry to scare you. ATF."

The man retreated backward down the hallway, mumbling,

"Ok, man, really, ok. Will leave you to it."

Cal continued his search. In the makeshift bathroom, he found a damp sliver of soap. It smelled of rosemary and mint.

At one of the huge windows, he gazed into the dusk. In the park, under the light of the street lamps, two dogs enthusiastically rough-housed. One of them was a pug.

A mixture of disappointment and relief flowed through him. He had lost her.

On the desk, he noticed a piece of paper. It was a baggage claim ticket from 30th Street Station.

Down on Cresson Street, Beam called Odom. "It's clean. She's gone."

"What did you see?"

"He was inside checking it out. It was a big loft. Spotless. No sign of life. Except a mattress on the floor."

"She's flown. Damnit. Ok, keep on the agent but from a distance."

There was silence down the line.

Beam spoke again. "Maybe she's finished, Sir"

"Maybe she is."

New York, NY

Freda watched the MSNBC newscast on her screen. An excited reporter stood outside Capitol Hill. He gushed, "We've just learned the Senate has passed the Assault Weapons Ban!" Behind him on the lawn of Capitol Hill, a crowd holding a vigil threw up their arms, hugged each other. Whoopie horns blared and cameras flashed. The camera panned wider. The crowd started chanting, "U-S-A! U-S-A!"

Freda glanced up. Jack stood in her door. He smiled. She smiled back. He turned and walked down the hall.

RESOLUTION

The Weeping Woman's right ear has turned into a bird sipping at her tears, a sign of new life. Her hair flows like a river. She has a flower in her hat. But this moment of hope does not erase the fury of the painting.
- Jonathan Jones

I am no bird; and no net ensnares me:
I am a free human being with an independent will.
- Charlotte Brontë

54

New York, NY

Penny softly closed the door to her apartment behind her. The smell of grass and soil from dirty cleats tickled her nose. She leaned against the inside of the door, listening to the silence; the boys weren't home from school yet.

In the kitchen, she poured a glass of water and took a long sip, the cold hitting the lump in the back of her throat.

She found Kenneth in bed in a t-shirt and boxers, unshaven, unbathed, typing on his laptop. He didn't look up.

"Kenneth."

"I'm right in the middle of some killer dialogue." He purposefully kept typing.

She waited.

He finally looked up.

She swallowed. "I'm not going to let you follow this Peter Pan dream anymore."

He lifted his fingers off the keypad, annoyed at the interruption, not taking her seriously.

She said, "I've been letting this go on for too long."

He leaned back, waiting.

"It's time." Her tone was sympathetic, soft. "I take part of the blame. I haven't done you any favors by allowing this dependency."

He rested his hands on his stomach and gave her a 'go ahead' look, taunting her to carry on.

She did. "While you've been able to chase your dream, Kenneth, I've had to work. But you know what? I have dreams too. We don't talk about them. You don't ask about them. But I have them." She shifted on her feet, took a moment to clarify her thoughts. She redirected. "It's not fair to blame you for not asking about or not knowing about my dreams. But it's also not fair to me to keep them buried. I need the space to let them breath. This is really, truly, about me. Not about you." She chuckled to herself, her relief now unfiltered. "That's such a line, but it's really true. This is about me letting me dream."

He finally spoke. "What are you talking about Penny?"

She took a large breath and exhaled slowly. "You have three months to find a job. If you don't, I'm going to file for formal separation. One of us will have to move out and get a second apartment. It's time."

Philadelphia, PA

Cavernous 30th Street Station was a cacophony of noise and movement. Late evening commuters rushed past Cal as he entered through the West doors.

He found the leave luggage counter, handed the baggage ticket to the attendant, who in turn returned with a white courier envelope.

Reaching for the envelope, Cal asked, "How long do you hold bags?"

"Only 24 hours."

"Then what?"

"We clean 'em out."

"So this has been here less than 24 hours."

"For sure." The attendant nodded to the envelope. "Actually, I remember her."

"The one who dropped it off?"

"Yeah."

"Blond, 5 foot 8, slender? Short bob cut?"

"Exactly. Nice lady."

Moments later, at a cafe table off the main station hall, Cal sipped a coffee and stared at the sealed package on the table. The train announcements blared loudly in the main hall. A policeman and his dog passed. An Amtrak employee laughed loudly to a colleague.

Cal opened the envelope and slid out a bulky pile of documents. The top document appeared to be a simple cover memo.

Final Operations Report - SFG Destabilization
Classification: *Need to Know*
Tags: *Rogue, Firearms, National Security, Fraud*

He began flipping through the stack. The package included a snapshot of one of the Picasso Weeping Women series. It included a photographs from the internet of a run-down tenement building captioned Harlem Polo House and what appeared to be the former Newtown elementary school. There were the three photos of Neil Koen sitting across the restaurant table from Congressman Peters. Cal recognized these as the same photos the New York News had been sent.

Next in the pile were the four Blue Lantern cables. They were followed by a photo of the raid on Scimitar taken from a local newspaper's website. In the photo, up on the hill, Cal stood to the right of Sheriff Soloman.

Deep below the station a train churned to the platform. A forlorn bell announced its arrival, followed by the whistle of brakes. The air pressure changed slightly as the train pushed fully into the station.

Cal turned the pages. There was the 'post-Newtown strategy' email from Neil Koen to Charles Osbourne.

Each of Stacia DeVries's *New York News* articles on the SFG had been neatly clipped and included.

Dora Maar - whoever she was - had compiled a full, final report on her entire operation.

Toward the end of the pile, Cal found a black-and-white photograph. His hand hovered over it. In the photo, a man was lying on a bed in a dark room. A yellow sticky note was attached to the right top corner: "Your 'get out of jail, free' pass."

His eyes narrowed on the photo. It was his apartment. It was his bedroom.

Across the bottom of the photo she'd written in Sharpie: *CIA Case Officer Frank Odom: birth name - Thomas Apostle: DOB: 8.20.68, Cincinnati, OH: SS#: 405-80-1329*

Maar had given him proof of a CIA officer undertaking a domestic op against an ATF agent.

The last page in the pile was a short, hand written note on clean, crisp linen parchment.

"Cal, I know you're probably in trouble with your boss. This should help that. But I wouldn't use it further than that. I'd recommend a safe deposit box in an international bank. But in the end, you decide what's best for the country. Be careful, they're watching you right now. - Dora Maar"

Across the busy station hall, Beam stood in a corner with a cell phone to his ear, watching Cal. "He's finished looking through the documents. Now he's looking around."

Odom barked, "He's looking around?"

"Yes."

"Looking at faces?"

"Yes."

Odom yelled through the cell phone, "Abort --"

" — Christ he's seen me - recognizes me from the loft — "

" Abort now! Abort now!"

Beam had already hung up.

Manayunk, PA

Mac stepped across the threshold and into the bar.

The small restaurant was fairly crowded. There was an open kitchen at the far end where the bartender chatted with the chef. Deep red walls were crammed with framed reproductions of famous paintings. Was that a Picasso? Yes. *La Muse.*

At the bar, Joe held his book with one hand while the other slowly lifted a forkful of food to his mouth.

Silently she stepped forward and slipped unobtrusively onto the bar stool next to him. He took another mouthful, didn't look up.

The bartender noticed her from the other end and she indicted she was in no hurry.

Next to her, Joe continued to read.

Steadily, slowly she turned on the stool so her knees faced him and propped one elbow on the bar. It was an intimate position.

He looked up over his book, eyes widening, then softening.
She smiled hesitantly.
He closed his book and set it on the bar.
She sat frozen.
His voice was gentle. "About fucking time."

Acknowledgements

This was, without doubt, a collaborative effort. A very special thanks goes out to my editing team who provided substantive input and emotional support throughout: A, K and J.

A sincere, personal thanks goes to those who have and continue to battle for common sense gun control every day.

If you would like to learn more about the gun control debate or the amazing people and groups working to find sane solutions to America's gun violence epidemic, please visit the novel's reference page: www.hnwake.com/books.html

www.hnwake.com

Made in the USA
Middletown, DE
22 December 2014